# Give It to Me

Sexy Tales About Women Getting the Good Loving They Deserve

Angelina M. Lopez

Angelina M. Lopez

# Table of Contents

proaches her childhood friend and town bad boy for sex lessons. Deleted scene from *Full Moon Over Freedom* each other in their vineyard after two long weeks spent apart after the end of ***Lush Money***

14. (pg 236) **Star 69** – The couple from ***The Phone Call*** finally get to enjoy their first time. Can their desire overcome their nerves?

***=first time in print**
**See Trope List at back for list of tropes**

# CHAPTER ONE

# The Phone Call

This is the first romance short story I ever wrote. The way it turned out made me fall in love with romance short stories. I'm proud to say that the amazing Leslye Penelope let me know this story made her cry.

If you've read **The Phone Call** before, it might be because it's the story I offer for free to all my newsletter subscribers. If you haven't read it, now might be a good time to subscribe to my newsletter!

***Content warning: Mentions death of a spouse***

***

**Part 1: The Phone Call**

"Hello?"

"Hi."

"Hey. Hello there." Rosemarie could call Sam three times a day, and he always sounded so wonderfully pleased.

"What are you doing?"

"I'm finishing up a site. What time is it? ... Damn, it's six. No wonder I'm starving."

"Do you have anything in your fridge? Besides week-old pizza?"

"Yes, I have *day*-old pizza."

Rosemarie laughed, as she knew Sam wanted her to.

"What're you doing?" he asked.

"Nothing," she said quickly. Too quickly. "I just...was wondering if you've got plans next weekend?"

"Valentine's Day weekend? Hell, no. I'm staying home and out of the crosshairs."

"I thought I'd buy you a plane ticket and force you to come out."

"I'll come but you're not buying the ticket."

"Yes, I am. My finger is hovering over the mouse, and I just have to hit the 'Charge' button."

"Well, you'd better haul that finger back right now."

"No. Can you come?"

"Not if you buy the ticket."

"Don't be an ass. I've got a reason."

"What reason?

"I...I want to use you."

"On Valentine's weekend? That sounds promising." The grin in his voice was clear. "What am I going to be doing? Wait. You're not going to make me paint again? You didn't pay for my ticket that time."

"You wouldn't let me. I bought you dinner."

"Chuck E. Cheese does not count."

"The girls needed out of the house. And I gave you tokens. See, this is exactly why I want to buy your ticket. Then I don't have to feel guilty if you're...uncomfortable."

"Uncomfortable?" He stuttered a laugh. "What are you going to make me do?"

"I think we should have sex."

The silence after their rapid-fire conversation was deafening. Its roar filled Rosemarie's ears. But she couldn't have proposed it any other way. It had to be quick, like ripping off a Band-Aid. All business, like suggesting lunch. Instantly and without thought was the only way she could ask for what she needed.

At Sam's continued quiet, Rosemarie began to panic. She couldn't even hear him breathe. She'd coached herself to give Sam the time and space to react however he needed to—as long as he didn't say no. She looked at her computer screen, where the arrow throbbed over the "Charge" button. She clicked her mouse. *Screw it*, she thought. She'd guilt him into having sex with her.

"You know..." His voice, when it rumbled through the phone line, quiet and measured, made her stomach clench. "When you first said...what you said...I thought you were joking. I was waiting for the punch line." Now she could hear him breathe, a whopping inhale. "Rosemarie, what is going on?"

She laughed nervously. "I think it's pretty obvious. I want you to have sex with me."

"Fuck! Stop saying that."

His bewildered anger, complete and hurting, stabbed at her through the phone.

The realization that she had offended him crawled over her. She had never heard him angry at her. She'd almost thought it was impossible.

"Sam, I'm sorry. Please don't be mad at—"

"Jesus, Rosemarie, you throw this thing at me—"

"I know, just listen—"

"God—"

"I'm sorry, listen," she pleaded. She took a second, a second to relax the muscles that had locked. "So...I've been feeling...the lack." The short laugh on the other end of the line had very little humor in it. "Look, you know how long it's been for me."

"No, I don't." His petulant answer dared her to disagree.

"Why are you making this so hard?" she burst out. "I'm asking you because I wanted it to be easy."

"What?!"

She felt near tears and that was the last thing she wanted him to hear.

"I'm sorry. I screwed this up. I'm just going to go."

"Wait, *wait*." Patience was trying to strangle the frustration in his voice. "Don't go. Tell me. Tell me what you need."

And that was it. In the two and a half years since her husband's death, Sam had been there to give her whatever she needed. At first, it was a shoulder for her and her two young daughters to cry on. Then, when they'd started the long process of healing, he was someone they could share her husband and their father with. As her husband's best friend since kindergarten, his memories stretched farther than theirs. They made the treks across the United States—more often him to Boston than the three of them to the sunny shores of Southern California—because they all loved being together. He would visit to work on the house, celebrate birthdays, or to gift her some free babysitting.

And then there were the phone calls. The everyday, whenever she needed it, effortless phone calls to a man who made her laugh, a man who made her feel interesting and intelligent, a man who could talk her through fixing a garbage disposal and who allowed her to talk him through the book-keeping for his website development company. He'd call at any moment, answer whenever she rang. She restricted her phone calls to him to daylight hours—he'd picked up twice while he was on a date and once, she was pretty certain, while he was engaging in post-dinner activity. But there had been many nights when he'd called her, when his deep, slightly scratchy, always teasing voice was the last thing she heard before she drifted off to sleep.

She'd hung up quickly the few times she'd felt a hum of electricity over that line. She didn't want that. Her loving husband, Philip, had given Sam to her, in a way, had given her his best friend to hold her together when she wanted to fall apart. On that horrible night—the one-year anniversary of Philip's unpredictable, unfair car accident—Sam had held her on her living room couch and muffled her weeping in his chest so the girls wouldn't hear. He'd stroked her hair, kissed her cheeks, whispered into her ear. But he'd never kissed her lips.

Now Rosemarie had given a good twang to the lovely, silken tightrope that was their best friendship.

She took a deep breath and structured in her head what she would say. There were reasons, good reasons, that had led to him as her only answer.

"You know I haven't been with anyone since Philip. I haven't wanted to be. But lately… God, all of this would be so much easier if any need for sex had died with him."

"Oh, sure, that's definitely what Philip would have wanted. You throw your hot thirty-something body on the pyre of widowhood." Thank God he was starting to sound normal again. "Why don't you go on a date?"

"You know better than anyone that people don't go on dates anymore. They go on Tinder. You want me to swipe right until I find some guy who wants to come over and do me? What time did you go to that girl's house, that *stranger's* house? Two a.m.? That's romantic."

"Christ, no, don't…I mean, don't they have a ChristianSingles.com or something?"

"Sam!" she wailed.

"All I'm saying is maybe you should start dating again. Stop being so interested in my love life and get one of your own."

"I don't want to date."

"Why?"

"Do you know who I am?" she asked, exasperated. "I'm a thirty-three-year-old widow with two girls in grade school. I'm a downer. And, thanks to my unfortunately endless curiosity about your love life, I know way too much about what single people do to each other. I don't have the time or the energy for the stuff gorgeous guys like you put women through. I've got to concoct a healthy dinner for two girls who don't eat anything but apple slices and chicken tenders shaped like dinosaurs. And I have no interest—I repeat, no interest—in putting my girls through the drama of a parent who is dating. You know the hang-ups I have about the revolving door in my mom's bedroom."

"You wouldn't—"

"I know, I know. Look, if there was one male in the whole of Boston that I was even remotely interested in, I would probably take your advice." She continued talking over his scoff. "But look what I have to compare them to. Philip. He wasn't the perfect man, but he was the perfect man for me. Every other man is too smiley or too weak or too Master of the Universe or too everything compared to him. Except you. You don't get compared."

She stopped for a moment to catch her breath and gather her reserves. "So that's why I need you to help me take care of this little issue I'm having. Think of it like a household chore. You cleaned my gutters last spring."

"God," he guffawed.

She charged ahead. "It's a basic biological need. We'd both know what we were doing and why we were doing it, so it shouldn't be uncomfortable. Just a friend doing a favor for a friend. So please say yes."

He huffed a breath. "Rosemarie, I really don't think..."

The sea of mortification she'd been treading was about to pull her under. "I'm dying here, Sam. I couldn't be more humiliated, but I didn't—"

"Fine. Fine, God, I don't want you to feel bad. Yes, I'll...yes."

"Really?"

"Yes!"

"I haven't forced you?"

"How am I supposed to answer that?"

"I mean..." She would rather swallow her tongue than say what she was about to say. "You're not opposed to the idea because you find me...unattractive, are you?"

Her heartbeat thudded in her ears three times while she waited for his answer.

"Are you a complete idiot?"

Her heartbeat receded to its normal silent rhythm. "Phew! Good." She waited a second. "I do think we should have some rules."

"Rules? Wait, you didn't say anything about rules."

"I just think we should set some clear boundaries so that things don't get confused."

"What? No kissing on the lips? You're going to make me feel like a whore."

The words "kissing" and "lips" coming out of Sam's mouth sent a sizzle of sparks down her spine. That particular brand of fireworks had been lighting up more and more during their conversations. But it had nothing whatsoever to do, she told herself, with her decision to have sex with him. In fact, she hoped the sex would serve to extinguish any niggling embers of curiosity.

"No, we can...kiss, but no sleeping together."

"I thought sleeping together was what this phone call was about."

"No, no sleeping. You have to go back to your own bed."

"I'm going to fly out there to be your personal stud and you're going to make me sleep on that torture device you call a sofa bed?"

"I just don't want any confusion."

"Yeah. And what are the rest of the rules?"

"After you go home, no talking to each other for a week."

He went silent again. This time, she could hear his slow breathing into the phone. It sounded like he was trying to restrain himself.

"I'm sorry." She could feel the urge to babble. "I just don't want sex and our friendship getting mixed up. I think it's easy for people to mistake feelings about sex for feelings...about something else. I don't want any—"

"Confusion. Yeah, you said that. So, me sleeping in another bed and us not talking for a week will somehow keep everything straight even though *I've been inside you*." His last four words hit like shots out of the dark.

She lowered her eyes to her lap, the phone still pressed to her ear. Her body felt leaden. It was like she spent all day dragging it behind her. She remembered a not-so-pretty day during a cold and wet fall when she and Philip and the girls had entertained themselves by tossing a tennis ball over a volleyball net. She remembered leaping off her toes to catch the ball one second and then diving to the cracked pavement to catch it again. That body could have hopped right over that volleyball net into Philip's arms.

"What else can I do, Sam?"

The silence was heavy before he answered.

"I don't know." He sighed, a seriousness she was sad to have put in his voice. "I don't know why I'm giving you such a hard time about this. We'll keep it light and..."

"It's just biological."

"Right, biological. And I'm buying my own ticket."

"Too late."

"What?"

"I've already pressed the button."

"Goddammit."

"I'll send you an e-mail. See you Friday."

She hung up on him.

***

**Part 2: The Text Message**

The text that Friday afternoon, on the eve of Valentine's Day, shouldn't have come as a surprise.

But it did.

They never texted each other. It was something Rosemarie had realized a year into their phone calls. Even if it was just a quick, "My plane is going to be late," they always called each other. It was something she loved about their friendship, the quick rasp of his voice that was never impersonal. She'd decided not to analyze too deeply why it pleased her so much.

But Sam had sent this message by text when he should have already been in the air on his way to her.

"*I can't,*" the message said. "*I'm so sorry. But I can't. I'll send you the money for the plane ticket.*"

She actually laughed when she saw it. The plane ticket. She could lose the money for the plane ticket; Sam could burn it for all she cared. What she couldn't lose was her best friend. But her hasty, ill-conceived, poorly delivered phone call might have done that. It might have lost her her best friend.

Where could she send money to get Sam back?

***

**Part 3: The Return Call**

Late in the last hour of Valentine's Day, Rosemarie sat in the bay window seat of her living room, rain pattering against the three dark windows surrounding her, staring at a ginormous bottle of wine and a one-pound box of chocolate when her phone rang. It was probably her mom, who lived on the West Coast and could never seem to get her head around the time difference. She picked up the phone without looking at the ID, too busy contemplating whether to start with the wine or the chocolate. Both were getting demolished.

"Hello?"

"So you didn't get a date for tonight?"

At the sound of Sam's voice, joy, shock, and anger sluiced over her all at once, along with a rushing torrent of relief. She dropped her face into her free hand and began weeping.

"Rosemarie..."

"Shut up," she whispered, trying to control her voice and her tears so she wouldn't wake her girls, sleeping upstairs.

"Aw, sweetie..."

"No, just...just give me a minute."

She should offer to call him back. But there was no way she was letting his warm, scratchy voice out of reach. Taking deep breaths, she worked to calm her tears. "Fourteen messages, Sam." She shuddered into the phone. "I left fourteen messages. I know your voicemail by heart now. Do you know I'd never heard it before?"

"I know. I'm sorry, sweetie. I just had to—"

"Don't, Sam. *I'm sorry*. I'm so, so sorry. I should have never put you in that position. I should never have asked...that of you, or worry you about our friendship, or make you feel uncomfortable, or...do anything that makes you feel—"

"Rosemarie," he cut into her babble.

"Just, please forgive me, Sam. Please say you'll forgive me."

"Always. Of course."

The sweet benediction almost started her crying again.

"And know that I won't ever discuss…that with you again," she reassured him. "That issue is *off* the table. We'll just pretend that conversation never happened."

"No." His voice cracked like a whip through the phone.

Rosemarie recoiled as though it had flicked her.

"Sam?"

"We can't keep going like we were before."

She slowly raised her hand over her trembling mouth. "What?" she croaked.

"Everything is different now."

A hole opened up inside her and all the gleaming hope she'd gathered over the last minute, the tiny light of it she'd held onto while leaving fourteen voicemails, drained away. Left behind was only endless, infinite black. She'd done it. With her callousness, her thoughtlessness, her lack of gratitude, she'd destroyed the second biggest reason she got out of bed every morning. This second biggest reason had made it so, so much easier to get out of bed for the first biggest reason.

"You remember, when we met, I didn't like you very much." His voice rumbled over the phone like a death knell.

"Yes," she said dully. It was actually one of her favorite stories. How, when she quickly fell in love with Philip her junior in college, she soon met his best friend, the embittered and sarcastic Sam. Sam had just ended a four-year relationship and wasn't a big fan of pretty girls or couples in love. His sarcasm, now mellowed to a grin at the whole world, was back then a precisely sharpened weapon he used to cut the protective layers off anyone he met. He'd regularly stripped a piece off Rosemarie.

"You were such an asshole," she said with none of the past verve she used to tease him with. "I always think it's funny that that guy became my best…friend." She had to swallow the tears in her voice.

"Philip asked me once when he took me aside to demand for the twentieth time that I back off if the reason I was so mean to you was because I had a crush on you."

Rosemarie gave a humorless huff at the ridiculousness of that suggestion.

"I didn't. I was a dick to everybody back then," he said. "It wasn't until a few years later that I wanted you so much it hurt."

***

**Part 4: Hanging Up**

Rosemarie's heart stopped beating in her chest. Her breath paused in her lungs. Everything strained to re-hear those words, to hear them correctly over whatever had warped them into the shape they took; maybe the bay windows or an echo or the sudden rush of the blood in her veins. But there was not another sound in the room except the soft flick of rain against the windows.

"We were all out at that old-fashioned Italian place, and you were leaning over to put the baby in her car seat...and I got hard. Right in front of my best friend and my godchild, I'm having a 3-D vision of smoothing my hand over the ass of their wife and mother, warming it, and then grabbing a handful to bring her to me. I couldn't even look at you the rest of the night."

A hazy memory penetrated Rosemarie's shock. "I remember that," she said, hushed, unbelieving that this conversation was happening. "You were acting so weird. You shook my hand when you left."

"Yep. No way was I going in for our kiss and hug."

Rosemarie leaned back against a cool, rain-spattered window, her brain a useless, heavy brick on her neck.

"I told myself that I just needed to get laid, that I was suffering from—what did you say—the lack? But no matter how many women I slept with, you kept showing up: in my car, in my shower, in my dreams. Who does that? What kind of scumbag falls asleep thinking about how sweet his best friend's wife must taste between her legs?"

Rosemarie sat straight up, a forbidden bolt rocketing through her.

"Sam—"

"I stayed away from you guys as long as I could," he continued. All humor and tease had left his voice; her Sam was a stranger in her ear, a determined stranger with a leather-tanned voice drawing erotic pictures in the dark. "The next time I saw you…I don't think you noticed, but I couldn't stop from touching the shiny soft ends of your hair."

His sigh held mountains.

"So, I finally decided, 'Fuck it. I'm in love with Rosemarie.' It's not like I was ever going to do anything about it. I could handle it as long as I had you and Philip and the girls in my life. I'd accept the attraction and reject the impulses. And that's what I've been doing for the last eight years, and what I'd planned on doing for the next fifty."

Her voice broke on his name as she clung to the phone, her emotions rattling her like an earthquake as the continents of the last eight years of her life moved into new positions. She was as terrified by his revelation as she was made deeply, deeply sad by it. Her dearest, most deserving friend had gone without what he wanted for eight long years.

She felt shame in her very foundation.

All that she had asked of him, all that he had done for her and the girls, the trips and the babysitting and the household repairs. Oh God, and all the phone calls.

He was thirty-seven, four years older than her. She had assumed, because it was convenient for her, because her life would have shattered if something had changed, that he had gone without being in a serious relationship all this time because he just hadn't found "the one."

And she'd asked him to fly 2,700 miles and, essentially, be her dildo on Valentine's Day.

"I can't believe I asked you to have sex with me the way I did," she gasped, breath stolen by her own callousness.

The so-soft huff he gave was full of irony, full of pain.

Then she heard the steel in his voice. "I'll make love to you, Rosemarie. I'll fuck you six ways to Sunday. No one's going to be able to do it better than me. Every time you've liked the feel of something against your skin, every pleasurable stretch, every moan, I've remembered it. I've got a doctorate in what gets you off and, gorgeous girl, I'm ready to put it to use.

"But let's be clear. Once you invite me into your bed, I'm not leaving."

Rosemarie's heart pounded with a full-body throb like a prisoner beating on bars.

"I love the girls like my own." His voice grew gentler, stroking her ear. "Right or wrong, I've loved you like my own for two years. If you'd gone on a date like I suggested, if another man had touched you—I would have found him and torn his fucking head off."

She closed her eyes as his primal claim swept through her. There, in the dark, she could also hear his frustration. His weariness. His loneliness.

"I can't pretend anymore, Rosemarie. I'm sorry. I wish I could. But this pseudo-relationship is keeping you from putting yourself out there again. It's keeping those little girls from having a father in their lives. I understand why you asked me for sex: I give you everything else without making you risk anything, why not an orgasm?"

"Sam, no," she gasped through tears. But there was no denying her cruelty.

"If I'm not the man for you," he forged on, his voice dead as if he already knew her answer, "then we have to end this so you can go find him. Philip wouldn't want you to be alone. Love"—she heard him swallow thickly—"I don't want you to be alone."

Wasn't that just like Sam? Putting her first. Giving her exactly what she needed.

Rosemarie wiped at the tears on her cheeks as she gripped the phone closer to her ear, her quaking emotions settling into a new reality.

"Sam?"

"Yeah," he echoed back tonelessly.

"Sam," she urged.

"Rosemarie?" A spark of curiosity lit his voice.

"Do you ever think that Philip gave you to me?"

He was quiet a full, deathly five seconds before his breath whooshed into the phone, like he was giving life to it. "Holy shit," he said. "I think that all the time. I mean, that Philip gave *you* to *me*."

"Right," she said, accidentally shoving the pound of chocolate to the floor. "Because our conversation has always been so..."

"Exhilarating," he finished for her.

"Yeah, and our connection feels so..."

"Effortless."

"It's like we've been blessed somehow."

"Yeah, blessed," he rumbled slowly, as if he was processing what she was saying. She heard his slow inhale. "I think he knew, Rosemarie. He trusted me. But I think he knew."

She smiled, filled with sweet melancholy for all she'd lost and the sweet memories of all she'd been given. "Not much got past that brilliant, loving man."

"Not much at all," Sam said, and she loved hearing the mix of joy and sadness in his voice, the realization that they would never, ever have to push the memories of her adored Philip to the side.

"But, Sam?"

"Yes, Rosemarie."

"*I* never knew." Her voice strengthened with her words. "And you had two and a half years to tell me."

"I...I didn't want to push you."

"Or you were afraid." She was beginning to realize that she was a little pissed. "I might have been clueless and inconsiderate—"

"I never said that," he returned with his own heat.

"But I had a right to know that I was the thing keeping you from moving on with your own life. I don't want *you* to be alone, either."

"That was...different."

"No, it's not. You help me and I help you. You protect me and I protect you. That's how this thing works. And, Sam?"

"What?"

"When I touch myself at night, I think of *you*."

Thunderous silence echoed back at her.

"I never allowed myself to think of you that way during the day," she continued, more shy now that it was out there. "But at night, in my bed, you've been finding your way in there with me. I told myself it was, you know, a fantasy, like choosing an actor or a rock star. But, Sam, I never choose an actor or a rock star. It's always your name I moan."

"Jesus," he breathed, hunger and pain all there in his voice.

"I think my body has known for a long time what my brain was too cowardly to admit."

She wanted to say this clearly, but she couldn't keep the tears out of her voice. "I'm in love with you, Sam. I called *you*, I asked *you*, because I love you. I don't want to date anyone else. I don't want to Tinder anyone else.

"I want *you* because I'm in *love* with you."

She heard him shudder into the phone. She wasn't the only one crying.

"Sam?" she said with a watery voice.

"Baby?"

"I'm really, really afraid."

He laughed, deep and tear-clogged. "Me too, love."

"Sam?"

"Love?"

"Why couldn't you have gotten on that stupid plane?"

"Um...sweetie?"

"Yes?"

"Open your door."

She scrambled off the window seat and ran to her front door, phone still up to her ear. She flipped the lock, threw the door open, and there he was, stepping out of the rain and onto her porch, his rental car parked in front of the next-door neighbor's house. Her Sam. Her Sam made new with his overnight bag slung over his shoulder, Gerbera daisies—her favorite—bobbing in one hand, and his phone at his ear. His smile grew slow and wondrous as he looked at her.

He took a step toward her.

A clench of sudden fear made Rosemarie stick her hand out, against his T-shirt-covered chest. She looked at her hand, clenched it into his shirt and skin and muscle. Even this simple touch was different now. This chest, this incredible man, now belonged to her.

"Will you still sound excited when I call?" she asked into the phone as she looked into his eyes, unwilling to let go of the tenuous safety the device provided.

His smile softened, as if he understood her fear, knew what she was trying to do. He also spoke into his phone, creating an echo that surrounded her in his warm voice and loving words.

"Rosemarie, my love, my heart, you're the first person I want to see every morning. You're the last face I want to see every night. So will I be excited to get your call? Absolutely fucking not. Because it will mean I'm not close enough to touch you. I'm tired of bottling up my love for you and squeezing it into a weekend visit or a thirty-minute phone call. This all might have happened on Valentine's Day, but I want to love you fully and intensely and gloriously every single day of the rest of your life."

Sam let go of his phone. It dropped to the stone porch with an audible crack.

As he stepped closer to her, her free hand traveled up his strong chest to wrap around his neck, her body wiser than all of her anxieties. Then, with his breath on her lips and his eyes staring into hers with the same impassioned look he would give her for the rest of her days, Rosemarie's best friend in the whole world slid her phone out of her hand and ended the call.

## THE END

Loved *The Phone Call*? Read about Sam and Rosemarie's happy ending in the concluding story of this book, **Star *69**.

# CHAPTER TWO

# First Date

*L*ike many romance couples, my enemies-to-lovers, grumpy-sunshine, bartender-and-professor pair from **After Hours on Milagro Street,** Alejandra "Alex" Torres and Jeremiah Post, jump into fucking then fighting then loving then saving a town together (as you do) while missing the traditional steps of courting. What would happen, I asked myself, when these two finally go out on an actual date?

This is the answer to that question, set after the conclusion of the story. If you're concerned about the book being spoiled, you can always read **After Hours on Milagro Street** first!

**Content warning: filthy talk, edging**

***

The nerdiest guy Alex Torres had ever met and the hottest man she'd ever known just kept surprising her.

A month after Jeremiah Post accepted her offer to build a home and a life with her, he was sitting across the desk that was becoming less Loretta's and more hers, initial drafts for their house's layout and a huge wishlist for the Hugh Building remodel and invite samples from their wedding planner covering its wide surface, when he looked up from the Johnny's burger he was hoovering and said, "I've never asked you out on a date." His beautiful green-brown-gold eyes were big and horrified behind his tortoiseshell glasses.

Alex had swallowed her instinct to say something caustic. That was a muscle she might've overworked during the last decade. She was trying to let other muscles grow stronger. So instead of pointing out that going he was a little behind the "first date" ball since they'd been fucking like bunnies-bent-on-making-baby-bunnies since the moment a month ago when she'd proposed, she simply smiled and said, "Ask now. I'm pretty sure I'll say yes."

He'd brought up taking her to the elegant New American restaurant on the Dupen College campus. They scrolled Yelp to look at all the highly rated craft breweries and restaurants in downtown Tulsa. But ultimately, he surprised her by taking her out in Freedom.

It was kinda perfect that their first real date was in the town they were going to save together.

They had dinner at Schmitty's Family Tavern, and although this restaurant spot at the corner of Main and Penn seemed to change names and owners every year or so, the chicken fried chicken wasn't half bad. They even had an okay wine list. Alex split a bottle of cool, grassy Chardonnay with Jeremiah and gave him her last bite of Texas toast to soak up his gravy and was even nice to the owners, new folks out of Atchison, who approached their table cautiously. Like everyone, they'd read the newspaper articles about how Alex was gunning for the west side and every misbehaving Hugh.

The day federal police had arrested Doody-meyer, Alex invited everyone to Loretta's, uncorked a few bottles of Poor Eddie's Treasure, and got everyone appropriately and expensively hammered.

When Alex complimented Paul Schmitty on his breading, Jeremiah gave her the kind of smile that made her belly flip-flop.

It was when they went down the street to Turbo's for the second part of the date—beers and karaoke—that Alex had given her future husband way too much ammunition. Turbo's. Jesus. She never thought she'd be at this neon-and-beer-soaked honky-tonk on Main Street again, much less having a good time at it. She'd been leaning a little heavily with her chin in her hand after he said he was going to the bathroom, maybe daydreaming about the way his forearms looked in the rolled-up-sleeves of his shirt, when she'd heard the opening guitar churn of a song, and to her shock, watched her man saunter to the front of the room, toss his tie over his shoulder, grip the mike as confidently as his dick, then, with a mind-blowing hip swivel and chin thrust, launch into, "Are You Gonna Be My Girl?"

The packed crowd at Turbo's screamed in appreciation as they sang and stomped along. Alex felt like a hysterical Elvis fan. She was close to ripping out her hair and flinging her panties.

When he'd sat down next to her, red-cheeked and sweaty and triumphant, Alex told him, half drunk and half sobbing, how she couldn't stand the fact that she could never pin him down. How wild in love it made her. How awed she was by his dependability, his kindness, his sweetness. How he still surprised her nightly with his filthy, smart mouth. She told him she couldn't stand it when he teased her in bed. She told him she hated it. It made her crazy. She never wanted him to stop.

Jeremiah had gotten a peculiar and dastardly expression on his face. Then he'd called her cousin Zekie, who had the night off and had promised to give them a ride if they had a *really* good time on their date.

Now those careless words, words Alex would never have said if he hadn't had her reeling in surprise, were why she was in more physical pain than she'd ever endured in her life.

Okay, maybe she wasn't in pain. But she ached.

"Fuck this," she groaned into the mattress. Naked, she lifted her face from the sheet and her pussy from Jeremiah's mouth and began to crawl to the edge of the bare bed. They'd shoved the summer-weight down comforter and 1000-thread-count linens and pillows stuffed with mulberry silk to the floor hours ago.

"Hey," that voice growled behind her, that horrible, deep, I-can-wait-all-day-for-an-orgasm voice that made her quiver. "Where do you think you're going?"

Then a big, hot hand, fingers tacky from all the times they'd entered and fondled her, grabbed her ankle and jerked her to a halt. It fit around the skin and bone like a cuff, made ankles that supported her all day on a job that demanded she be on her feet feel delicate and small.

Her pussy did that awful fluttering thing again.

She kicked out behind her, tried to yank her ankle away. "Gonna get myself off," she gasped on her knees, clinging to the edge of the mattress as she stared desperately at the closed door. She just had to get to the door. She wouldn't make it to the vibrators in her room. Why hadn't she stashed some of her vibrators in here? She just needed a second away from him, a second without him stopping her hips or stilling his hand or moving his tongue away or pulling out. Around the corner and out of his sight, she could make herself come in a heartbeat. She'd hump the doorjamb if she had to.

"But, sweetheart..." And, oh God, that purr, while his big hand effortlessly trapped her and his warm, strong thumb rubbed into the valley between her ankle and heel. "You said you liked it when I tease you."

She'd created a monster.

She kicked again, much weaker than she normally could because her thighs were trembling, and he laughed—laughed, that asshole—then yanked and dragged her like she was a little tossable thing back toward the center of the mattress. Before she could escape again, he crawled up behind her and around her, caging her in with his big, strong thighs and thick, bulging arms and heavy, hot chest and huge, swinging dick.

"I'm not done with you yet," he said directly into her ear like he could enter her there too, and she heard the animal sound she made. She felt the liquid drip down her wet thighs.

He bent to kiss a wet, shivery line down the length of her neck, and she stretched her head up, let him have it, while she arched to rub her ass against his cock. If she could get him distracted, maybe she could tip up just enough to get him positioned and...

"Not so fast, angel," he said before he bit with those perfect teeth where her shoulder met her neck. She groaned her desperation into the sweat-soaked air.

"Why?" she cried. It was more plea than she'd ever given any man.

This time when he moved, it was to press his chest to her back, his arms close to hers, and his thighs and cock, that hard, heavy dick, against her ass. She was wrapped and safe and protected in the promise of his heat and muscle.

"Because when I'm inside you, I want to see you," he whispered against her. "Turn over."

She heard the words. She understood the command. But she was paralyzed by the promise of him, the weight of him, the threat of him. For the rest of her life, she'd have this. This terrifying, tempting, teasing, gentle man was going to spend the rest of his life fucking her up.

"I said—" And then there was a shock of cold but only for an instant as Jeremiah moved away, then she was lifted and spun and whammed onto her back and she lay there, stunned, breath knocked out of her not by the movement, but by the surprise. Jeremiah had flipped her as effortlessly as a hot dog on a grill.

"Holy fuck," she breathed. Staring up at him, seeing him, she reached between her legs. Just as quickly, he grabbed her wrists and shoved them to either side of her head.

"You are relentless," he said, smiling, that dark hank of hair wavy and damp, his face like the sun had wandered into their room and was shining down on her. He was burning her to a crisp and she was happy to go.

His crinkle-eyed smile was gorgeous. Glorious. He was so, so, so happy. His entire wide, heaving, sweat-sheened torso was a glorious rose of barely hanging-on desire and to-his-bones happiness. She'd done that. She'd made him desperate and panting and sweaty and so stunningly happy as he planked above her and held on by the tiniest thread. He wanted her as desperately as she wanted him, and this glorious man, because she said she loved it, because she said it drove her insane, was denying them both.

She made another pathetic *gah* sound and let her thighs fall wide.

"Good girl," he whispered and her hips helplessly thumped up to him. She was nothing but the wanting he created.

Staring into her eyes, still holding onto her wrists, he lowered his hips between her thighs, positioned his cock, then impaled her in one hard, impatient thrust.

She instantly started coming.

"Jesus," he grunted, letting go of her wrists to wrap his arms around her, to haul her close as he buried his face in her hair, his cock shoving into her to help out. "Holy God."

"I...ah, ah, ah," Alex said, riding it out, writhing against him, everything of her trying to rub against everything that was him. "I tried—" Her teeth were chattering. "I tried to tell you."

"Sweet darling," he crooned into her hair, thrusting so good and hard and deep. "My good, good, good precious girl."

His love words made her want to die.

As her orgasm started to fade away but the mind-blurring pleasure remained, she loved that finally, finally, he ran out of his limitless patience and began to use her as mindlessly as she wanted to be used, pistoning hard and fast between her thighs because he knew she could take it, knew she was made for him. She hooked her legs around his strong thighs and planted her feet on his rock-hard calves and arched up to take him even deeper and rougher.

"Get in there," she groaned, digging her nails into his flexing lower back. "Give it to me."

"You want it?" he gasped against her. "You want me?"

She didn't stop humping up her body to take him in, to squeeze and grip at him, but she grabbed two handfuls of his thick, sweaty hair and yanked him back so he could look into her.

"Always," she said, meeting his precious gaze. "I will always want you."

Then she pulled him down to her mouth and kissed him, as deep and wet and hard as he was fucking her, and the thrill of their tongues, their biting, their tasting, and their knowing that it was forever, lured the first hot spill of him inside her. That look on his face, that slight widening of his eyes and the thrill in the smile of the good, good man who'd never been loved right until he came to her hometown, had her coming too, holding on and kissing and making sure he knew she was never, ever, ever going to let him go.

Maybe she was going to spend the rest of her life surprising him a bit too.

**THE END**

Learn more about ***After Hours on Milagro Street***, named top 10 romance of 2022 by *Entertainment Weekly*, *The Washington Post*, and the *Fated Mates* podcast.

*"Bar none, one of the best contemporaries of the year"*—Sarah MacLean, co-host of Fated Mates and *New York Times* bestselling author of **Knockout**

"Guapo pobrecito" her grandmother calls him. The "poor handsome man." Professor Jeremiah Post, the poor handsome man, is in fact standing in the way of Alejandra "Alex" Torres turning Loretta's, her grandmother's bar, into a viable business. The hot brainiac who sleeps in one of the upstairs tenant rooms already has all of her Mexican American family's admiration; she won't let him have the bar and building she needs to resurrect her career too.

Alex blowing into town has rocked Jeremiah to his mild-mannered core, but the large, boisterous Torres clan is everything he never had. He doesn't believe Alex has the best interest of her family, their community, or the bar's legacy in mind. To protect all three, he'll stand up to the tough and tattooed bartender with whom he now shares a bedroom wall—and resist the insta-lust they both feel. But when an old enemy threatens Loretta's and the surrounding neighborhood, Alex and Jeremiah must combine forces. It will take her might and his mind to save the home they both desperately need.

**Order now**

# CHAPTER THREE

# Twelve Drummers

*W*hen I was invited to participate in the erotic **Twelve Naughty Days** anthology, which is no longer available for purchase, I was assigned the "twelve drummers drumming" theme. Me! In an anthology of sizzling hot authors like Sierra Simone, Skye Warren, and M. Malone, the little trad author who had only written twosomes was given twelve drummers. Do you know how many limbs that is?

I decided to make the most of it. I rolled up my sleeves and got to work figuring out how to make the decidedly European countdown (up?) into a story that reflected mythology and seasonal celebrations I'm interested in. In the end, this powerful, magical, orgiastic story is one I am most proud of.

I was deeply honored when the hosts of the Whoa!mance podcast decided to do a whole episode about **Twelve Drummers**. Isabeau's quote has become a favorite in our household: "I was mostly surprised by every sex scene. I just walked in to each one like, 'What're we gonna do next?'"

***Content warnings: Consensual magic makes them do it, multiple partners, gangbang, anal, stranger sex***

<u>Author's note</u>: During the darkest month of winter, the Mexica celebrated Panquetzaliztli, a 20-day event rejoicing in the rebirth of Huitzilopochtli, the god of the sun and war. On the final day, around the winter solstice, people would honor Huitzilopochtli with effigies and amaranth cakes and a mass wedding, and he would be reborn and bring back the warmth and light of the sun.

This rejoicing of a birth on the twentieth day of a long celebration in winter had such symmetry to the twelve days of Christmas that I wanted to share it with you in **Twelve Drummers**. The Mexica believed the teponaztli, the drum I feature in this story, held the spirit of a beautiful court singer. When it was played, the powerful sound brought forth supernatural forces.

I hope you enjoy this story about the power of our bodies and beliefs to carry us from the dark into the light.

***

The woman whose paycheck identifies her as Sabrina Ramirez is invisible.

She's also prompt, focused, quiet, diligent, patient, and excellent at her job. In the blue dress and white shoes the museum forces on the all-brown female cleaning staff, she makes the most nightmarish bathroom stalls shine like Sèvres porcelain. She eradicates the lobby accidents of ill children, ensuring the air smells as sweet as the scents that dripped off the Romanovs.

She observes the rhythms of security guards so closely that she knows when they're going to take their next breath and injects subtle kinks into a security system until the guards no longer trust it. Her lifelong invisibility—of the six foster homes she lived in, not one person could remember that her name was Anna and not Anita or Maria or *that Hispanic girl* that they dismissed her with—has transformed her into an expert at extracting the diamonds in the rough from mid-sized regional museums.

So why this invisible, focused, great-at-her-job woman is creeping down the hall of the east wing when the emerald necklace she's spent three months prepping to steal is in the west wing is anyone's guess.

But there's a sound.

*Tic...tic...tic.*

Soft and rhythmic.

*Tic...tic...tic.*

Hollow but soul deep.

It's tapping at her breastbone and echoing in her gut. It sounds like the first raindrops after a drought. Or a wife's lover beckoning at the window. Anticipation makes her fingers tingle and creates a delicious buzz in her brain as she continues the wrong way down the low-lit hall. It's the same electric sensation she first felt on her eighteenth birthday, when she discovered her foster home had been locked against her; her birthday present was scaling a tree and popping a latch with a bent paperclip to reclaim her things.

It's a sensation that freeing jewels from their cases hasn't given her in a long time.

She pulls back her black cuff to look at her watch. This part of the east wing will be clear for another eight minutes. She has time to find the source of the sound and then return to her jewel heist.

Her renegade feet don't care if she doesn't. *Tic...tic...tic.* She's being yanked by a rope anchored into the core of her.

The room she enters is a little-visited antechamber as far east as the east wing will go. Mesoamerican Art reads the plaque above the archway. She does little more than dust and vacuum when she's assigned this section; the good people of this Nebraskan city seldom press their noses or fingertips against these cases. And while the indios who carved these masks and created these onyx figurines and painted these bright scenes of worship and sacrifice are her ancestors, she has resisted her curiosity. She excels at her job. Sabrina Ramirez must stay focused and seldom noticed.

But now Anna follows the sound—tapping and teasing and beckoning at the wide-set collarbones beneath her black shirt, at the wings of her shoulders and the peaks of her small breasts, at the little pearl humming between her legs—to a beast. No, not a beast.

A drum.

Her heart leaps and her pussy squeezes with an unwarranted excitement.

It's a wooden drum, the size of a baby if she laid it across her lap, carved into the shape of a crouching jaguar with snarling teeth. A Teponaztli, the sign says beside it. Its snarling teeth are still sharp, the spots carved into its rosewood surface still defined, belying its five hundred years of age.

Anna pulls off a black glove and, breaking every one of her rules about anonymity and discipline and respect for the sanctity of the pieces she steals, she strokes trembling fingers across the ancient wood.

She gasps as she is slammed with knowledge she's never had before.

Inside the teponaztli, where no one can see, where the wood was hollowed out and cauterized, there are fissures and cracks. It's barely holding together. Dawn is coming and it may not survive this longest night.

She presses the back of her still-gloved hand to her lips to restrain her sob.

The teponaztli's song is seeping away.

That single, hollow rhythm begins to beat frantically in her veins, crying out in her blood.

*Tic...See me. Tic...Touch me. Tic...Make me sing.*

On top of the teponaztli are two wooden mallets tipped with rubber. Their name, olmaitl, simmers to the top of her brain. Who would just leave these here? It's five days after the new year, in that frozen dread of winter, with lightless days and to-your-bones cold, when she usually takes herself to the sun and unleashes months of loneliness on anonymous lovers, when museum visitors are light and school groups have yet to begin their field trips. Still, why would the curators just leave these...?

Logic takes flight as she rips off her other glove to take the olmaitl into her hands, to feel their balanced weight in her palms, to see the pale wood against her dark skin in the spare, after-hours museum light.

She twirls one of the mallets in her hand like it's a slim-jim. Like she has the grace of years of use. And doesn't she?

The olmaitl are like any other tool Anna has used to unlock something precious from its cage.

Slits are cut into the top of the fine, heavy wood of the teponaztli, creating two tongues of percussion, and when she hits one—*tic*—it rings inside her heart, high and beckoning. With an eagerness she hasn't felt in years, she bounces the mallet on the other tongue—*tak*—and the tone is denser. Harder. She taps against the body of the jaguar, against the spots carved into the rosewood, and it is the densest, hardest sound of them all. *Tok.*

The tongues are the tune of a hip sway, a shoulder shake. But hitting the body is the beat of bare feet stomping the earth, demanding, summoning...

A dark-haired man she knows well comes slowly through the archway, hand on his still-holstered firearm but the retention strap released as the olmaitl begin to slow dance in her hands. She drums to the beat in her heart, *tic...tic...tic...*, then adds a touch of the deeper tongue. *Tak...tictictic...tak...tictictic...taktak.* A jolt of the body. *Tok.*

Anna is freeing the teponaztli's song.

"Sabrina?" he says deeply, with all of the confusion she's forgotten to feel. "What are you doing?"

This is the first time that Juan Carlos Pedron, this security guard she knows well, has spoken to her. She's surprised he can put a name to her face. She should be alarmed; she's worked hard at being invisible, at receiving the same lack of notice or care as the other hardworking Latinas on the cleaning staff.

But Juan Carlos is prompt like she is. Focused like she is. He knows her name on the roster because he, too, excels at his job. He covets the night guard position, even with its poor training, inconsequential pay, unrealistic expectations, and racist supervisor, because it allows him daylight to focus on his degree. His dreams are bigger than hers, and he is more hopeful than she could ever be.

Juan Carlos no longer wears his wedding ring, but his thumb still strokes over its absence, in moments of forgetfulness. She wonders about the person who would let him go. Juan Carlos is dark-skinned and hook-nosed, strong and compact with black eyelashes as thick as a painter's brush. His hair is sleek and black and long to his shoulders, although he restrains it in a neat low ponytail.

"I..." *I don't know*, is what she's about to say as she continues to play the teponaztli, the beat still slow and mesmerizing, *tictictak...tictictak...tictictaktok*, even to her, the drummer, a woman who has no more musicality than the smack of her hand against her steering wheel, when instead she says, "Can't you hear it?"

And then, as if she'd licked the words into the shell of his ear, his eyes widen and his strong shoulders arch back in his dark security shirt. His right hand clings to the holstered gun like a railing. The hand with its missing ring trembles as it slowly, haltingly, slides down the front of his uniform trousers.

Yes. He can feel the grip of the drum's rhythm now.

Heat like a July noon flares through her and from her.

"What's happening?" he groans, closing his eyes tightly, those black lashes fanning in pleasure like agony against his skin.

*I don't know*, she tries to stammer again. But words escape her as she watches him cup himself. She watches this good, decent man roll his hips, once, against his hand that bulges with the strain of resistance.

"Come play with me," she begs instead.

His lash-heavy eyes shoot open and on her, and they are full of fear and fight, even as he squeezes himself to the rhythm of her drumming. She misses a beat. She's accustomed to him distracting her from her discipline; she repeatedly had to rewind the security tapes when he spent too long on screen.

"Sabrina, please…stop," he says through gritted teeth. "I want…." He lets out a groan, shakes back his hair to stare at her fiercely as he struggles for control. "We have to get you out of here."

His concern makes her lose her focus, makes the olmaitl skitter over the rosewood.

Juan Carlos excels at his job. She should be invisible to him, or at the very least, indistinguishable. Uninteresting. He shouldn't care about the consequences as she stands there in a thief's all black, beating at a 500-year-old wooden drum in a way that—outside this bubble of heat and magic—would bring armed men and violence and retribution.

But he does care. And in that moment, in that continued flow of knowledge she's never had before, she understands they each have a choice.

Anna has been chosen to make the teponaztli sing. But she needs him to unleash the magic in the song. Only together, and with the drum healed, can they celebrate this sacred day, the darkest day of the year, when their god is reborn and the sun begins its return. Only together can they give homage to the old ways and provide another year of strength to their people who are mistreated or dismissed in this new world.

Or they can choose to walk away. They can let those cracks become fractures. They can let the lack of notice and care bleed the teponaztli's magic dry. They can let the sacred ways of their people go as dark as the sun one day will.

They each must make a choice. They are not captives here. She is fully conscious that she is an anonymous jewel thief with no better understanding of her heritage than the visitors who ignore this room. He is fully conscious that he is a protector who excels at his job.

But she is tired of bearing the weight of cold, lifeless rocks that attract more attention, devotion, and love than she does. When she thinks of all the invisible Latina cleaning women she's worked beside, her grip on the olmaitl firms. Every lonely step of her life has led her to this one purpose.

She taps a hard defined rhythm over the jaguar's spots—*toktoktok*.

"Leave or stay," she murmurs as she toes out of her soft shoes. She squares her stance, plants her feet solidly on the earth. Meets his dark, beautiful gaze and lets him fully see her, if it is her only and last chance to do so.

Anna picks up the rhythm and gives him a soft smile of goodbye.

Juan Carlos raises that firm guardian's chin at her. He gives one punishing stroke down the front of his pants. His other hand clenches on the butt of his gun.

Then his hands fly free as they rise to his head.

He reaches behind himself to pull the band from his hair and shakes the shimmering black weight around his collar. "I won't leave you alone to this," he says, striding boldly toward her.

The goddess burgeoning in her goes weak in the knees. This man will offer his heart to the cuauhxicalli vessel before he relents to something he doesn't want to do.

He comes at her with the force and fire of a rocketing star. When he stands on the opposite side of the teponaztli, she smells the sweet scent of burning copal. When he picks up the olmaitl that suddenly appear next to her thrumming mallets, she tastes the amaranth cakes kneaded with maguey honey. When he stares into her with the eyes of a priest and hair that must enrage the devil and begins to drum a complementary rhythm that matches their shared pulses, she hears a low long blast, a wail and a call to arms and a warning all at once. She knows, with this memory of knowing new things, that it is the blowing of a quiquiztli. A conch shell.

In this low-lit room of museum artifacts in a mid-sized city in Nebraska, they are joined by ten shadowy shapes that glint and glimmer behind objects and display cases. They are now at the apex of a large circle of twelve.

These twelve will celebrate and acknowledge and renew.

His soul-deep gaze is unrelenting as they drum together, as she sees the simple gold cross vibrate in the shadow of his collar, as she feels the impact of his beats up her arms, as she smells his clean soap over the copal, as she feels his body's heat through the warmth of hidden ancient fires pulsing around the room.

Anna startles when she feels a touch at her hip.

Standing next to her is a man, a huge man, whose dark eyes burn down at her through the black and yellow paint on his face. Two long, green feathers dance in his headdress. His thick glistening chest, his massive thighs are revealed more than they're covered by the beaded short cape and elaborate loincloth.

He smells of musk and smoke as his warrior-rough hand pulls the cap off her head, then buries his fingers in her hair. His firm mouth dips toward hers.

She resists her impulse for violence—she is skilled when the rough world sees her—but clutches the olmaitl protectively against her breast as Juan Carlos maintains their rhythm. Panicked, she looks to him.

"What do you want?" Juan Carlos asks softly. She feels his words in the depths of her, as alluring and strengthening as his hand stroking the small of her back. "I'm here. For whatever you want."

He, too, seems to be in possession of knowledge not entirely his own.

She is a thief and an adventurer. But while her bedroom explorations are numerous, they've been restrained by Sunday school teachings of unwarranted guilt and perpetual angst.

She huffs a shaky laugh and offers Juan Carlos a tremulous smile. But it's the warrior whose fingers trace the shape of it. It's the warrior's iron taste she savors when she licks his glassy calluses with her tongue.

Anna lets the olmaitl go and doesn't hear them clatter to the ground.

This huge man's kiss is skilled and beckoning, with plush lips and a soft tongue exploring her mouth as if searching for amaranth crumbs. There is a reason this decorated warrior was the first to resolve from the shadows. She compels her heavy eyes to open, to look at Juan Carlos. The way he is watching is as seductive as the warrior's fingers curled into her short hair. Curious, emboldened, she lets Juan Carlos see her suck on the warrior's tongue. He grits his teeth and shoves his hips once against the hard wood as his mallets fly over the teponaztli.

Heat flares in her at the unexpected pleasure of teasing.

But her bravado flees again when the warrior dips his fingers into the black band at the top of her sleek pants. She stiffens and the warrior stops but nips her jaw, like a stallion settling his mare. Heart racing, gripping the warrior's huge bicep in her hands, she again looks to Juan Carlos.

A bead of sweat meanders down his sharply planed jaw as he continues to drum frenetically—*tictictaktok...tictictaktok...tictictictictoktok-tok*—maintaining the power of the magic. And although the mystical copal has filled the room with a warm haze, the magic won't do all the work for her. She's not a captive here.

"Whatever you want," he says again, with so much tenderness, with that cross shimmying in his collar. "I will support you."

She has a flash of an image, of a willing sacrifice flung over the snarling jaguar, the teponaztli accepting the heart's blood. But blood isn't the only life force that will renew its magic.

She digs her short nails into the warrior's solid bicep and sees Juan Carlos watching her as she widens her stance.

The warrior pushes his huge hand into her pants and between her legs with a grunt. But his touch across her clitoris is gentle. Anna's body welcomes him wetly, with no hesitation at all. He slicks the tip of his finger with her soaking arousal, fondles her entrance, then retreats to her clit, plays with it to Juan Carlos's rhythm.

She never takes her eyes off Juan Carlos as pleasure shivers up her spread thighs and the man sinks his thick finger into her body. She opens her mouth and lets Juan Carlos see her moan at the luxurious shove and slide. She arches her hips into his mighty hand; he tugs her head back by her hair and she gasps. The warrior cups her and pulses one finger, then two, deep and hard into her to the beat Juan Carlos sets.

For tonight, Juan Carlos—this god-touched man—will be her voyeur and protector and partner. She cries a call to all the gods when she comes spectacularly into the warrior's hand.

The warrior grips her hair hard and claims her mouth for a kiss all his own, a kiss Anna gives him willingly and thankfully. Then he retracts his hand from her pants, closing his fist as he pulls it out, and draws his hand over the teponaztli, saying a prayer she does and doesn't understand as he rubs her release into the wood.

The red heat of the room pulses and flares and chanting that she'd known but hadn't heard becomes audible.

The warrior, her warrior, reclaims his shadowy spot in the circle but adds the rhythm of the huehuetl, a large upright drum with ocelot skin drawn over one end, to Juan Carlos's rhythm, slapping at the skin with those mighty hands. She feels her strength renewed, her thighs firm, as the teponaztli weaves its song with its new bombastic companion.

The new drummer strengthens the magic.

Two shadows leap from the circle as ferociously as the warrior was gentle. Young men—one clothed in the soft skin of the jaguar, his face eager and hungry as it emerges from between the animal's teeth; the other in a finely netted cape, his body seen through the weave sleek and hairless and strong—grab her and yank her out of her clothes, twist her head possessively to lick into her mouth, grip and suck at every morsel of flesh revealed. She kicks and shoves them away before they can rip seams.

"Do you like it?" Juan Carlos demands fiercely, those saint's eyes promising retribution if she doesn't, his protectiveness making him a giant, hovering force in the room. He grits his teeth to hold himself back as he continues drumming and waits for her command.

Anna grins at the boys, who are panting for sex and war, and sucks the taste of them from her lips. "Yes," she growls, stepping out of her pants as she flings her bra. She plants her bare feet in the commercial carpet and displays herself naked for them, for him, and—for herself—she closes her eyes. Not to hide. But to savor the feel of her hands on her hairy mound, over her wide hips, up her ample waist, and over her small breasts to pinch her sensitive nipples. Her body is power and ability and life and magic. Even if others have never seen it, she always has.

Anna has always known her value.

She opens her eyes and stomps her feet to the rhythm of the weaving drums and shows them what she's always known. Then, licking her lips as she stares at a sweating Juan Carlos, the gleam on him bronzing his beauty like gold, she beckons the young men to her.

They attack.

She is bountiful, with enough flesh for both of them as they kiss and fondle, suck and stroke, bite and grab with all of the eagerness of the young heeding the call of their bodies. She sparks under their hunger, allows them to feed to their hearts' content. The jaguar soldier rubs his fur-covered body ardently against her as he tongue-fucks her mouth while the caped young man grips bruises into the handle of her hips as he sucks on her nipple. The soldier imprints eager bruises down her neck until they're both at her breasts, licking, sucking, biting with all that first fascination, and it's an ecstasy Anna's never had, one she doesn't want to end soon as she grabs their dark hair to hold their mouths at her tits. The mostly naked young man grunts and yanks away, petulant and disrespectful, earning a dangerous growl from Juan Carlos.

She croons her forgiveness into the musk-soaked air when the young man slides down, down to his knees, his skin and strong muscle shining through the linen ties of his netted cape, licks up her thigh, and shoves his tongue—rough and ardent and hungry—into her pubic hair. He makes a sound of happiness when he gets her taste and works her without skill and with wet enthusiasm as he pulls himself from his loincloth.

The goddess in her swoons as she looks down at him, young and golden and beautiful, brutal face buried in her pussy as he licks hard and quick, like a hummingbird catching nectar, and he harshly strokes his straining penis. The jaguar soldier grunts at being ignored and forces her hand into a slit in the fur. She wraps her hand around his warm, hard cock and feels it leap as she pulls it out.

The young man on his knees leans across to take the head of his companion's penis into his mouth, to lick then suck, and she almost loses her legs at the surge of pleasure.

When she sees the ravenous expression on Juan Carlos's face, she would be on the floor if not for the soldier's strong grip. He notches her against him while his young friend's mouth travels between them—using his tongue, his lips, biting their thighs, making them moan and thrust—while she feels the prick of the jaguar's teeth against her face as she lolls against him and lets him exert his will on her mouth.

"I'm close," she gasps, and the young men suddenly grin and go wilder, pushing her toward the teponaztli while they jerk themselves, the jaguar soldier fucking her fast with two fingers while the young man on his knees spreads her hair to waggle his tongue wildly over her clit. Anna lets out a wail just as he pulls away, and her orgasm sprays from her, the first time that's ever happened, and trickles down the drum. With ferociously prideful grins, the two young men aim their cocks and shoot.

Their orgasm doesn't even have a chance to drip to the carpet before it's absorbed. As the heat flares again, as the hidden fires seem to blaze brighter and the chanting grows louder, the two young men pray and cross the threshold into full manhood. They re-take their places in the circle, this time with two additional huehuetl. The pounding of their strong hands against the animal skins shakes the floor like an erupting volcano.

Their drum circle of three has become five. She can feel the cracks inside the teponaztli beginning to mend. The bites and bruises on her heal. The sweat whisks away.

While Anna feels as fresh as if she'd just stepped out of the steam of the bathhouse and rinsed herself with cool water, Juan Carlos looks like he is one raving second from smashing the wooden drum, the only thing that's separating him from her. He beats at it hard as his hair shakes around his face. She feels burned by his saintly gaze.

She hears them before she sees them. The rattle of the chachayote, the ankle bracelets made of hollow tree nuts bound together, sounds like rain falling as they approach. Three beautiful women, court musicians, approach her with red stripes painted across their faces and their black hair twisted up into horns at the front of their hairlines, proudly drawing up and pulling off their long, ceremonial tunics and skirts to reveal dark flesh and thick waists and full hips, the chachayote at their ankles rattling both a welcome and a warning.

The air throbs with percussive rhythm. It's the first time she surrenders to the floor.

One of the women, with emerald plumes in her hair, leads her down with kisses and soft touches, then spreads her thighs with strong yet gentle hands. Anna is awestruck by the look of the musician—knowing, bold, focused—and knows that this is what others see when she is fully acknowledged. She is knowledgeable; she is courageous; she is unwavering. Her invisibility isn't ordained.

But then she is beyond thinking when the other two women press their warm, soft, fragrant bodies against her on both sides, bathe her in kisses—to her lips, her neck, her shoulders, her stomach, her breasts that ache with sensitivity—while the feathered court musician lowers her mouth to Anna's pussy.

The focused, knowing, devouring of it is something beyond pleasure, beyond skill. It's adoration. She feels herself slump to it, fall helpless to the suck and lick and hum all over her pussy, over her skin and breasts and lips, fall helpless to her inexperience. Until she realizes she, too, is hungry. She, too, is eager. She opens her eyes as she reaches for the women, slips her fingers into heavenly warm wetness as she looks down to see the woman's gaze burning up at her as the mouth works ardently at blood-red, glistening flesh.

When she glances up from the floor at Juan Carlos, he looks down at her like the universe has collapsed on him. The throb of the percussion in the room is thick enough to slice; duty is all that keeps him upright.

One of the women leans up to demand her mouth and arches into her learning fingers and all she can think about then is the miraculous taste, smell, touch, and feel of women. How fortunate they are to be these creatures of sensation and temptation, of emotion and knowledge, of strength and heart, of mother earth and magic. Anna comes screaming into the woman's mouth, under the warm blanket of silken, searching female flesh, but she immediately surges up, out from underneath them, and takes her place as a leader and goddess here, lays them out and lines them up, hip to hip to hip, and tastes and takes them, drowns herself in their salty, soury, feminine flavor that wells up from the richness of their bodies, soaks her fingers in hot holes that clench and spasm, rubs her lips and hands and hair against all that decadent skin, and sobs in wonder at their perfection as they each cry out in pleasure.

They, each, are perfect. These women that some may abuse or negate, that may go unnoticed and ignored or scrutinized and fetishized, are a miracle.

She mourns when she untangles from them. But as they rub their faces and fingers and pussies against the jaguar drum's smooth spots and silky teeth, praying and singing and humming, as Juan Carlos stares in awestruck worship, she can actually see the drum glow. She can actually hear the rosewood vibrate as it heals from their attentions.

She presses them close and blesses them with goodbye kisses before they walk away, their chachayotes shaking around their ankles, and they take their places in the circle, adding another huehuetl, a hand drum, and ayacachtlis—hollow gourds filled with seeds—to the celebration.

Five have become eight, and she weaves her arms above her head and twirls her naked body in a pattern to their magical music.

When she swings back to look at Juan Carlos, he is breathing like he's midway through a battle. His uniform is soaked with sweat and his hair gleams with it.

"Are you okay?" he whispers, his eyes running desperately over her. She feels like she is glowing with health, like each orgasm has fed and nurtured her. He looks like he's been hit by a truck. And yet, he asks, with all of his humanity and innate goodness and desire to protect, about her well-being.

"I'm fine," Anna whispers back, that sense of knowing tickling her brain. "I can't wait until..."

The four priests who break away from the circle are there to ready her for the final rite.

Although they span ages and experience, the four men are dressed the same: in simple white loincloths and fine black capes edged with red over their shoulders. Their long hair is tied back and red stripes bisect their faces. They pass a vial, pour the oil of the cempasúchil—that vibrant orange flower that captures the sun and ushers the dead—and warm it in their cupped palms. Their devotion and discipline seem to calm Juan Carlos; his strong shoulders ease and his stance settles as he watches them lay hands on her naked skin.

Anna raises her chin and lets her eyes go lazy with pleasure, a small grin on her face as she watches Juan Carlos watch her, as she enjoys the stroke of eight hands running slowly, worshipfully, over her breasts, belly, shoulders, thighs, calves, ass, and in between, making her brown skin shine and leaving none of her unexplored.

She holds the excitement in the center of her, doesn't let it vibrate out to her limbs. Calm and ease is what is asked of her now.

She raises her hands to the oldest man with his heavy shoulders and thunderous brow and brings him close for her kiss. He is *her* priest, they all are, tasked with assisting her in healing the teponaztli and preparing her for the celebration of this darkest day and the return of the light. His devotion must be rewarded, and Anna kisses down his thick, strong body until she is on her knees.

His cock is a delicious mouthful, heavy on her tongue. She smiles around him—dear Lord, it's been months—and urges him with a push of her hands. Gently, with sacred movement, he begins to pulse in and out. He is salt and musk on her palate and strength between her hands and a pounding rhythm in her ears and—if not for her eagerness to discover what the final rite is—she could suck him deep and long and for hours. She could suck out his well-pleasured soul.

But a hand urges her thighs apart, and she feels the silk of hair slide between them as supple lips surround her nipple and a hand rubs oil over her palm and wraps it around another priest's cock. She is filled with a blessed tongue, but it is not enough. She is suddenly ravenous.

She pulls off the cock in her throat, squeezes the cock in her hand, thrusts her breast into the mouth. "More," she groans. "Give me more." They pick her up, all of those deity-directing hands on her, controlling her and lifting her, and position her further down the younger priest's body. She is surrounded by hard flesh. She is covered in worshipping hands. As she kneels above him, the drumming gets more violent, more rampant. The chanting grows louder.

She looks up into Juan Carlos's burning eyes and finds that he, too, is now chanting. He sees her clearly. He will protect her. They are both here with a job to do, out of choice, and they will do it with the same aim for excellence that they do all things. An excellence that people glance at them and assume they can't achieve.

Juan Carlos's eyes flicker down to where she has the priest positioned, high and hard beneath her. She sinks down, rolling her hips to take the priest into her weeping pussy, and Juan Carlos changes the rhythm to the beat her body sets.

The slide up inside her is wondrous. Her thighs—those thighs that support her as she cleans and cleans them out, thighs that are strong and reliable and steady—move her, squeeze him, work that lovely penis inside her when all she's had for months is her fingers and her imagination.

In her imagination, Juan Carlos has taken her this way.

As two of the men move closer to surround her, to beckon her mouth and hands onto their hard cocks, she feels fingers behind her, fingers coated in that pungent cempasúchil oil, and she leans forward so they can find her entrance, so they can tease the muscle then relax it. She closes her eyes and allows the pleasure of a cock sliding along her tongue, a cock pulsing in her hand, to loosen and relax her. The priest beneath her grips her hips and distracts her from the sting with a miraculous movement of his hips.

She sucks on one head, then the other. As the roll of her pelvis sets the rhythm of the music, as she gets those dicks good and deep inside her, she feels a hand push her forward. She arches back her hips.

Relaxed and oiled, the muscle worked, the priest's penis still burns as it slides inside. She breathes deeply, her pussy clenching and clinging around the man beneath her. When it is settled, she breathes out a sigh of relief. She has never been so full before. She licks up the penis closest to her face. Slicks oil from her breasts to jack the untended cock.

Back arched, thighs wide, jaw relaxed and hand fervent, she takes control of her priests, pleasuring them all at once, and hears their prayers. Through their groans and pants, she hears their plea for renewal and healing. As they thrust and shake inside her, she hears their hope for strength. As they clutch her close and beg her body, she hears their demand for acknowledgement.

She is the master of their ecstasy. Through her, through the teponaztli that is connected to the old gods who still listen, she is the maker of hope that will give their people another year of fortitude in a hard world.

She does not come. But one by one, the priests untangle from her, trembling and gasping and desperate, and stumble to the teponaztli to groan their orgasm out onto it then bless it with her fluids: her wetness, her saliva, the cempasúchil oil that drips off her.

The younger priests rejoin the circle, adding more drums and the flute-like sounds of the tlapitzalli to the thunderous song. But the oldest priest circles to Juan Carlos and takes the olmaitl from his hands.

Now they are twelve. It is time. It is time for the final rite.

As Juan Carlos circles the teponaztli to stand in front of her, she is surprised to hear the orchestral, pounding rhythm recede. The bright hidden fires dim. The copal smoke thins and all she can smell is him. Juan Carlos. He smells of evergreen, of bright new things growing.

The infinite time of sweat and drumming and arousal doesn't show on him as he begins to take off his uniform.

"What's your name?" he asks her as he steps out of his pants, revealing a body that is firm and compact, with a thin line of black hair that trails down his torso to circle his flushed red cock. He folds his pants, puts them neatly on top of his folded shirt.

The drum sings its most beautiful song.

He is wise enough to know that her name is not the Sabrina Ramirez he saw on the roster. She sighs with the enjoyment of his wisdom and his beauty as she beckons him with a smile and a finger.

He smiles back while his hands, one with a missing ring, slide along her hips, her waist, the smooth skin of her lower back as he pulls her naked body close. For all the touches of this endless night, his is the one that feels the most foreign, the most exhilarating for its newness, like a bite into an unknown fruit that tastes strange and delicious. For all the kisses and copal over hours, his is the most drugging.

She rubs her hands into his long, silky hair, caressing his head and the brain inside it.

"I dreamed of doing this with you," she says against his mouth.

He sucks on her soft bottom lip and she never knew she liked that. "I've been trying to figure out how to talk to you for weeks," he murmurs back.

His words aren't meant for ghostly ears. His words are just for her. Although they are surrounded by thrumming magic and they have a job to do and they complete a circle of twelve drummers and they are watched by the chanting other ten, it is—within their circle of arms and bodies and kisses—just the two of them.

She pulls him to the floor.

"Like this," Anna demands, pulling him on top of her. "I want you to feel me. I want you to see me."

"I do," he says, stretching over her, kissing her nipple, her shoulder, her mouth, but too eager to linger as he presses inside her and against her, naked man to naked woman. He holds her head in his guardian's hands and looks into her eyes. "I always have."

The sudden hard thrust of him inside her is as animalistic as it is sacred, his pull of her wrists over her head and his ensnaring grip is as shocking as it is pussy drenching. He licks her ear then pulls back to look into her wide eyes.

"You think your pussy's weaving magic now?" he whispers to her, his grin hungry and his black hair licking around her face as he thrusts. "Wait till I get you in bed. We're going to make sparks fly out of your michi."

The goddess has *never* been spoken to this way before.

The goddess claps in excited glee.

The goddess must be appeased before she lets them go.

This woman who is not Sabrina Ramirez, who has been seen and valued, who has the power and will and skill to succeed at whatever she desires, twines her thighs around her lover's hips and lets him pleasure her. Lets him learn how to make her come. As his orgasm pulses inside her, and her orgasm soaks him back, she holds him close while he sobs his ecstasy into her neck, murmurs the prayer that she will forget, watches the teponaztli shine blindingly as every tear is mended, and hears its song reach its zenith. Her ten mighty drummers slowly sink to the ground to kiss the earth in her honor and then—as the incense and heat and music and magic fade—disappear.

In the otherworldly realm, the celebration will continue. Their god is reborn. The sun, bringing all of its hope and fortitude, will shine again.

On the carpet of a seldom-visited room in a regional museum in Nebraska, she caresses Juan Carlos's face as he looks into her eyes.

"Anna," she says. "My name is Anna."

She is invisible no longer.

**THE END**

# CHAPTER FOUR

# Too Old for You

*My longtime readers may know that for about six years, I had a pretty intense obsession with the show* Supernatural *and its star, Jensen Ackles, who played the older brother, Dean Winchester. My crush has waned, as crushes do, but I'm still pretty proud of the fanfiction I wrote during that time. For liability's sake, I've changed the names in this fun, hot story set in the world of supernatural hunters. But IYKYK.*

***Content warnings: age gap, off-screen death of parents mentioned***

***

Gina had been fifteen and feral when she'd arrived at the Hunter Academy, snarling at the people trying to help her after two years of ripping out the throats of the things that killed her parents and baby brother. The folks at the Academy had been her enemies, then her teachers, then her friends. By the time she graduated and decided to stay in the hunting life and go back out on the road, the friends and mentors she'd met at the academy were her family.

But she'd never known quite where to put Sean.

He'd rolled into class on a day when she'd still been trying to break out and insisted everyone call him Sean. Not the "professor" or "ma'am" or "mister" that the other instructors used. Just Sean. His don't-give-a-fuck command and the easy black-and-white of his instructions—do this or die, ain't no skin off my back—had been the first time she'd paused from counting steps to a window she could jimmy.

His green eyes and crazy-soft lips had distracted her too. He'd been thirty-one to her fifteen—a fifteen that hadn't gotten to mature naturally, to have crushes and stare at beautiful boys on a screen—and she thought the bubbling feeling low in her tummy had been a sickness. She'd been prepared to puke up whatever they'd probably poisoned her with. There'd been wild rumors about Sean: That he'd sacrificed himself to bring his brother, the Academy's lorekeeper, back from the dead. That he'd gone to hell and back. That he'd eaten four pies at one sitting and kept them down.

She wondered how he could live through all of that and still have those gorgeous laugh lines around his eyes. She wanted to stroke her fingers across that tender skin. Being around Sean, thinking about Sean, made her feel something new and weird. It fit as well as shiny wrapping paper under her skin.

The feeling had been hope.

Her final year, Sean had been her advisor for her thesis project—Could Día de los Muertos celebrations be used as recruiting events to get one-day-a-year spirits to convince their restless brethren to leave with them? There'd been long nights in libraries when Sean would sit close and read over her shoulder, and cold nights in graveyards when he'd sling his jacket around her shoulders. He'd never, ever, ever looked at her the way she looked at him. Still, Gina had thought...maybe. Someday. Maybe.

Well, it was ten years later, and Gina had returned to the Academy as an instructor to teach Mexican monsters and lore. Sean was forty-four and more beautiful than ever—he'd let his hair grow out, he had a beard, and his chest and biceps were massive—and it was now.

The time was now.

She'd asked him out on her first day back, right after he wrapped her up in a big hug and a bigger smile. His eyes almost bugged out of his head (how did he not know?) before he'd scowled and said, "Hell no!" and that he was too old for her. Gina was a successful hunter because she never gave up. She was twenty-eight and might as well have been thirty-eight for as long as she'd been making grown-up decisions. She knew her own mind. She knew what she wanted.

She made Sean buñuelos and empanadas de piña and arroz con leche just like her mother had taught her, jars of salsa that could make a grown man cry, and tortillas that were soft and airy, dropping by his class to give him one just off the plata, rolled up and dripping with butter. She'd watch him chew grimly while his eyes closed in the throes of pleasurable food and his trainees looked on with huge grins. She wore shirts that brought out her eyes and jeans that brought out her ass. She saved his life—twice—but that was canceled out when he saved her life three times.

Then she stabbed a mesquite stake dipped in holy water through the hairy chest of a racist rancher a second before his mano pachona, his de-mon hand, could crush Sean's brother's trachea on the other side of the sprawling estate. They'd been part of a team sent to El Paso to investigate a series of mysterious immigrant deaths.

A week later, sweaty and with no makeup after a hot Pilates class, she'd run into Sean in a hallway of the teacher's dorm. Strands of pure silver shone in his beard like Christmas tinsel. "Fuck. Fine. One date," he'd growled. "I'm driving. Don't even think about paying."

"I'm only doing this to show you that I'm not all you've cracked me up to be," Sean said when he knocked on her door the next night, every instructor in her wing making some excuse to be hanging out in the hall or leaving their door open. Gina hadn't been shy about her admiration for the man. Life was short. She had no time to be coy. Danny, Sean's brother, had said it was Sean's decision, but he thought Gina could be good for his brother. He made too many excuses to be alone.

Gina knew Sean wasn't alone. She knew who would always have the bigger piece of Sean's heart. She just wanted whatever pieces the dedicated brother could spare.

Sean wasn't going to dissuade her with the way he looked for their date—he'd worn a denim shirt tucked into jeans and worn-in boots, and he'd put a little something into his hair to keep it from flopping into his eyes. When he opened the door of the GTO for her, when the reality that this was finally happening as she settled into the creak of his classic car and was surrounded by his man heaven smell as his driver door closed, she had to press her fist hard against her galloping heart.

She brushed his sleeve before he could start the car.

"Thank you," she said, looking down at her lap. "Thank you for taking this second to see me as a woman and not a girl."

"Gina, I—"

"If this is the only night I get with you, I want to savor it," she said over him, still staring down at her lap, still jamming her fist against her heart as a light from the training center trailed over her simple velvet dress with its long sleeves and sweetheart neckline. "But I'm going to be so distracted by my hope that you'll kiss me goodnight. Could you kiss me now and get it out of the way?"

"Gina, let's not—"

"Please?" she said, finally looking at him. He was so beautiful in the half light that it was hard to keep her gaze on him. "How many women have left this car without at least a kiss?" She wasn't above begging. This was Sean Salinger. Women begging of him was the norm.

His heavy sigh created a cloud in the car, and Gina dropped her eyes to her lap again. She'd ruined it before their date had even begun. She did that a lot. Those lost two years before the hunters found and saved her had knocked askew parts of her that no amount of lore expertise and lifesaving could straighten. Or maybe she was just born this way. Born crooked and wr—

A creak of the seat and hot fingertips against her chin evaporated all thoughts from her brain.

"Just one kiss," he said, suddenly so close, puffs of his breath against her skin, his capable and callused hand sliding over her jaw. Those lips, his fabled mouth, touched hers, smoothed over like the slide of silk, then pushed forward, making her feel softness and heat, the tiniest wet cling of the inside of his lips against hers and the brush of his soft beard against her cheek. She remembered then to kiss too, to kiss back if it was only just this once, and when she did, a shock of heat bloomed like the first ray of sun over her lips until it seared her brain. He made a low, surprised sound in his throat, then let go of her chin and jerked back into the driver's seat.

As the GTO started up with a grumbly roar, she slid one hand into her shoulder-length wavy hair while she fingered her lips with the other hand. "A kiss has never felt that way before," she said.

"Jesus." Sean flipped on the radio and squealed out of the parking lot.

It was something that he turned down the volume by half several miles later.

The restaurant he pulled up to was something too. The parking lot where he parked in the far, far back roared with life, and the outside of the restaurant was a big thatched roof. It was a tiki hut over the heads of young, happy hipsters totally unaware of what went bump in the night. Inside, it was lively but still...romantic. Low lit with goofy tiki flares and strings of lights and people drinking out of coconuts but still special.

He gave his name for a reservation and the Hawaiian-shirt-wearing hostess led them to a round corner booth with two tiki torches and an elaborate island backdrop. She couldn't have been more surprised if he fucked her on the table.

She wanted to fuck him under the table.

"Danny likes the potstickers here," he said gruffly, not taking his eyes off the menu. They were about a foot apart on the round bench. It would be nothing to slide even closer. "They got a kick to 'em, but I know you're not against that. I usually get the bowl of fries, they got a kick too, and the burger. Most of the stuff's meant to share, but if you don't like that you can—"

"Thank you," she said, staring in wonder at his firm nose, his heavy-lidded and shy eyes, watching him do something as mundane as looking over a menu. "Thank you for bringing me here and—"

He put down his menu and gave that rain cloud sigh again. "Stop that." He scowled sideways at her. "Stop acting like I'm so special."

"But you are," she said. She was only telling the truth.

"Then stop acting like you're *not* special," he snapped back.

She closed her mouth without a response.

When the waiter came to ask them what they'd like to drink, Sean ordered for them both. That surprised her.

"What did you get me?" she asked.

"It's a rum drink," he said, looking down at his folded fingers. He had a fresh cut over one big knuckle. "They put fresh pineapple and cinnamon in it."

"I can order for myself."

He cocked her a glance from under his heavy eyelashes. "Maybe I didn't want you falling all over yourself thanking me for letting you have a glass of water," he said. The slightest edge of a smirk was how they'd been in training, out in the field, since she'd gotten back. They both put away what she so obviously felt for him when there were lives to be saved. "And I wanted you to try it. It reminds me of those empanadas you make. You don't like it, get something else."

She smiled at him and nodded. She was special. She knew that. This man, even when she'd been too young for him to want her the way she wanted him, had been a big part in helping her believe that.

"So how in the world did Danny convince you to step a foot into this place?" she asked.

Sean laughed, throwing his head back—they weren't going to fool themselves about the kind of diners and dives he preferred—and when he stretched his arm over the top of the booth, even though it was stretched away from her, she was immensely glad to see him relax.

They chatted for the next half hour about Danny's obsession with Yelp, now that they were settled in one place, about the trainees who had promise and the ones who'd probably walk away once their nightmares got better, and about where to get the best carne asada in Mexico City. Gina did like her drink, was pleased that it reminded Sean of her when he'd had it in his mouth, but got herself a good tequila with lots of ice and soda and lime for her next drink. She needed to keep her head about her. She went ahead and let him order food for her too, since he was on a roll, and was wide-eyed at how many dishes were set on their big table.

"Try a little bit of everything," he told her gruffly, a flush of color peeking up above his beard as he grabbed a green-onion-flecked meatball with his chopsticks. He must have realized he'd overdone it. "It's all good."

Again, if he was trying to drive her away with this date, he was doing it all wrong. He'd changed from the young, hip-rolling, side-smirking daredevil she'd fallen in love with when she was a girl. The thoughtful way he listened to her while he pulled on his beard, the reactions he let loose with his laugh lines, the meaning he put behind *we* and *us* and *ours* as he spoke, the trained talent and creative impulse she'd seen in his fight—declaring that the daredevil hadn't gone away—made him more devastating now. She swallowed her urge to say *thank you* again and dunked a fry in fiery hot chili oil.

"You ever think about settling there for good?" Sean asked. She'd been telling him about the city of Guanajuato, about heading to that beautiful canyon city to deal with a restless mummy in its famous mummy museum and staying for six months. "Leaving the life and maybe getting a faculty position in Mexico?"

It's what her mother would have wanted. Sean and Danny had been the ones who'd encouraged her to back up her lore training with a college degree. She'd cobbled together a few of them.

She traced her thumb over the small silver cross that always hung against her sternum. "You haven't left the life," she said. The foot of space between them on the round bench hadn't shrunk only because it allowed her to see his whole beautiful face. "And as you keep pointing out, you're much older than I am."

He wouldn't be distracted by her tease. "No, but we've settled down." He and his brother had a little house on the Academy grounds. A garage for Sean's baby. "There's gotta be someone...special there. You've been in Mexico a long time."

She traced the tip of the cross over her skin. Did her absence seem long to him too?

"There've been a few someones," she said quietly. She could feel the etch of her mother's metal. "No one special enough for me to tell them who I truly am."

His eyebrows furrowed deeper as his eyes dropped to her cross.

"No one special enough for me to share all my secrets."

Sean was the only one who knew that this tiny piece of silver was the only thing she had of her family. When she was young, after a forlorn cemetery ghost had reminded her of the people she'd lost, she'd sobbed in his arms and told him then that she'd pulled the cross from her mother's bloody hand.

If this had been the point of his date, if he'd planned to convince her to settle down and away, he'd failed spectacularly. She let go of the cross.

His brows slowly went thunderous. When she'd let go of the cross, his eyes had followed its descent to where it settled in between the full softness of her boobs rising above the body-hugging black velvet of her dress. If he needed confirmation that she was no longer that girl, that she was a full-grown woman who knew what she wanted, he had it.

He ripped his eyes away and took a long pull on his beer.

Her eyes widened when she heard the rattle of a steel drum in a side room. "Do they have a live band?" she asked, grabbing his hand. "Let's dance."

His eyes widened too. "I don't—"

But she was already dragging him out of the booth with her hunter's strength and pulling him to the side room. She was able to find a breath of space in the crush of bodies as the band played something that swung the hips, and there was no choice, in the press of people, but to move along with them, Sean's knee forced between her thighs and his hands going to her hips if he wanted to watch her back and she'd known—she'd known—that a man who fought like him had moves.

Madre de Dios, did he have moves.

All but pressed against his chest in the crowded room, she watched him scan the people behind her as they swayed, then look at the silver hoop in her ear as they dipped, and finally meet her eyes as he rolled her against him. She smiled, beyond thrilled. She was essentially riding his jeans-covered thigh and his hands were splayed around her waist. He gave a heavy-lidded smirk back.

Yeah, she was a brat who demanded her way and got it.

With the dance giving her permission to touch, she smoothed her palms up his strong, denim-covered chest. The heat in the room had loosened his hair product and a thick lank of dark blond fell onto his forehead. She finger-combed it back for him, taking the opportunity to wreck the rest of his style and make his hair hers.

"You've let your hair get so long," she said, breathless against the hard, hot, muscular reality of him.

"My dad would've dragged me by the ear to the barber," he said, smiling down at her, his words deep and low and just for her.

She ran her fingers over his ear and tugged on his lobe. "I'll cut it for you, if you want."

"You don't like long—" A couple bumped them hard, nearly teetering Gina off her heels, and Sean moved instantly to steady her. He grabbed her bare thigh.

His leg between hers had hiked her dress so high, the black velvet barely covered her ass.

Sean went preternaturally still, except for his hand. Like he couldn't help himself, his hand stroked over her thigh where it was the fullest. Gina had thick, strong thighs, but his engulfing hand made her feel overwhelmed. He could effortlessly hike her up around his hips if he chose to.

She gave a tiny helpless moan that should have been hidden in the blare of the band.

"Fuck," he muttered. He stepped back and she swayed without his support. Everyone made a lane. "C'mon." He turned and barely stopped to throw money on the table before she was following him out to the once-boisterous parking lot. It was quiet and half-empty now, the GTO lonely out in the hinterlands away from the parking lot lights. Sean's stomps in the gravel pounded like a drumbeat. Her heart banged in her ears.

As they reached the passenger side of the GTO, backed up against a row of trees, Sean jammed his hand into his pockets for his keys.

Was that it? Was that her only shot? "Sean, I..."

He spun on her as fast as the monsters they chased. "You gonna thank me again?" he demanded, big and hulking.

She'd stopped shying away from things that scared her when she was fifteen. "If that's what you want." She notched up her chin. "I'll go down on my knees and show you how grateful I am."

She started to do it too, sinking down, staring at his widening eyes as she slowly lowered.

He grabbed her biceps and yanked her up. "I want—" His glare went thunderous as his fingers flexed into her flesh.

The full moon caught the silver in his beard and the fire in his eyes. "I am soooo sorry..." she hissed softly. "That my decade-long desire for you is such a *big goddamn* imposition—"

He swung her around and shoved her back against the door, shocking her. The car was his baby.

"One time," he snarled, his fingers digging into her velvet-covered biceps. "We do this one time, work it out of your system, then we never talk about it again. You hear me?"

He was a huge, heaving predator looming over her in the moonlight, a killer who could snap her neck as easily as looking at her. He was the only man since the death of her father who made her feel safe. He was the loveliest creature she'd ever seen.

"Fine," she spat, hating the tears that leaped into her eyes. "Fine, you stupid cabrón, if one time is all you'll give a woman who's in love with y—"

"Goddammit." He wrapped his hand around the cross at her neck and thumped his knuckles against her sternum, between the soft rise of her breasts and against the bang of her heart. "You going to let me do this?" He searched her eyes. He was breaking her like a bronco. "You going to let me take care of you?"

She could feel then that he was gently rubbing his knuckles over the soft skin that rose above her neckline. Sean Salinger was touching her skin. At last. Finally. She could see every speck of color in his wild, sea-green eyes. She desperately wanted him to kiss her. "Yes, Sean." At last. "Please."

He was the one who made it to his knees. He put his hands on his precious car and slid down, tracing his nose down the middle of her as his joints popped and his palms squeaked over the car's surface. She stared in astonishment as Sean Salinger kneeled in front of her and rubbed his nose against the black velvet at the apex of her thighs.

"Fuck, you smell good," he said in a whiskey-soaked voice that sounded like it came from a dream.

Then his hands, those huge, scarred, callused hands that taught her how to hold a gun, pushed up the form-fitting velvet, stroked hot up her naked legs. He grunted like she'd kicked him in the balls when he saw her underwear: black and high-cut, bought just for him, her trimmed black bush framed in the see-through lace. He held her wide hips and stared. He looked at her like he'd been the one begging. Then he leaned close and...oh God...he inhaled. Breathed her in, eyes closed, those thick lashes sooty on his cheeks, like she was his favorite pie.

Had he dreamed of her too? She felt a bubble of giddy hysteria burst in her chest.

He pursed his lips, that gorgeous lush mouth she'd get in trouble for staring at instead of listening to the words coming out of it, and rubbed them tenderly over her lace-covered mound. She must be hallucinating. His tongue came out, pressed wet and soft against the lace, and there was just enough light to see how pink it was.

She gave a soft sob into the warm night air. Hopefully their waiter hadn't been a djinn. She didn't care if he had been. She'd happily stay in this moonlit parking lot until she was drained dry.

Sean Salinger, her teacher and mentor and friend, the only man she'd ever been in love with, looked up and met her eyes as he lipped at her through her panties, hooked fingers into the band, and pulled them down just enough to reveal her dark curls. "You going to let me take care of you?" he asked, a rumble as low as the GTO's engine, his heavy-lidded eyes on her.

She nodded desperately. If she tried to answer, she might cry.

Holding her gaze as securely as a devil's trap, he leaned in and pushed through her curls. She bit her lip—hard—and watched his tongue, Sean Salinger's soft, experienced tongue, rub across her hard, wet clit as he let her see who was doing this to her. He licked in deep and got a long, slow taste, his fingers pulling her panties down to just below his beard.

Then he closed his eyes and tilted his head, and she watched in helpless amazement as his glistening tongue moved. Against her clit. Against her cunt. She felt herself drip and started to shake and clutched at the car to keep herself standing, the sensation of what he was doing—Sean was licking her pussy—slamming into her pelvis like a witch's curse and making her lurch against those big hands still holding her.

He looked up at her and grinned, striking those priceless lines around his eyes, as his tongue moved and created shocks of pleasure. He knew how good he was. He knew exactly what he was doing. Then he yanked her panties farther down her legs, making her *meep*, yelp, then spread her thighs as he tilted his head to wedge his tongue deeper in, helping until the lace dug into her flesh. His hand rubbed up the inside of her leg and his thumb stroked at her.

She gave some crazy sound when she felt him push inside.

"Your pussy's so sweet," he growled against her, separating her curls with his free hand and moving his mouth against the shining, burgundy flesh. "Who knew baby girl had such a sugar-sweet pussy?"

"Chíngate, pendejo," she cursed. He was *inside* her, his thick thumb working inside her as he kissed and licked and sucked, luring the orgasm out of her, and it was all going to happen too fast. Was this her one time?

He grinned again as he moved this thumb in a circle, twisted his hand so he was cupping her ass, urging her to pump against his face. "Who knew baby girl had such a filthy mouth?"

Ohgodohgodohgodohgod. She didn't want it to be over so soon.

But his thumb was so thick, so, so agile, and she couldn't—she was dripping; she could hear the wetness of him fucking her. He had his lips pursed around her clit and he was sucking, rhythmic, warm sucks while he nursed at her and shoved her against his mouth like he was hungry, like her cunt was what he'd been starving for and she wanted to come like breathing but she didn't. She wanted to watch his face between her legs forever, but then he pulled out a butterfly knife hidden in his boot and sliced through the lace of her pretty new underwear and pulled her freed thigh over his strong, denim-covered shoulder and tilted his head so he could taste her insides and that was it.

She came riding Sean Salinger's face and Sean Salinger held her ass in his hands and forced her harder against his mouth and made grunting, growling sounds as he did it.

As her moans were about to die away, he shoved in another finger and aimed his wicked mouth back against her clit, and she burst into an orgasmic scream she barely suppressed.

The pleasure was otherworldly. The pleasure was why the things they chased said yes to the dark. She rode and rode and rode and barely realized minutes later that she'd stopped coming, propped back against the door, both legs on the ground but spread, as Sean kept the pleasure voluptuous, softly bringing her down licking and fondling and kissing all the wet, sensitive flesh. She felt like cream from her chi-chis to her knees.

Without strength, without muscle or bone, she put a hand over her eyes and started to cry.

"Hey," he said, immediately standing. She heard the scrape of his beard against his sleeve before his arms slid around her. "Hey—"

"No!" She shoved him back and opened the door behind her, sat down in the passenger seat, then she grabbed him by his belt and dragged him closer. Still crying, she worked to free the thick leather.

"Gina." He surrounded one of her hands. "Don't—"

"Ignore it," she said, sniffling and pushing his hand away. "Just let me." When he made another protesting sound, she said, "You said you'd take care of me."

She pulled the warm leather out of the dented silver buckle and went to work on the button at the top of his fly. She put her fingers inside the waistband and Sean's stomach, his vulnerable flesh, was warm and soft with silky hair against the back of her fingers. She shivered involuntarily and wiped at the tears on her cheek.

"Gina." His voice, soft and shamefully understanding, beckoned in a way that made it painful to deny. She didn't want to look up at him. She didn't want to see that her time was up.

She carefully pulled down the zipper against the bulge that pushed against it. In the moonlight, in the open fly of his jeans, against his black boxer briefs, he was beautiful. She leaned forward and nuzzled him through his underwear just like he'd nuzzled her.

He grunted when she did it. One huge hand gently stroked over her skull. "Girl," he said. "Sweetheart."

She opened her mouth—wide—and tilted her head to rub it over the ridge.

"Baby girl," and it was lovely to hear his breath picking up to a pant. "I never did anything. Did I? To make you think... To make you think that I..."

She didn't want to sob with him in her mouth. She pressed his hand against her hair and turned to kiss his palm. His calluses were as sleek as glass. "Never," she said fiercely. "You never. If you had, I wouldn't love you the way I do."

"Aw, baby," he said, full of regret, and she didn't want him to be sorry. She wasn't.

She pulled his briefs down and drew him out. He was singularly perfect and she held that perfection in her hands. She kissed that tiny, puckered mouth and licked the perfectly cut head, then she put her mouth around him and tasted. Sean Salinger was over her and around her and inside her. She put her hands inside his shirt, against his tense sides, and savored him. She relaxed her throat, slowly slid down his cock, and felt his fingers dig into her curls. She moaned deep in her throat.

"Fuck," he groaned. "Girl..."

She liked doing this—she loved him best, but she'd loved other men too, some only for an evening—and, when she took him deep, she liked the weak knees and the spasmed grip it caused. He gave a little thrust with his hips before he jerked back. Out. She licked her lips, smiled at his groan, watched him glisten from her in the moonlight.

Every fantasy she'd ever had was topped by the reality of him. "Your cock is better than I imagined."

"Jesus, fuck," he said. "You imagined this?"

She licked at his head, sucked at it, as she ran her fist up and down him. "Every time I touched myself."

She took him down again and he made a choked sound. She heard the door frame creak where he gripped it.

She worked him into her throat and loved the helpless sounds he was trying to swallow. This close to his body, he smelled like steel and forest. He smelled like the essence of her dreams.

"Sweetheart," he gasped. His touch was so sweet in her hair. "Honey."

She was going to drink him down.

His fingers gripped a handful of hair, not hurting, but it could have. "Gina." She stopped but kept him in her mouth.

He was breathing heavily. She heard things in the deep, dark woods sound like him. "I'm not as young as I was. Getting head. In my car." She heard him swallow. "From *you*." He swallowed again. "If you want anything else to happen..."

That had her letting him go. The head of his cock bumped her bottom lip as she looked up at him. She'd never learned to hide her hope from him.

He was still panting as his thumb ran down her cheek. "What?" he asked, smile lines appearing around his eyes. "You thought one piddly orgasm was all you were gonna get?"

Piddly? From any other man, that orgasm could have kept her satisfied for weeks.

He let go to put himself back in his briefs, then ran his thumb over her wet bottom lip. "I told you, Gina. We're gonna work this out of you." He put the tip of his thumb in her mouth and she ran her tongue over the pad. "Hard."

She gripped it with her teeth.

He bent down, leaned in, and replaced his thumb with his tongue. He pushed her back against the seat, scooched her halfway across the bench, and kissed her, deep and rich, one elbow beside her head, one big hand holding her face, and pressing in between her hitched-up thighs.

He lifted away so he could meet her eyes. A lock of hair was hanging down. She brushed it tenderly back. "I get to have you this one night," he said. "You giving yourself to me?"

She could smell herself on him. She'd marked him.

She would give him the rest of her life. But, for the first time, she let herself fully understand why Sean Salinger—her teacher and mentor and friend, who'd been to hell and back, and whose number one job was to watch out for his brother—might never be able to accept it.

She would give him what he could take. "Yes, Sean. This one night."

With eyes too full of emotion, his mouth began to descend to hers. Right before their lips touched, she breathed, "It's always night somewhere."

He huffed a surprise laugh against her mouth. When he kissed her again, when he restarted this endless night, he did it smiling.

All those years ago, he'd saved a feral girl and given her what no one else could.

Now she could give him hope too.

**THE END**

# CHAPTER FIVE

# The Proposal

*When I turned in my first draft of **Full Moon Over Freedom**, my second-chance, childhood friends, super steamy romance with a touch of bruja magic, I had several flashback scenes. My editor felt my focus on the past between my good-girl heroine, Juliana "Gillian" Armstrong, and her bad-boy, Nicky Mendoza, took away from their current love affair.*

*I cut those scenes but refused to leave them tucked away in my computer. The following scene takes place thirteen years before the events of **Full Moon Over Freedom** and will not spoil the book.*

**Content warning: discussion of parent's alcoholism**

***

Through the flames of the bonfire in front of the abandoned house on County Road 95, Gillian watched Nicky Mendoza and counted the sips of liquid courage she took from her red Solo cup.

*Fourteen. Fifteen. Sixteen.* She grimaced at every sip as she hid in a corral of friends.

She hadn't needed liquid courage when she'd given the valedictorian speech in front of the entire senior class and half the town, or when she'd sat in front of the three alumni from Brandeis who'd interviewed her for college admittance. She'd gotten a standing ovation for her speech and a full ride to the almost-Ivy outside of Boston.

Having dressed for the occasion—she wore a short pink skirt, white polo, and the only push-up bra she owned—she expected similar successful results when she spoke to Nicky.

Still, they'd barely said five words to each other in five years. And in those four years of high school and one year while she was away at Brandeis, Gillian hadn't acquired the expertise that would make it easier to approach her childhood friend and ask what she planned on asking of him.

Nicky had all the skills.

Looking over the rim of her cup, Gillian triangulated Lacey Mellon's slow perusal of Nicky through the shifting flames. He was worth perusing—standing near the keg, he leaned back on one big motorcycle boot, his black short-sleeved shirt hanging open, the bonfire's glow occasionally highlighting his smooth, brown, muscly torso. His dark hair fell into his face and past his shoulder; he laughed with Tommy Costa as he handed a bottle of water to Matt Hugh and took back his bloodied shirt. Fifteen minutes earlier, an obviously drunk Matt had been giving Tommy, who had a stutter, a hard time until Nicky intervened. Nicky had shucked his T-shirt to give Matt something to staunch his bloody nose.

Only Nicky, Gillian thought.

The excitement had died down and now Lacey, who Gillian knew from gossip had already had a turn with Nicky, was looking at him the way Gillian had looked at prestigious internships before she'd decided to return to Freedom for the summer to fix her family.

Gillian had to get to Nicky before she lost her chance. And her nerve.

After taking two big, shuddering gulps...*seventeen, eighteen*...she ducked out of her semi-circle of friends and poured out the rest of the beer as she walked just outside the light of the bonfire. The air beyond the heat of the fire on this early June night was a relief; inside the abandoned house—with its empty window frames, missing doors, and holes in the walls—it also had been sweltering. All the kids dancing in there now howled along to "Friends in Low Places."

Gillian thought longingly about her Friday night study group at Chum's, the campus coffee shop, and the acoustic indie artists that would sometimes play there.

Nicky stood alone, the keg just behind him.

She marched up to it on bare legs that wobbled, grabbed the tap, and aimed it into her cup.

"Hey, Nicky." It came out softer than she meant it to, trying to draw his attention without others noticing.

He turned around slowly and smiled at her in a way that made her feel like an ember had drifted inside her clothes.

"I was wondering if you were gonna say hi," he said low, his voice entirely different from the last time she'd heard it. His hair covered half his face, but one eye caught the firelight.

"You were?" This time, it was her voice that cracked.

Beer gurgled into her cup.

His grin grew on half of his full, soft mouth. She wanted to run her fingers through his hair then tuck it behind his ear and out of her way. She wanted to stare.

"Surprised to see you here," he said. "I heard you were in Boston."

She and Nicky had stopped hanging out once they got to high school (he certainly wasn't in her Honors and AP classes or attending student government meetings), so it had been on some mysterious day when she'd turned around and seen a long-haired boy all in black with cheekbones that could cut glass smile at another girl. She'd stopped dead in the crowded hall a minute later when she realized that the boy was Nicky. The metamorphosis of her shy, devoted friend to this beautiful bad boy with a dirty grin had been as fascinating as it had been shocking. When she'd seen glimpses of him loitering in the parking lot or hanging out under the bleachers at football games, it'd been like watching a dandelion seed grow into an orchid.

There seemed to be no ceiling to how hot he could get.

When she'd heard girls laughing and cawing in the locker room about Nicky's "talents," she'd had to give herself a peppermint-steeped limpia that night to focus. She'd been in the middle of midterms and needed her head on straight.

The fact that he'd noticed her now and knew she was at a college in Boston shouldn't surprise her in this town with so much gossip and so little to talk about. But it did.

"Watch it," he cautioned just as she felt beer splatter her sandal. Her cup was overflowing.

She let go of the tap, put the beer on the ground, and shook off her hand. She hated beer, which was unfortunate when everyone in your family expected you and your sisters to take over a bar one day.

"I'm just home for the summer," she said, tucking a curl that had escaped her headband behind her ear. She wished her hair had the soft shininess of Nicky's.

He straightened and shoved his hair out of the way. "Heard about your sister," he said softly. That little concerned crook above his dark eyebrows was the first familiar thing on his face. "How's she doing?"

There was only one sister everyone heard about. The baby, Sissy, kept to herself.

Last summer, her middle sister, Alex, had been forced to move to Chicago to avoid getting sent to juvie. The drama had worsened their parents' already shaky marriage.

But the last thing she wanted to discuss with Nicky was her family. That wasn't what she needed him for. Gillian smiled swiftly. "She's fine."

He bit the corner of his full bottom lip as he watched her. That habit had looked...different when they were kids. "Your dad doing any better?" he asked quietly.

She stiffened. Tucker Armstead's drinking was something that was not discussed—not by the town who admired the aspiring writer and home-town boy, not by her large and gregarious family who loved him, not within the four walls of her home. But Nicky had still been walking her home most days in middle school when her dad's erratic behavior started and had seen the high highs of the normally pleasant introvert rushing outside to play with them and the low lows of finding her dad on the couch and impossible to rouse. They'd smelled the sour sting of alcohol on Tucker's breath together.

With Nicky was the only time she'd ever cried about how angry she was that her mom wasn't doing more to help her dad stop.

She was here instead of improving her resume for grad school because Sissy had called to whisper that their dad's drinking had gotten worse since Alex had left. Her first day in town, Gillian had borrowed her cousin Joe's truck to take all the bottles she'd emptied to the recycling plant. She'd been furious her mom allowed them in the house. She woke her dad every morning for a three-mile walk, and she'd bought him a huge water bottle that she filled for him every day. She was going to fix this.

But those were things you discussed with a boyfriend. All she wanted from love-'em-and-leave-'em Nicky was what he was giving to so many girls.

"Everyone's fine." She lowered her voice to a whisper, hiding it in the roar of the bonfire and the shout of the music and the twang of drunken conversation around them. "I was wondering if I could ask you something?"

"Yeah." He stepped closer, close enough for her to see that perfectly shaped teardrop scar beneath his eye. "Anything."

He made her feel like there was an intimacy between them, even though they hadn't talked in years. But she didn't want others to notice Nicky working his come-hither skills on her.

"Not here." She nodded into the field, where the full moon lit up a row of old hay bales melting into the ground. "Meet me in a few minutes."

She had every confidence that Nicky was the right man for the job and would be interested in what she was offering. Still, by the time she saw him in the bright moonlight in the aisle between the hay bales, Gillian had shredded strands of straw into fifty-two pieces. She dusted off her hands, then motioned for him to step into the shadow of the bale with her in case others wandered back.

"You okay?" he said, leaning his shoulder into the bale. His shirt was still open, and all that smooth skin and lean muscle was just inches from her. He smelled like the bonfire. It wasn't a bad smell. "What's going on?"

Looking at him from this close sapped all her determination. If you didn't know that Nicky stood up to bullies and assholes, that he defended the kids who had a hard time defending themselves, you might think he was too pretty to talk to.

She dropped her eyes to the decaying hay around her feet. "I...um...I want to be with you." She couldn't hear anything but her pulse in her ears. "I haven't been with anyone else. I mean...I haven't gone all the way." She never allowed the unknown to dissuade her, but this was awful. "I'd like to go all the way with you," she whispered miserably.

"What?" he spat out. "Why?"

She wanted to hide behind the hay bale.

"I like you," she answered, honest and pathetic. "I trust you." She still did, even though it'd been years since they'd talked. "I..." He'd either say yes and give her what she wanted or he'd say no and she'd never see him again, but right now, she was asking this boy to be the first inside her, and she had to at least look at him.

She raised her eyes to his face, saw his black hair hanging in front of it, and reached up with a weak hand to push his hair behind his ear. His hair was so silky soft. "I think you're really gorgeous."

The muscles jumped in the hollow beneath his cheekbone. "Aren't you going back to Boston?"

What did that have to do with anything? She dropped her hand from his hair and gripped her fingers together. "Yes. But not until the end of August. We'd have all summer."

She didn't understand the look in his eyes and she didn't want him to say no. "Not that...not that I expect you to be with just me this summer. I know you don't do girlfriends."

He turned and slumped back against the hay. It was a relief to get a break from his eyes.

"So what are you asking?"

"For lessons. In...sex. I want you to teach me about sex."

He laughed, sharp and loud. "Are you fucking serious?"

She'd never in a million years thought he'd *laugh* at her.

"Virginity is a construct, but why should my first time be with a boy fumbling around in the dark?" she demanded, shoving off the hay to face him. He was looking down the row, not at her. "I don't want that. Why should I settle for that? Why shouldn't I learn from the best?"

"Jesus fucking Christ."

The way he said *fucking*, glaring away from her, was really hot, which humiliated her more. "I don't want anything from you that you're not already giving to a bunch of other girls."

She had a horrible, stomach-punching thought.

Gillian had never been without a date for a dance or a sorority event. She'd made out a little. But in Freedom, her overwhelming passion had been to be more than another high school girl who got pregnant. At Brandeis, she learned that who you knew could change your life. She wanted to know the right boys and Nicky could help get her ready for them.

In middle school, Gillian had known that Nicky had had a crush on her, even though he'd never said anything. It'd been nice, being looked at that way with no pressure for a response.

But what if he looked at her now and felt nothing? What if that crush she thought she could rely on had been a kid thing and now Gillian was just making a fool of herself?

"Fine," she shot out. Humiliation swamped her. "I'm sorry to bother you. I'll let you go back to the party so you can find a girl you're actually attracted to."

She turned to stomp off and get in her car and never, ever, ever again attend one of these stupid bonfires when he grabbed her elbow. He swung her back to face him.

He stared at her, long and hard and angry. Then he snatched her hand and pressed it against the front of his jeans. "This feel like I'm not attracted to you?"

His...penis, Nicky's dick, this part of Nicky, was thick and hard behind the soft denim, in the nest of her fingers he created with his hand. She startled when it kicked in her palm like a heartbeat.

"This is what you wanted, right?" he said, glaring at her as he shamelessly held her hand to him. "Why we're back here in the dark?"

Even through his jeans, this part of him was hot. She imagined that heat inside her. Her stomach did loop-de-loops. "You can sleep with everyone you want and be praised for it," she whispered, her voice shaky. "But girls are called sluts." Nicky with the homecoming queen...the news would burn down the gossip vine. "I trust you to protect me. I trust you to keep this private."

He yanked her between the bales and lifted her—lifted her—onto a shelf of hay.

He leaned against her knees, his hands near her hips. "You want me to be your dirty little secret?" he asked. The height of the bales hid them in the shadows. "How's this for dark? Not even La Llorona could find you back here."

She inhaled quickly, as much fear as excitement.

He'd been about to tag her on the playground the first time she'd seen Nicky stop short, launch himself backwards, and trip to the ground with his hands over his eyes. She'd known instantly that he was seeing something that wasn't there, just like she sometimes saw or heard La Llorona near the Viridescent River when no one else could. When he'd come back to school a couple of days later, she'd told him about the wailing ghost. Wide-eyed, he told her about the phantom black dog, and the medicine the doctor made him take that didn't chase the cadejo away but only made Nicky sleepy.

During their friendship, he'd begrudgingly followed her to the river to fish or jump off the rope swing or catch crawdads. She refused to let what they were afraid of make them afraid.

His saying *La Llorona* felt like it was summoning what haunted them to watch these two old friends dare to do what they were about to do.

"Spread your legs," he whispered, a hazy outline giving off heat, and she sucked in a breath, shocked and overwhelmed by what he was saying to her in the dark. Shakily, she did as he asked, felt the old straw slide and prickle against her skin.

He moved closer, the warm denim at his hips sliding between her knees, and put his hands on her thighs.

She shivered like a ghost had walked over her grave.

His thumbs raised goose bumps as they slowly smoothed back and forth over the inner curves of her thighs. "No one knows your body better than you." She could feel the rough scratch of calluses against that tender skin. "I know some stuff…" He leaned forward, and she lifted her chin for his kiss—finally, she'd get to know what those lips felt like—but instead, he kissed the underside of her jaw, and it made her stiffen and shiver and shift at the same time.

He licked and she made the weirdest sound.

"But only you know what feels good for you. You gotta talk to me." His voice was like nectar a bee would follow. "Can I touch your pussy?"

She gasped out into the night air as he licked a spot on her neck. The inch of skin he was stroking on the tender insides of her thighs felt as sensitive as the wet flesh between them.

The bees following his honeysuckle voice had set up shop in her brain. And her pelvis. She shifted against the hay.

"Gillian?"

"Hm?"

"Can I play with your cunt?"

Everything between her legs surged and got wet. Her knees spasmed around his hips and she grabbed onto his biceps to have something to cling to. "Yes, please, please, oh God…yes, please, Nicky."

He pressed one finger against the warm, soft, wet center of her cotton panties as he bit the tendon of her neck, his hair against her cheek, and she squeaked and jumped and shoved her hips against his finger all at once.

"Good," he breathed.

She sucked in a breath, gripped his muscled arms tight, as he rubbed his finger up and down, up and down her crease through her panties while he kissed the sensitive skin just above her collar.

"You smell as sweet as a peach."

He bit her like she was the fruit he was going to sink his teeth into. She widened her thighs, wanted that finger inside.

"Gillian?"

She dug her nails into his arm with a whimper.

"What do you want, girl? I said you've got to talk to me."

She rolled her hips against that blunt fingertip.

That fingertip pulled away.

Teeth pulled at her earlobe. "Does that feel good?" She could feel his voice in the pit of her stomach. "Do you want me to keep touching you?"

He flicked his finger over her, and she nodded so hard her dangly earrings chimed. She had magic, she knew magic, she recognized it in others.

This was Nicky's.

"Then use your words. You want to be good at this, right?"

Just because she wanted to be methodical about sex didn't mean she wanted it less than other kids her age. She thought about it *all the time*. It was like Nicky knew and heard and understood her quietest, dirtiest wishes.

She wanted to be *great* at this.

"Touch my... Touch me. Right there." His finger flicked again. "Please, right there. I've never...I mean, not with anyone else. Only by myself." He sucked hard on her neck and she moaned out into the night. "Kiss me."

He did kiss her. As he dipped beneath her panties, he kissed her neck like her pulse kept him breathing. When he touched between her folds, when he touched her clitoris and made her jump at how sensitive it was, he made her ear feel pornographic. When he pushed a finger into just the opening of her, made her gyrate her hips up against his hand and rubbed light then hard, fast then slow, with his thumb, he bit at her nipple through her polo shirt and bra.

His touch would lighten whenever she went silent, so she whispered out gasps and moans.

"Yes...there...no...a little over...it's so...I'm so wet...ah...no, no cir-cles...deeper...god, yes...Nicky, please, please, kiss me..."

But he didn't kiss her mouth. And her lips kept hoping as the crest she could reach in bed with a lot of work and concentration kept moving out of reach.

She panted against his jaw. "Kiss me, kiss me, I can't unless you—"

She heard voices and stiffened.

"You're so hot," a girl said, slurring, then another girl said, "No, you're so fucking hot."

They were giggling and thumping off the hay bales like pinballs as they bounced closer.

"They're coming back here," she whispered, panic at the edge of her voice. "They might see us."

His stroke on her clitoris was softer but hadn't left her. He panted against her neck. Then he turned his hand and slid in another finger along with the first, crooking them both up deep inside her.

"What are you doing? They might find us," she gasped through her teeth. She felt voluptuous warmth flood out and, by the evil huff against her neck, so did he.

"I think my good girl might like being a little bad," he growled into her ear. "If you don't want them to see, you better come before they do."

He did some filthy, sucking thing to her ear as his free hand covered her mouth and he gave her what she'd begged for.

He gave her a lesson. He showed her what her body could do.

Biting into his palm, she came all over his hand.

Then he picked her up, threw her over his shoulder, and ran farther back into the field, only the moon witnessing their escape.

**THE END**

Learn more about **Full Moon Over Freedom**, named top 10 romance of 2023 by *The Washington Post*.

*"Lopez works her own brand of literary brujeria in the second vibrantly written addition to her Milagro Street series...by crafting a scorchingly sensual love story."—Booklist,* ★ Starred Review

Gillian Armstead-Bancroft—class valedictorian, Pride of the East Side, and once-perfect bruja, wife, and mother—is going to spend her summer getting good at being bad.

The first time she left Freedom, Kansas, behind, she did it by doing everything right. This time, she'll hide from the large Mexican American family welcoming her home and work in secret to break the curse that's erased her magical life. Only by doing it all wrong can Gillian get herself and her two children away from the ghosts of her hometown by summer's end.

Nicky Mendoza is an answer to her prayers. He was the practical solution to the problem of her virginity when they were younger, and now, as a gorgeous artist only in town for a weekend, he's the ideal man to launch her down the path of ruination.

But Gillian isn't the only one who's cursed. Nicky has been plagued by his furtive, enduring love for her as long as he's been haunted by his cadejo, the phantom black dog that stalks his psyche. He'll stick around to be whatever Gillian needs him to be this summer—but he won't touch her. Touching her, then watching her leave again, will ruin him for good.

**_Order now._**

# CHAPTER SIX

# Hot Pockets

*This story is a favorite of mine. It's probably the most "real people" love story I've ever written. I wrote it for **Best Women's Erotica of the Year, Vol. 7** in 2020. The annual erotica collection regularly highlights some of the best and hottest writing in romance, and when they asked me to contribute, I knew I'd made it!*

*I'm not the only one who loves this story. It's highlighted in this podcast with Best Women's Erotica editor Rachel Kramer Brussel. And if you want to listen to it in audiobook, Rose Caraway does a great narration on her podcast, Kiss Me Quick Erotica.*

P.S. The short stories in this collection were written over a span of ten years. I realized when the collection was edited that the heroine of this story has the same name as the heroine in *The Phone Call* and *Star 69*. I'm going to maintain the names, but they are different people.

***

Rosemarie took a final tired look around the baby's room and was about to turn off the light when she noticed smudges on the switch. Chocolate? She rubbed the switch clean with the bottom of her nightshirt, then turned it off. She leaned over to scoop up the kids' dirty sheets and groaned when she straightened. That groan was becoming more common.

She tossed the sheets to the bottom of the stairs and then looked through her bedroom doorway.

The last room to tackle.

The mid-morning sunlight warming the room and the halcyon call of the rumpled bed made tackling it the last thing she wanted to do. Right now, their little chaotic house was calm and quiet and almost clean.

Five minutes, Rosemarie told herself as she dropped the bucket of cleaning supplies and collapsed facedown on Jacob's side, her bear-claw-slippered feet on the floor and her blue-satin-undied ass poking out. If she crawled all the way onto the bed, she'd be out. Just like this, halfway on and halfway off, for five minutes, with the sun on her face, her eyelashes still tacky with the mascara she hadn't gotten around to removing after work and Friday night pizza and a Disney movie.

The squished-up sheets gave off the clean-skin scent of her husband, who always smelled like fresh-cut grass, even when he'd been camping in the Blue Ridge Mountains for four days.

She kind of resented how good he always smelled.

She was so grateful Jacob had started taking charge of Saturday morning sports and birthday parties, leaving her to get to the housecleaning. She was grateful their therapist had recommended it. When she was young and envisioned growing old with Jacob, she imagined they would only fight over impossible stuff: the billionaire who wanted to steal Rosemarie away, the movie star who Jacob would ultimately resist.

She never imagined getting into scary hissing matches—hissing because they wanted to scream but didn't want to wake the babies—over the dishes. She never imagined Jacob storming out because of a disagreement over a closet rack. She'd thrown a dried flower arrangement at him when Naomi needed to be picked up in the middle of the night—again—because she didn't want to stay at the sleepover she'd begged to attend.

The cut under Jacob's eye from the distressed wooden flower box had been Rosemarie's last straw. They needed help.

It wasn't that one of them hadn't been doing enough. They were both doing too much: work, kids, house, parents. Jacob's dad moving in had been necessary but awful in the beginning. And there'd been no clear delineation of duties, so they both felt they were half-assing and doubling up and overseeing and being analyzed on everything.

It was embarrassing to be in your early thirties and need a chore chart.

That chore chart had saved them, giving Rosemarie her husband back. But in some ways, it took him further away. Because now, as a hard-working, double-booked mom of three kids, she never got to see the hard-working, double-booked father of her three children.

Much less fuck him.

"Date nights" the therapist said. Rosemarie and Jacob looked at each other and thought about his father's slow slide into dementia and their bank balance and their therapist bills. And they laughed.

"Patience," the therapist then advised. "This is just a period in your lives."

"Find pockets of time."

Well, their pockets had been coming up empty. And they'd promised forever.

Rosemarie curled her husband's sweet-smelling sheets around her face and gave herself two more minutes.

She blinked awake when she heard a groan. She hadn't slept long, but she'd slept hard, and waking up was like swimming through tub water. She heard quick steps and then a thump directly behind her, in the direction of her exposed blue-satin bottom and oversized slippers.

"Jacob?" she mumbled groggily, hoping the kids weren't standing in the room with him, but too cozy to fuss much or even bother to open her eyes all the way.

"Shhhhh," he hushed her, an urgent note in the sound. Then she felt her Snoopy nightshirt sliding up, and lips, warm lips, giving soft, wet touches to the small of her back.

Bursts of heat, like those fast-motion images of flowers opening, bloomed where his lips kissed. "Jacob, what..."

He straightened, and her husband—her mild-mannered, assistant-coach, moving-company-manager husband—grabbed two hard handfuls of her satin-covered ass.

"Gotta..." His tongue licked at the base of her spine and liquid heat shot down her thighs. "Forgot the juice boxes. Libby's watching dad and the kids. Just let me ..." Then his mouth—his lips and his tongue and even his teeth—followed his fingers as they dragged her panties down, abandoning them at the bend of her knees.

Rosemarie wondered if she was still dreaming when he ran his tongue back up between her thighs, anchored both hands at the small of her back, then licked, stroked, swirled, and burrowed his tongue into her.

Her arms were buried beneath her, and her head felt heavy with shock and sleep, and she was making helpless *uh-uh-uh-uh-uh* sounds into the mattress.

Her husband was making her fuck his face; she'd never felt so bonelessly out of control.

"God, Rosie, your taste. Forgot how creamy you are." There was the soft clink and clang of belt and zipper before his strong, baby-catching hands bit into her hips. "Let me, Rosie, you gotta let me..."

She slid her trembling thighs as wide as her panties would let her. "Please," she begged, feeling needy and bountiful at the same time.

Jacob pushed into her, slow and hard, until he hit deep. He held himself motionless and she heard his heavy breaths.

"It feels so good in here."

Rosemarie couldn't be bothered to move her warm arms from underneath her or even lift her face from its nest in the sheets. But she arched her spine, letting her muscles grab at him. He gasped low.

The mattress shifted as he dug his fists into it. He started to move, pushing his hips into her, and although he'd screwed up his back helping with the neighbor's roof, he still could do that thing, that rolling thing that hit that spot, that spot that made her shriek the first time he'd touched it when she was nineteen and made him look at her with shocked pride. She moaned into the sheets as her body gobbled him up, gripped every inch of him, rippling and flowing around him. His panting breath sounded like it was coming through his teeth. She could smell the clean sweat of his morning in the sun, and it had her straightening her legs around him, pointing the stuffed claws of her slippers into the wood floor and using her thighs and ass to squeeze him harder, love him deeper. She was melting over him.

He moaned helplessly, "Ah...don't...I don't want to...God, you've got me...please..." His words—pleading words from a man who owned her everything—sent the orgasm rolling over her like a drowning wave. She squeezed him mercilessly, and he grabbed her shoulders, shoving hard inside her and yelling. It shocked her, that primal sound in their sweet house, and she jolted, squeezing him until he groaned, and the cock that she'd never had a disagreement with kicked, and she gasped and shuddered and he yelped and she laughed then he laughed and then... Oh God, they were going to suffocate and die like this.

They'd be found dead and cold with his cock in her cunt and crazy grins on their faces. And her in her bear slippers.

She giggled so hard she shook him where he'd slumped on top of her, also laughing. His dick trembled out.

"Get off," she gasped. "I can't breathe."

He slid to the side with an *oof*.

She finally lifted her face from the sheet and the air was cool and smelled of sex and Pine-Sol. She turned to look at him.

He was staring up at the ceiling with a goofy grin and awed-wide eyes. "I'm gonna stop declaring my hatred of Saturday mornings."

She frowned. "Do you hate Saturday morning?"

She thought he liked the T-ball practices and stalking the Target toy aisles with the kids for sales so that the birthday party gifts didn't bankrupt them.

He turned to look at her. His lashes were so thick, they felt like kitten fur when she rubbed her thumbs over them. "No," he said softly. "But remember what Saturday mornings used to be like?"

Long mornings in bed that often blended into early afternoons. Some Saturdays all they'd accomplish was ordering a supreme pan pizza. They hadn't had a TV in their room but hadn't lacked for entertainment. Their twin bed meant that only one person could lie on their back at a time. They'd slotted together like a peg and board.

"They'll be like that again," she whispered.

"This is just a period in our life," he said.

"We'll find pockets of time."

"This was one hell of a pocket."

She felt almost dizzy with possibility.

"How hard was it to get away?

***

The next weekend, Jacob found her in the living room, finishing the vacuuming. He told Libby he'd forgotten the Goldfish this time.

As he was squeezing her nipple through her nightshirt and backing her toward the ottoman, he murmured, "God, I love these little cotton nightgowns."

She pulled her mouth from his earlobe with a wet suck. "You do?"

His big hands smoothed down the plain yellow nightshirt with white buttons, over a waist that wasn't so small anymore and hips that weren't as sleek. "Yeah. Why wouldn't I?"

"Just…" He pushed her down on the ottoman and kinda loomed over her, and her voice went weird and breathy. "I thought you'd like sexy push-up bras or crotchless panties or…"

He smiled right into her face. She suddenly felt like a little lamb about to be eaten, like she didn't have fifteen years of bossing him around at her disposal.

"Rosie, I don't need anything fancy."

But then he showed her fancy when he twisted her on the ottoman, flipped her head where her hips used to be like she was an arrow in a spinner game, and buried his head between her legs, getting her panties nice and soaked with teasing before he ripped them down her legs and really went to work.

Rosemarie helplessly thumped at his jeans with her hands before he was nice enough to unzip and get his cock out, put his knees up on the ottoman, and carefully and gentlemanly fuck her throat.

She came with a wail and Jacob had to shower and Rosemarie had to find the fabric cleaner for the ottoman.

Libby was not too happy with him when he showed up. Without Goldfish.

***

For the next six days, Rosemarie felt seventeen again.

Her husband flirted with her. He gave her long, lusty looks from under his kitten-soft lashes. She put on lipstick for him and left kiss prints on his side of the mirror and on his lunchbox Tupperware and centered on the crotch of the boxers at the top of his underwear drawer. They sat too close on the couch, and his dad privately warned him that if he knocked up the Thompson girl, there'd be no college for him. Jacob gently reminded him that he'd already knocked her up. Three times.

Each kid individually asked in their own unique way for them to stop acting so weird.

They didn't have sex during the week for the same reasons they normally didn't have sex—too busy and too tired. But whether she was crashing into sleep or tossing and turning with her standard worries, there was a low hum in their bed that grew as every day passed. When her husband gave her an exhausted smile right before he turned off his bedside lamp, she knew he was thinking the same thing she was.

*Six more days till Saturday.*

*Five more days till Saturday.*

*Four more days...*

*Three more days...*

*Two...*

*One...*

But when Saturday came, Rosemarie was taking forever to put the cleaning supplies back under the sink and thinking that, really, she should have changed out of her nightshirt and into real clothes already when she got the text from Jacob.

*Rosie.*

*So sorry.*

*Libby didn't come to game.*

*At second birthday party.*

*We'll be home in an hour.*

*I love you.*

Well, she had an hour.

Rosemarie sat on her kitchen floor in her nightshirt and cried for thirty minutes.

***

Then, as is the way of things, just when they thought they were geniuses who'd figured out what no one else could:

A kid was sick and home the next weekend.

The other two caught it and were home the following week.

A spring thunderstorm soaked the ball fields the week after that.

And then, terrifyingly, Jacob's dad fell. It was only a broken wrist, but Rosemarie and Jacob had to have a serious conversation about whether they were providing the best care and whether they could afford anything else. The doctor reassured them that, yes, they were doing a good job. But, for two weeks, it felt evil to want anything for themselves.

The next weekend, when Rosemarie was helping load the fruit snacks and juice boxes into the minivan in her knit pajama pants, Jacob grabbed her pinkie with his through the driver-side window. "Maybe that just wasn't our pocket," he said, shaking her hand. "We'll keep searching."

She smiled but saw the same suck-it-up sorrow on his face. Because when? When would they have the time to look?

***

So it was one hell of a surprise the following weekend to hear everyone banging home just twenty minutes after they'd left, and the TV come on, and then to watch her wild-haired husband charge through the bedroom door to grab her and shove her back against it.

He kissed like he'd been slowly suffocating since he'd gotten in the van. He kissed her like it was the only way he could breathe.

"Jacob." She trembled against his mouth, tasting his breath and the familiar steam of his tongue.

He shoved her nightgown up to her shoulders. "Fuck pockets, Rosie," he growled against her nipple before sucking on it and sending her up on her toes. "Let's just rip a hole in the material if we have to."

She let out a sob that she hoped was drowned out by *PAW Patrol*'s latest rescue.

She got her hands in his jeans just as he buried his hand in her panties. They could jack each other off as well as they could do themselves—they'd never lost those terrified, furtive arts they learned before they visited Planned Parenthood—but she wanted so much more than that. She was all but crawling up him and pushing down his pants with her bare feet when the door tried to come open at her back.

"Mommy, can we…"

Two fingers inside her, his callused thumb rubbing so good and sweet, Jacob shoved her back to keep the door closed. Her man had love handles and big, strong arms.

He paused as she took a gulping breath. "You need anything, baby?" she called.

"Can we open the doughnuts?"

Their eldest knew the doughnuts were for Sunday, and he had the kind of sweet tooth they were trying to put a kibosh on…

"I'll make sure to share with the girls, and Papi only gets one."

Their eldest was the wiliest kid and the best big brother around.

"Yeah, baby. Thanks for asking."

Her husband looked her in the eyes, smiling, knowing, as he slowly worked those two fingers in her, swirling, testing, then pulled them out. He slid her a little up the door, put his cock to her pussy, and let her slip slowly down onto it.

She bit her lip, and his eyes went heavy at the thick, liquid, tight, full, hot sensation, like they were both feeling the same thing. She arched up high on the ball of her foot while the other thigh gripped his hip. He squatted to push in deep. They weren't going to be able to do it like this for long.

They wouldn't need long.

Jacob was rocking into her, into her, and thank God for old houses and not being able to find a plumb line anywhere because the door stuck in the jamb just enough to keep it from thumping.

Still, Rosemarie made a sound and Jacob groaned "Rosie," before pushing their mouths together as tight as the stuck door, and here, she suddenly realized, here they'd found their pocket. Here, she could be as loud as she wanted. Here, he could be as filthy as he could dream up. Here, in the rips that they would tear, in five seconds here and five minutes there and twenty minutes when they got really spoiled, they could celebrate with their mouths and minds and the magic of their bodies what they had, and have, and would have for years to come.

She cried as she came, and Jacob kissed away her tears.

They swiped clean with washcloths. Rosemarie pulled on the first thing she could find. Then they walked downstairs holding hands and took their family into the summer sun, letting the screen door close on the dirty house and the blinking phones and the birthday presents, and, instead, filled this little tear with only what they wanted to carry.

**THE END**

# CHAPTER SEVEN

# In the Stacks

*I wrote this story for for Read Me Romance, a podcast featuring steamy romance audiobooks hosted by the* New York Times*-bestselling author-duo Alexa Riley. We authors are invited to suggest audiobook narrators for our episodes, so I grabbed the chance to have my first male narrator. Narrator Gregory Salinas knocks the steamy scenes out of the park! Go here to listen—the narration begins after some chatting!*

**Content warning: Exhibitionism, voyeurism, stranger sex, dirty talk**

***

She was too old for this.

At thirty-two years old, Rosalia Salvador felt too old for everything she'd been doing: quitting her job as in-house legal counsel, going back to school, moving into a tiny two-bedroom place in Pilsen with three people. Rosalia had been thrilled to get into Loyola University's prestigious Latine Studies program. Talking and learning about her people lit her up in a way that terrifying the workers and protecting her bosses' asses hadn't. Then she'd been instantly freaked out by the new student loans.

She was deeply grateful that the university had hooked her up with three other non-traditional graduate students who were trying to keep living costs low, but the woman who slept in the other twin bed in their tiny room meant that Rosalia was now doing what she was way too old to be doing back in the stacks of the massive university library.

It wasn't just the smell of books, the privacy of this nook, and all the knowledge swirling around that turned her on. An overpacked class schedule, never-ending assignments, no downtime, lack of privacy, and the occasional burst of rough men's voices as they worked on the library expansion on the closed floors above her conspired to make this study nook at the far end of the stacks with its fifties-era wooden desk and pull-chain lamp a perfect spot for a little me time.

She hadn't been able to resist on Tuesday when she'd come across some inspiring pictures while reading López Austin's *Sexuality in Mesoamerican Tradition*. To make it easier today, she'd worn a skirt.

With her books and notes piled high around her, and her knee up on the desk edge, Rosalia bit her lip and, eyes closed behind her glasses, imagined being a beautiful *ahuianime* giving pleasure to a group of victorious warriors returned home from battle. Her finger worked faster as she fantasized that a jaguar warrior devoured her between her thighs, the teeth of his pelt brushing her skin, while another man, smelling of copal and wildfires, thrust between her—

"Hey."

She ripped her hand out of her panties as she opened her eyes to see a man in a white T-shirt and jeans standing beside her, a hard hat under his arm and both hands held out. Although he looked like one of the dark-skinned, hook-nosed, black-haired warriors out of her fantasies, that didn't stop her instinct to scream.

"Shhh, shh, hey, hey, hey, I'm sorry, I'm not gonna hurt you," he whispered urgently, eyes wide. "Just—quick, put your knee down." He actually touched her knee.

The searing heat of his finger made her lurch upright, her foot stomping to the tile.

"Shh," he whispered, then put down his hands.

"What's the commotion back here?" A squinty-eyed male librarian shoved a book cart around the corner, scowling. Rosalia had had a run-in with the man before when she'd tried to check out a mislabeled reference book; the little Napolean had acted like she was stealing the crown jewels.

She straightened and made sure her skirt was pulled down over her thigh-high tights.

"No problem, sir," the construction worker said quickly. He pulled a yellow meter out of his back pocket and held it up, his full mouth stretching into a wide, convincing smile. The glaring halogens glowed in his short, dark hair brushed back into neat waves. "Just down here taking sound readings and I startled this poor lady."

The librarian's eyes narrowed into suspicious slits. "Don't make me talk to your foreman again."

The worker's smile went wider. He had a dimple and the whitest teeth. "Okey dokey. Don't worry."

The librarian gave her a dark once-over before he continued pushing the cart down the long aisle, the squeal of one wheel mocking his demand for silence.

Rosalia kept her eyes on his rust-colored cardigan until he turned the corner, her humiliation rising to her tortoiseshell glasses.

"Sorry," the worker said beside her. His voice was velvety soft. "I didn't want that asshole catching you doing that."

She planted her elbows on the desk and covered her face. "Oh my God," she moaned, beyond mortified. "I would have been banned from the library and charged with public indecency." The banning from the library would have actually been the worst part. She didn't have to start her thesis until next year, but she needed these resources. "I am so sorry." This poor man. What a thing to stumble upon. "You're just trying to do your job and you come down here to find some pervert—"

"Hey," he said gruffly. "Look, I was sent to this floor on Tuesday to take sound readings and I...saw you. But today, when my foreman tried to send one of my buddies I..." He cleared his throat. "I volunteered."

She spread her fingers and looked between them. "You were watching?" she whispered shrilly. She'd seen more people today in Section 972 than she'd seen since she'd discovered this preciously private nook a month ago.

"Yeah," he said. His eyes met hers cautiously. He had the darkest, thickest lashes. "Yeah, I was watching you."

He held her gaze. He was younger than she was, probably in his late twenties, but as she watched the muscles work in his jaw where an afternoon shadow was already appearing, she thought that maybe he wasn't that much younger. The way he was watching her certainly didn't make her feel old.

He pressed his lips together—they were really good lips—and her mouth went dry.

Rosalia lowered her hands and pulled again at the edge of her corduroy skirt.

He leaned on one work boot and lowered his hard hat to tap it against his thigh. "On Tuesday when I saw you...doing your business, I turned around and left. Coming back in here today to find you"—his voice dipped low—"touching yourself again..."

The side of his mouth cocked into a wary smile.

"Honey, I'm sorry but my halo's a little too bent to be that much of a saint."

What would she have done if she'd stumbled upon this creature enjoying what he thought was a private moment? She could just imagine him with his eyes closed and strong chest heaving, stroking himself through those worn jeans.

She blinked away the steam in her eyes. "What's a sound reading?"

He handed her the meter. "Part of our contract with the library says we have to keep construction noise below a certain decibel level. We walk through and check it."

As she reached for the meter, he hung on a second too long. "I'm going to be taking all the sound readings from now on."

She huffed an embarrassed laugh. "All future testing will be uneventful."

"No judgment, sweetheart, but is your man not taking good care of you?" he asked as he let go of the meter. His gentle *sweethearts* and *honeys* were sprinkles on the way he was looking at her. She couldn't remember the last time she'd been looked at that way; her high-paying corporate job hadn't allowed any more time for it than her academic poverty.

She ran her thumb over the gauge of the meter. "There's no time for a man." She put the meter down and began rummaging through her stack of books. "There's no time for anything but classes and classwork and..." She told him about her small, shared room and sleeping roommate and packed schedule, about the barely treading water feeling she hadn't shared with anyone, as she found the book she was looking for then flipped to the right page.

"On Tuesday, I saw this." She handed him the open book. She watched him take in the ancient illustration of a feather-capped woman enjoying her place as the filling in a Mexica soldier sandwich.

He gave a wide-eyed *huh*. Then he shifted his hips and cleared his throat.

"Who knew this filth was hiding in the library shelves?" he mused. "Maybe I *should've* invited my buddies down to—"

He looked up with a devilish smile when she made a sound. "Totally kidding, sweetheart." He smiled like a naughty altar boy. "Only kidding."

He took another long look before he closed the book reverently and handed it back to her. She put it on top of her stack then handed him his meter. When he took it, their fingers brushed, and the spark raced all the way up her arm.

"My cousins are on this job too, and we're all living together to save money to start our own construction company," he said, returning the meter to his back pocket. "I got to build my private time around their food-and-beer runs. Doesn't make for a very satisfying experience. I'm sorry if I ruined yours."

He put the hard hat under his bulging brown bicep. It would be a short trip to returning to his head.

"Thank you for protecting me," she said softly. She lowered her eyes to her lap and hoped he'd leave without making her watch him go.

The hot jerk just stood there.

"I want you to know," he said quietly, "when I saw you touching yourself, your eyes squeezed tight behind your glasses, so lost in making yourself feel good, I thought I was hallucinating. My cousins say I walk around with my head in the clouds, but you—truly—are a perfect fucking fantasy."

Life had been so real lately. It was a good real, but it underlined the fact that adulting was hard. The last thing Rosalia had thought she had the capacity to be in all her good-but-hard realness was a decent man's perfect fantasy.

She pushed up her glasses before they slipped off her nose. "Really?"

Hope, happiness, and heat flashed over his face. "Hell yes." He swallowed, the motion obvious in his strong neck as he stood close in her little nook. "You know the only thing that's missing?"

She shook her head, her ponytail swishing against her sweater.

"Seeing you come."

She put her hand over her mouth without looking away. His velvety words floated like bath bubbles in the tiny space. She couldn't believe this was happening. She couldn't believe what she was contemplating.

The delighted smile he gave her echoed the one behind her hand.

"Sweet Jesus, baby, look at the way you blush. Smart *and* sweet *and* hot as fuck." He slowly lowered himself to his knees on the tile. "Look, I'll shut the fuck up," he murmured as he shuffled closer. He smelled like plaster dust and the last whiff of aftershave. "I'll go back to my hiding place. You won't even know I'm alive. But please, please, please, baby." Each *please* got a little more groany. "Please finish what I interrupted."

She shoved the words out of her mouth before she chickened out. "Do you want to stay here and watch?"

He fell back onto his heels and closed his eyes. "Fuck," he groaned. His lashes were thick and black against his skin. He adjusted his hard-on in his jeans, not even trying to hide it, before he dropped his hand. He opened his gorgeous eyes. "Yeah. Please."

"I like the way you talk to me," Rosalia said, her fingers curling on the desk. "No one's ever talked to me like this before."

This time he did give himself a good stroke. "You like a dirty mouth?" he asked. "You like the words?"

She nodded again.

"Good God damn." She winced as he flicked the pole of his cock like he was keeping it in line. "Okay." He got back up on his knees and slid closer. He put his hard hat on the old tile, then reached for her right hand on the desk. He stopped just before his fingers touched her skin.

"May I?" he asked, serious as he met her eyes.

He'd seen her masturbating in public. She'd just given him permission to watch her do it again. Yet he still asked before he touched her. The moment felt loaded with something she couldn't untangle as she nodded then verbalized, "Yes."

His workman's fingers slipped over her pen calluses as he lifted her right hand from the desk and, again, the heat from his touch was uniquely heart-shocking.

"Because I'm wired special," he said, stroking his darker thumb over her index and middle fingers, "I haven't forgotten that while you were covering your face with your hands then touching my meter then showing me the dirty pictures in your book, these two fingers were getting tacky with your pussy juice."

Oh God.

"Let me just…"

Rosalia saw his intent the second before he did it, and her eyes went wide as he slid her fingers in between his soft lips. He watched her as he sucked, slowly pulling her fingers out, and she could feel the stroke of his tongue between her legs, like the world's most erotic acupressure.

With her fingers glistening, he closed his eyes to swallow her taste down and murmured, "Sweet honey girl."

He licked between her fingers and she squirmed.

"That tickle?" he asked, smiling hungrily.

She nodded. "I bet you know all the ticklish places on women," she panted.

"What women? There's just you." He tongued the pads of her fingers. "You, tasting like ink and paper and big fancy words." He tilted his head and gently bit her knuckle. "I can't think about anything but your soft, wet, ticklish places."

Was he dreaming about what he could do with that mouth just like she was?

He swirled his tongue around her buzzing fingers one last time. "There. Your fingers are all wet and shiny again. You ready?"

She was. With her fingers quivering and her pussy weeping onto the hard chair, she was more than ready. But there was fantasizing and then there was actually touching yourself in front of a stranger.

"Hey, you want to put your knee back up on the desk?" he asked gently, like he could sense her hesitation. "You've got the prettiest knee I've ever seen."

"You've never seen my knee." He was handing her lines, but they were the distraction she needed. The sturdy wooden chair creaked as she leaned back in it, then rested the leg closest to him against the desk edge.

He stroked those strong fingers over her kneecap in reward. "These black tights make it better than seeing your leg naked. I feel like I'm getting away with something in the middle of mass."

Church on Sundays had always seemed strangely sexy to her too. She put her other knee up on the desk edge and he grunted, "Yeah," in appreciation. He licked his bottom lip as he looked at her thick, black stockings and brown corduroy skirt, and it had her stroking her hand up the inside of her thigh as he watched. Her skirt bunched up at her wrist, preventing him from seeing her fully when her hand brushed hair.

Suddenly, he said, "Wait, are those..." He was glaring at the thigh that faced him. "Are you wearing fucking thigh highs?"

A strip of brown skin showed between her skirt and the heavy black stocking. He stared like he'd been punched at a thigh that hadn't seen a gym in months.

"Well, that's it," he growled. "Now I'm gonna have to quit this job. I can't walk around with a hard-on every time I'm in the library."

She laughed and combed her fingers through her curls.

"You've got a great laugh," he groaned.

She separated her pussy lips and dabbed with a finger. She was juicy wet. "I love your voice."

"I'm glad you like my voice." He watched her face as she lightly stroked her clit. She tilted her hips—he saw that too—and brushed her finger over her entrance. "It gets lower when I'm—"

She pushed inside with the fingertip christened by his mouth. She heard how wet she was. Kneeling so close to her, he heard it too.

"Fuck," he huffed again. "I'm trying to keep my cool here, pretty girl, but..." He swallowed, staring where her hand and skirt concealed what she was doing. "Can I see?"

Potential disaster was right there on the horizon. "What if someone comes?"

He smiled but it was more like baring his teeth. "I promise you, someone's going to come. But no one is going to see you." She saw the oath in his eyes. "I won't let anyone hurt you."

It made no sense that she believed him.

She used her left hand to hitch up her skirt. She slowly slid her knees apart on the desk edge then took in what he saw: two perfectly serviceable breasts under a navy-blue sweater, brown corduroy skirt up around her waist, naked brown thighs cinched by black stockings.

"Baby girl." His voice came out strangled. "Did you forget your panties today?"

More aroused than she'd ever been in her life, Rosalia thrummed her clit. "I knew I was going to do this." Her heart pounded in her ears. "It's why I wore a skirt and thigh highs." She gave a little whimper as she hit the perfect spot. "When I was walking through the library, I was afraid I was going to drip down my leg."

She spread her pussy lips with her free hand so he could see everything.

With his gorgeous face a foot away from this glistening heart of her, he grunted like she'd punched him. "Look at the color of your cunt. It's so pretty. Your clit's so shiny and swollen."

Rosalia had been with good lovers. Kind lovers. Early in her career, she'd even been engaged. But she'd never been with a man so viscerally sexual. It was like he didn't know he was supposed to be ashamed.

"It's you," she moaned, the wet of her audible. "Your words. Your voice. Your face."

She could feel his warm breath against her skin. "Baby, you're so rough on that clit. What'd that sweet little thing ever do to you?" He had to know what he was doing. She pushed the middle finger of her left hand inside. "Yeah, get in there." The low register of his voice vibrated against her G-spot. "You touching something good in there, baby? Goddamn. Look at the way your work your hips."

"Bachata," she babbled.

But rather than laughing at her, he said, "Fuck you and your fucking bachata," and in this private corner in the back of the library, with this growling stranger shadowing her and staring at her exposed pussy like he was starving, his words shouldn't have been so overwhelmingly arousing.

"Listen to it," he groaned between gritted teeth, his chest now touching her rocking thigh as his eyes roamed over her. "Listen to that sweet, slapping wet… You beat that pretty cunt… I can smell you, fuck, I can smell you. I want to taste you so bad I'm drooling."

"Yes, please," she begged, and suddenly, his words, her hand, and the momentum of their bodies stopped.

He looked at her like she was handing him the incorporation papers for his construction company. "I wasn't going to ask, you're letting me have so much already, but yeah, baby, please, let me, let me taste you, *please*, baby…" like she hadn't already begged.

She turned her body so her left knee squeaked to the edge of the desk and her right leg lolled out for him.

"Yeah," he moaned with appreciation, slipping her right knee over his shoulder as she supported herself with her hands. Her butt was on the edge of the seat and she was spread wide.

"Fuck," he said, staring between her legs. "Is that all for me?"

She looked above his head and saw the rows of metal shelves, the endless spines of books, the pallid wall color that should've made the stacks depressing but just didn't. His huge, hot, callused hands stroked up her thighs, and she wondered if she'd had an aneurism. This had to be heaven.

"You sure all that wet, ripe, and shiny is for me?" he said, the puffs of his warm breath making her wetter and riper. "You sure there wasn't someone else under the desk getting you dripping? Maybe you were letting some another guy lick your cunt while I was dreaming about sucking those sweet hard nipples we haven't even talked about yet. Maybe we could get him to tongue-fuck you nice and slow while I gently feed you my cock."

It was exactly what she'd been fantasizing earlier, and she spasmed with a full-body shiver, making him chuckle.

"You're a tease," she whined, squirming to get closer to that beautiful mouth.

He grinned cruelly. "Sweetheart, I'll keep talking to this pretty pussy all day if it makes you shiver like that." He pursed his lips and blew against her wetness.

She'd never had time for guile. She looked him straight in the eyes, then stroked her knee against his jawline. "The thing I want most in the world is for you to make me come."

All the tease dropped out of him. "Tilt your hips up," he demanded.

Trembling, she did, used the leverage of the seat and the desk and his shoulder to raise herself closer as he hunkered down.

His deep, dark eyes met hers over the arch of her pelvis. "Now watch. You watch me. Don't take your eyes off what I'm doing to you." Gently, he spread her open with two fingers. She felt his panting breath against her. Then he leaned in and kissed her, soft and open-mouthed.

She had to tighten her lower body to keep her thighs from slamming closed with the pleasure.

He gave two, three, four soft, searching kisses, tilting his head, using his tongue, before he focused on her clit and sucked.

She moaned deep in her belly.

His hot hand gripped her hip. "Sweet sugar girl," he said, looking at the way he was making her drip. "Your clit's my sugar pop."

He lifted her higher to his mouth and bit the tender skin at the top of her thigh before diving back in.

She was entirely up on her hands, eyes squeezed tight and both thighs straddling his broad shoulders when she heard him command, "Cover that mouth."

She hadn't realized she'd closed her eyes. "What?" she gasped.

Oh God. His lips were shiny with her.

"You're getting too loud in the library. You can't keep quiet, I'm gonna have to drag you down here on the floor and give you something to keep you quiet."

She gasped and shook against his jaw.

"You like that?" He grunted. "You like the thought of me filling your mouth with my cock while I go to town on your pussy?"

She didn't need a gang bang of warriors. She just needed one. This time, she rolled her hips and stroked her pussy against his chin.

"Yeah," he said, triumph in his eyes. "Bathe my face."

He leaned in and licked at her entrance before thrusting his tongue in. She widened her thighs as his thumb massaged her clit.

"Yeah," he growled into her. "Poor baby girl's already spasming around my tongue. You close?" He thrust and sucked and bit. "What if I tickle my tongue like this? What if I..."

She swallowed her shriek and thrust her hips.

"Ride my fucking face, you dirty, filthy girl."

She did and she was close, so wonderfully, astonishingly, out-of-control close but then he shoved her hips back to the seat and he stopped eating her to stick two fingers in his mouth and then he was...he was...

He watched her relentlessly as he pushed then pulsed those two fingers into her desperate, clinging pussy.

"Listen to it," he hissed, tonguing her clit while he worked her. "Listen to the sound of my fingers fucking you."

She slapped her hand over her mouth because she couldn't keep the moans back anymore.

His eyes, the eyes of an empathetic priest and a pillaging soldier, met hers.

"Good girl, I'm going to make you fucking scream."

His muscles, his arm, his thrusting fingers, his opulent lips, his sucking mouth, his endless lashes, the sweat on his brow—everything went white, and Rosalia had the most explosive orgasm of her life with a stranger in the back of the stacks at the library.

When she was able to lift her head above the ocean of pleasure, she realized her feet were back on the floor. Her skirt had been tugged back into place. A gorgeous construction worker sat at her feet, his heart beating fast against her knee, his head resting in her lap.

Her fingers were combing through the back of his short, sweat-damp hair.

"Did I stay quiet?" she asked.

"Nope," he said without opening his eyes. "You really did find the most private spot in the library."

She relaxed back and floated, resisting reality. She didn't know his name. He hadn't asked for hers. They hadn't even kissed.

"Do you know the last time eating pussy made me come?"

She laughed, delighted.

His arms squeezed where they were loosely circled around her hips. "Laugh it up, giggles. Your skirt covers your sins. I'm gonna have to grab a clean pair of jeans out of my truck without anyone noticing I look like a happily-used cum dump."

He turned his head, buried his nose in her skirt between her legs, and inhaled deeply. "If you've got the time, I'll be ready to go again in a minute," he said, muffled, into the corduroy.

Before she could list all the ways it was a terrific and horrible idea, he lifted his head. Then she heard them too.

Footsteps were coming down the opposite aisle.

He held on to the bolted-down desk to get himself to his feet on legs that looked shaky, and she stood as well, put a hand on his chest as the world whirled, then stepped neatly in front of him and the large, wet stain on his jeans as one of her classmates turned the corner into the row in front of her.

"Rosalia!" the woman exclaimed. "Is this where I find the stuff on the Guachichiles' defeat of the Spanish? I'm glad you're here. It's so dark and grungy back in these stacks, I'm afraid I'm going to get mugged."

"Rosalia," he murmured behind her. From the corner of her eye, she saw him swipe at his mouth with his palm.

"Oh!" The classmate startled when she noticed him. "Hello."

She looked at Rosalia curiously.

"He was taking sound measurements of the construction work and we were..." Rosalia ran out of words.

What were they doing? What was *she* doing? What had she been *thinking*? She didn't know him, had no idea if she could trust him, and she was *waaaay* too old to be risking her new life on a handsome young man with dark eyes and a deep voice and a shared private-time problem and a gentle kink that perfectly matched hers—

"We were just making plans to meet for coffee," he said smoothly after too long of a pause. "Rosalia, if you can walk me upstairs, I'll grab my phone and get your digits."

He turned to walk down the aisle, keeping his front concealed from her classmate, and Rosalia had no choice but to follow him. When she glanced over her shoulder, the woman gave her two enthusiastic thumbs up.

Rosalia was glad the library was in its lunchtime lull. She was able to get him outside and to his truck parked in the library lot without incident while mentally drafting a firm, responsible, and entirely depressing message explaining why this could never, ever, *ever* happen again. Fall had come early this year, and leaves were already skittering on the ground.

"I'm busy," he said before she could open her mouth, putting his key in the lock. The truck was old but clean. "You're busy. Neither of us have much in the way of extra money or time."

That was the thing about fantasies—they were best left in the realm of make-believe. She hadn't needed to worry about her let-him-down-easy message. He'd been busy composing one of his own.

He opened the door, pulled a duffel from behind the seat, and retrieved jeans from it. His back to her, he also pulled a Wet Wipe out of the canister and, to her mortification, wiped his face with it.

He shoved the duffel back behind the seat, then turned to face her with a small smile and jeans in hand. "Job can get messy," he said.

She wanted the pavement to open up and swallow her whole.

He used the jeans to point over her shoulder. "There's a picnic table over there where I like to eat lunch. Sometimes it feels like the only place in the world where I can be alone."

She turned and saw a green picnic table under a huge oak tree with widespread limbs, the top of the tree already turning gold. A bed of yellow, red, and orange mums planted at that corner of the library was its backdrop.

It was a pretty spot, just far enough from the main thoroughfare to go unnoticed by the students streaming by.

"Even though you're busy, you gotta stop and eat, right?" For the first time, she heard nerves in his voice. "I'd love it if you'd join me. When you want."

Rosalia faced him and instantly threw away her firm and responsible answer. "I'd like that," she said, smiling at his relief.

"And…maybe…" He took a step closer and so did she. "I'm making no assumptions here…but…if you need some private time, you'll let me help you out again? Maybe we can find a place more private than the stacks."

This beautiful man was so sweet and young and obviously needed her wisdom and experience.

She turned to take a heated look at the crystal-clear solution to their problem, then looked at him with an eyebrow raised.

His smile grew as he turned to look inside his truck as well.

The big front seat was long and wide and welcoming.

**THE END**

# CHAPTER EIGHT

# Dream Man

When my debut book, **Lush Money**, came out in 2019, a story about a billionaire businesswoman who makes a baby deal with an impoverished Spanish prince, I had a clear, sequential line of which characters were going to get their love stories told. The prince had siblings, so his bad-ass winemaking sister, then his ex-military half-brother would get their turns.

Little did I know that it was the billionaire's bodyguard, a big-hearted goofball from Texas, who everyone wanted to see fall in love. Henry Walker is the big, burly Texas bodyguard with a naughty smile who we first meet protecting Roxanne Medina in  and who later becomes the best friend of Sofia de Esperanza in . This is his love story...

**Content warnings: Misunderstanding, one-night stand**

***

*1.*

Henry Walker didn't want anything getting between him and his whisky. Especially not the gorgeous redhead who sidled up to him at the mahogany-and-brass bar of the San Francisco hotel and laser-beamed him with her eyes while specifically ordering a bottle of wine produced by his world-famous best friend.

He might be known for his sunny Texas disposition and good ol' boy manners. But if she'd wanted to make his dark mood blacker, reminding him of his connection to Princesa Sofia de Esperanza y Santos, winemaker and owner of Bodega Sofia, was certainly the way. His best friend in the whole world was going to kill him. He'd just told that winemaker's sister-in-law—his boss, in fact—that he was quitting the job of his dreams.

He used all of his six-foot, three-inch height and healthy 260 pounds to glower away the pretty hanger-on. Then he finished off the double of twelve-year-old single malt Japanese whisky and signaled for another.

He needed to drown the image of his billionaire boss's hurt brown eyes.

Henry had been the head of security for Roxanne Medina, whose name was on the building right across the street, for the last eleven years. He'd protected her when she made brilliant business decisions and questionable personal ones, when she unexpectedly fell head over heels in love with a Spanish prince, and when she became a wife, mom and princesa of a small Spanish kingdom that adored her. Along the way, Henry had transformed from a former UT quarterback and former–Navy SEAL–slash–bouncer into the personal bodyguard for one of the most amazing, glamorous, and well-respected families in the world. These amazing, glamorous, well-respected people—his billionaire boss, her princely husband, their adorable twin kids, the winemaking princess sister, and her rock-star husband—had become like his family. He loved them and would gladly throw himself in front of a bus for each and every one of them.

But they weren't his family. He still went home alone most nights—even if it was to his personal suite in the castle of the Monte del Vino Real.

Three weeks ago, he had a birthday. At his party, the woman he'd been dating, a woman he thought maybe he could get serious about, suddenly jumped up on the table at a little taberna in the Monte's village and told him she had a birthday gift for him. As a warning tingle lifted his short hairs, she began to belt out a song. She never once looked at him. Instead, she spent the whole time singing to Aish Salinger, the rock-star husband of his best friend. Then she hopped off the table and handed Aish her card with a flourish. Backing vocalist extraordinaire, it read, when he hadn't even known she could carry a note. If it hadn't happened to him, in front of his very understanding friends, he would have admired her moxie.

He'd flown her back to the States and told her to lose his number.

The amazing, glamorous, and well-respected people he was always around shone too bright for a woman to see and value Henry for himself.

If he was ever going to have the real family he'd always wanted—a friend to grow old with, munchkins of his own, the kind of partnerships his boss and best friend enjoyed with their spouses—he was going to have to give up the fake family he already had.

He knocked back half of his expensive drink to ease the ache of his boss's hurt surprise. Roxanne Medina was tough, but she trusted him enough to let him see her tender places too. She'd assumed, just like he had, that he'd always be by her side.

He'd used weak excuses about "new avenues" and "unexplored opportunities" to cover up the truth that she was just...too much. They were all too much for Henry to compete with. He'd given her six months to find a replacement, and she'd promised to allow him to tell the rest of the family when he was ready.

He would never be ready to tell his best friend, because Sofia was going to kill him.

Tonight, Henry just wanted to drown his self-pity at the first bar he stumbled into after he left that meeting, the hotel bar across the street from Medina Now Enterprises, and pray that no one else recognized him.

Tonight, the last thing he wanted was to look up and see a short, bare-shouldered, brick house of a woman entering the bar from the hotel lobby and feel eyelash-melting insta-lust. The last thing he wanted was to watch her big brown eyes widen and see her totter back on her heels as if maybe she felt the same way.

## 2.

The woman stopped staring quicker than Henry did.

She looked around the room, her short, highlighted brown waves brushing over those gorgeous, gleaming, caramel-tan shoulders revealed by her black halter dress. A little skirt kicked out from her good, thick waist, and showed off thighs that were strong and dark and glowing, just like her shoulders.

Henry hoped she was looking for friends. He hoped she was meeting people so he wouldn't be tempted to approach her, to talk to her, to maybe pine for something he couldn't have yet while he was tied up with a boss and family so blindingly fabulous.

But this old-money San Francisco hotel bar with its low-lit shaded lamps, gleaming brass, and quiet jazz was pretty empty on a Tuesday night, except for the redhead and a couple of her friends in the corner. Henry looked down into the amber of his glass as the mouthwatering woman walked past and behind him, then he almost groaned as she sat at the other end of the long mahogany bar.

The bartender, whose lack of customer service had suited Henry's mood just fine, sure as shit perked up when he turned around and saw her.

"Hey!" he said. "Welcome."

Henry was not going to turn and stare. He was not going to turn and stare... He realized he could see her in the mirror, mottled with age, behind the bar.

"Hmm..." she said, and she was tapping her unpainted nails on the bar and running her tongue over her brilliantly white teeth as she looked over the liquor bottles. Her mouth was wide, her lips thin and delicate. "It's been so long since I've been out."

The bartender stood right in front of her. "Aren't you—"

"Yes," she said, cutting him off without a glance.

Wait. Who was she?

"Sorry," the guy went on. "I'm just a big fan of your—"

"It's fine," she said, and Henry could see the forced patience on her face. The bodyguard in him wanted to dive in where he'd not been asked to intervene. "Thank you."

"Then maybe I can show you my—"

"What are you having?"

Seconds from picking the bartender up by the collar and locking him in back, Henry realized she was talking to him. Her voice was lower, had a bit of scratch to it. She spoke to him with a straightforwardness he was used to from the women he worked with and protected.

He turned his bulk on the bar seat to fully face her. "Yamazaki. It's a Japanese whisky."

Before he could say more, she said, "I'll have that. Two fingers. Neat."

He wanted to intervene, but when the bartender opened his mouth, she tapped her fingers again on the bar and said, "Now. Please. It's been a long day."

Henry snapped his mouth closed and figured he'd ask the bartender—in private—to put the drink on his tab. Whoever she was, she deserved to have her whisky at the end of a long day without a bunch of men butting in.

She gave a soft "thank you" when the bartender set the drink in front of her. The man had the good sense to scurry away.

"Wow," she said, surprised. "This is delicious."

He smiled down at his drink, then watched her in the mirror from under his lashes. "I'm relieved you like it," he drawled, letting the Texas in his voice fly free.

"Relieved?" she asked. Her smile made her cheeks curl up into kissable balls. "Do you usually feel a lot of pressure when strangers bother you for drink orders?"

"I do when the drink costs forty-five bucks a shot," he said with a gentle grimace.

Her soft, throaty, goose bump–raising chuckle stopped his offer to pay for the ridiculously overpriced drink. "Whoa," she said, and damn, he liked her voice. He turned toward her. Catching her wide, white-toothed, ball-cheeked smile straight on was like getting a bat to the face. "No wonder it's so good."

That smile was the reason he spoke before he thought. "Also, if you didn't like it, you might leave."

Her smile calmed a bit. But her eyes—honey brown, black lashed—stayed straightforward and honest and excited on him.

Without taking those gun-barrel eyes off him, she picked up her glass and sipped from it. "I like it so much, I'm going to buy us another round."


***3.***

Gina Pérez's heart pounded as she set the glass back down on the bar. It truly was a spectacular whisky, one she'd wanted to try for a while. But it could have been bathwater for all the attention she paid to it while the gorgeous hulking blond stared at her with sky-blue eyes like she was the next shot he wanted to down.

She could spend all day long sipping on this big, muscular behemoth. His blond hair was short on the sides and styled on top, thick just like his strong neck in his open collar. Clothes shopping must be a bitch for him; the long, black sleeves of his quality button-up shirt looked like they could barely contain his enormous biceps and broad shoulders. She hoped the nice black slacks he wore could barely contain what they hid too.

Whaaaaat? she answered the imagined gasps of her mother, sisters, and heads of the various wine industry boards she served on. Her dirty thoughts were dusty with disuse—thanks to the divorce and the business and the girls—and she'd purposefully packed her little black dress for this secret trip to San Francisco so she could air them out.

Of course this bartender, in a city where everything was "artisanal" this and "boutique knowledge" that, would recognize her before her first flirt.

No one was supposed to know Gina was here interviewing to be the new cooper for the Monte del Vino Real, where she would work with the acclaimed winemaker Princesa Sofia de Esperanza y Santos to provide wine barrels for the historic wine-growing kingdom. It was a once-in-a-lifetime opportunity to establish her own cooperage and become part of the kingdom's exciting new winemaking revolution while tapping into its thousand-year history.

She didn't want the job just as passionately as she did want it. Not getting it would mean things would stay stable: she would continue working with her mother and sisters as the top barrel makers in California wine country, be the heir apparent of La Niña Cooperage and stay the poster girl for a highly specialized craft. She would go on raising her daughters in a community where she knew everyone and everyone assumed they knew her. She would continue to fight to maintain La Niña's dominance, while her mother constantly prodded her about the need to fight longer, faster, and harder as Mexican American women in a white male–dominated industry.

She would continue ceding control of her life and choices to her mother, Josefina Pérez.

Getting the job would mean blowing up her world. Leaving the company in the capable hands of her two younger sisters. Moving away from Sonoma County, where everyone wanted her to stay the pigtailed girl her mother had used to help build their brand. Allowing her daughters to determine their lives without the pressure of her mother's powerful influence.

Perhaps never seeing her family again. Josefina had cut people out of her life before.

Gina couldn't stay cooped up in a hotel room. She needed a distraction. And man, she'd found a giant one.

He had a nice dimple in his cheek to complement his easy, sexy grin. "If you're gonna be plying me with expensive drinks, I guess I should move closer to be..."

"Plied?"

"You mind?"

His check-in made her a little tingly. She was too busy to venture far from Sonoma County, except when she went on lumber-scouting trips, so it had been a long time since she'd been approached by a man who didn't want something from her or assume he already knew her.

"Not at all," she said.

He stood up from his bar seat, and he was even bigger than she thought. He was a tall, dense wall of a man dressed in black, the brushed-silver buckle at his flat waist teasing her like a target.

She really liked the feeling in her stomach when he walked toward her. "They grow them big where you're from," she said.

He grinned, pleased, as he sat on the stool next to her. "Texas," he said.

"I've never met a Texan who wasn't proud of it."

"You know many?"

"A few. We still have family in El Paso and Ciudad Juárez."

She realized she was talking about her family even when she didn't want to be.

The Pérez family fortunes changed when a Kentucky distiller went to Ciudad Juárez to escape Prohibition and taught Gina's great-grandfather how to make bourbon barrels. Her grandfather moved to Kentucky to continue the art, and her mother brought that whiskey-built knowledge to Sonoma County and applied it to wine barrels. In her late teens, Gina, the oldest, was sent to France to become a Master Cooper. Of the twenty people who started the four-year program, she was one of only four to graduate.

She didn't want to be thinking about this right now. She didn't want to talk about her family. She didn't want to answer questions about why the bartender had recognized her and probably wanted to make her try a bottle of wine he'd made in his garage.

Even when she was doing everything she could to free herself from her family and just be a different person for one night, they were right there on the tip of her tongue.


## 4.


Henry felt the mood dip with the mention of her people, and he watched her rotate her glass in little wet rings on the bar.

Up this close, she was even better-looking. Her skin was a golden tan, and her shoulders were so fit, the skin glowed. With her head bent, he could see the tight muscles dancing. She smelled good, like a campfire, and he would do whatever he could to get her smiling again.

He didn't want to talk about his people either.

The bartender had insinuated she was someone, and Henry couldn't have anyone, but, just for tonight, he sure wouldn't mind having her. Sure wouldn't mind being a regular ol' guy flirting with a beautiful woman.

"So, look," he said. "The bartender thinks you're someone to know." She stiffened. "What I know is that you're gorgeous and you smile easy, and I'd like to spend some time looking at your pretty face and listening to your nice voice. We're two strangers who enjoy expensive whisky, and it doesn't have to be more complicated than that. I'm not in a relationship, I'm not a serial killer, and I'm totally okay with sticking to first names. We don't have to know each other's life stories to enjoy a talk at the bar."

He liked the way her eyes got softer and softer as he spoke.

"Yes," she said, smiling. "I'd like that."

He put his hand out. "Henry."

"Gina," she said, taking his hand. "And I'm not either."

She had calluses, big, hard calluses as her palm slid over his, and it caused him to shiver.

"You're not either?" he echoed quickly, trying to cover up his reaction to her. Goddamn, her touch made him quiver like he was a little kid.

Her big, delighted, made-him-want-to-lick-it grin let him know he wasn't fooling anybody. "I'm not in a relationship or a serial killer either."

Goddamn. Calluses. Those shoulders. Those thighs. He'd just cut off his ability to ask her what she did for a living, but he was officially desperate to explore the rest of her and see where else toughness lived on her small, curvy body.

"Good to know," he said, clearing his suddenly dry throat with a good slug of whisky. "Drink your drink. You got some catching up to do."

*5.*

Even though they hadn't finished their current drinks, Gina ordered a second round so the bartender couldn't find an excuse to interrupt them.

Then she leaned back on her bar stool, eyed him thoroughly, and said what Sonoma County Gina never would. "So is this genetics or the gym?" she asked, admiringly waving her hand over all his "this."

He snorted into his drink, wasting at least a couple bucks of precious whisky, before he looked at her with his pearly white–and–dimpled grin. It was toe curling to see such easy humor on this bone crusher. She knew a lot of big men in her world full of loggers and coopers, but most of them had too much to prove to snort into his drink.

His cool-blue-water eyes wandered hotly over her bared shoulders.

"Uh...mostly genetics. Some gym." He didn't take his eyes off her as he chose every word. "I...played football. And was...in the military."

She rested her chin in her hand and let the big gorgeousness of him sink into her veins. "Thank you for your service."

He laughed again—big and in his chest—and shook his head, looking away. "Girl..." he drawled.

Who was this woman flirting with him? She felt like she'd untied the binds of everything she was—a single parent and a figurehead and a society darling and her mother's daughter—the instant she sat down at the bar. Now she was just a woman admiring a beautiful man.

"What?" she asked, grinning devilishly.

"You're a damn good pick-me-up."

She rested her temple on her fist. "Did you need one?"

He took a sip of his whisky as he eyed her. The big rocks glass looked small in his hand. There was no tan or line where a wedding ring might have been. Finally, he said. "Yeah. What do you need?"

"A distraction" popped right out of her mouth.

It wasn't meant to be a come-on. But the instant she said it, she knew what she wanted. She wanted to take this big bruiser upstairs. The way those sky-blue eyes grew smoky said he wanted to go.

She'd had exactly zero one-night stands in her life. Suddenly all those horrified voices—she was a mom!—grew a little too loud.

She took her elbow off the bar and put both hands around her drink. "That probably came out more honest than I intended," she said into her expensive whisky.

"Honesty has been a rare commodity in my life lately," he said, a little lower and gruffer. "Having a beautiful woman look at me like I'm a prime steak she wants to sink her teeth into—even though she doesn't know a thing about me—is not a hardship."

Despite herself, Gina laughed. She pressed the back of her hand to her mouth.

"Hey..." he said, his fingers catching hers. They were strong and hot and gently pulled her hand away from her lips. "Don't hide that pretty mouth. You say whatever you want to say. Whether we do anything about it...well, that doesn't need to be decided right now. We still got all this million-dollar liquor to drink."

His eyes twinkled at her. "And I'm happy to be a distraction, any way you want it."

## 6.

Henry put her small-but-callused hand down on the bar before he used it to tug her into his lap. The sudden blinding image of that—her straddling his lap, that flippy skirt and those golden thighs around his hips, those scratchy-soft hands rubbing all over the chest she admired—had him finishing off his whisky.

Thank the good Lord she'd bought him another drink. He wrapped his hands around his glass like it was a prison bar.

"Do you like steak?" he asked her.

They were in such a weird place. He couldn't ask her the usual questions that neither of them wanted to answer: What do you do? Where are you from? Is your family so glamorous and awesome that people use you to get access to them?

And he kinda didn't want to know that stuff about her, anyway. It was so...unimportant. He wanted to know what she did to be so fit. He wanted to know the color of her panties. He wanted to know if she thought tailgating before a college football game was fun and why her skin glowed like that and if she minded cantankerous old Texans who'd ask her way too many personal questions the instant she stepped onto their front porch. He wanted to know why she was so many fascinating contradictions—strong but soft, bold but hesitant.

She nodded enthusiastically as she took a sip of her whisky, not batting an eye at the weird question. "Love a good grilled steak."

"What's the best steak you ever had?"

She tapped her brilliant white teeth as she thought about it. He admired a woman who prized her meat. "São Paulo, Brazil," she said. "Templo de Carne. They cut it off the spit right in front of our table, and it was..." She put her hand to her forehead, and if this was what she looked like remembering a good meal, he couldn't imagine how incredible she looked when she orgasmed.

"Meat butter. It was meat butter. You?"

Henry had to wipe the corner of his mouth. "Not to try to one-up you or anything..."

She grinned. "This is San Francisco. One-upsmanship is mandatory."

Good Lord, he liked her. "Well, if it's mandatory... There's this little place in Jiménez de Jamuz, Spain. You can sit in a pretty cave room. And they serve you these ox chops..."

"Ox chops?"

"Ox chops. Man, my mouth is watering just thinking of them."

She smiled and he smiled, and there was something...nice...in realizing that they'd both had experiences like this. That her own work and money and life's journey had allowed her to enjoy some of the perks that Henry's life and work had allowed.

His smile dipped a bit when he remembered he'd just amputated himself from that life and work.

Sofia's new husband, rock star Aish Salinger, had taken Henry and Sofia to that exclusive restaurant as a bury-the-hatchet gesture, a way to say he was comfortable with the best friendship he'd been jealous of before he'd won the prize of his princesa.

Sofia was going to be so pissed. In six months, Henry's connection to Spain would shrivel and die.

Gina's small hand settled on his bicep. "And how was the wine that went with that ox chop?" He turned his head to look at her.

Stay with me, soldier, her honey-gold eyes seemed to say.

Because he could, because he didn't know how long he'd get a chance to, he reached across and rubbed his thumb over her warm, silky hand on his arm. This close, she smelled as comforting as a cabin's flickering fire. He met her gaze.

"The wine." He sighed, his smile saying he wished he were kissing her. "Don't get me started on the wine..."

### 7.

Talking about wine he'd drunk in a Spanish village led to Gina telling him about a dusty two-hundred-year-old bottle she'd sipped from when she was nineteen in Bordeaux, which led hilariously to a Fanta-and-Jäger experience he regretted when he was nineteen, which swerved weirdly to a solemn conversation about the terror of teens and binge-drinking.

As the mom of a three- and four-year-old, it was one of those far-off topics Gina easily worried about on any given day. Henry seemed as worried about it as she was. She refused to wonder. Or ask.

Binge-drinking suddenly leaped into a competition to name the most NCAA college athletic mascots—Henry won, but not by many—which led to a recitation of beloved family pets and the shared understanding that Where the Red Fern Grows was the most horrible, devastating, and awesome book about beloved dogs ever written. They both laughed and wiped the corners of their eyes and then laughed harder when they realized they both were crying.

Gina wanted to straddle his lap.

He was big and gorgeous and funny and made her feel...gorgeous and funny and fascinating. She was a mere mortal sitting next to a Norse god, and the god looked down at her like she was his favorite mortal in a millennium. And yet he didn't know one detail that made the rest of the world fascinated by her: that she was a female cooper, heir presumptive to the most esteemed cooperage in the United States, and had the ear of important winemakers throughout the world.

They were all attributes she was proud of. Kind of. Within her mother's iron grip, they were never attributes she could fully experience, grow, or claim as her own.

God, she hoped she got the Monte job. As much as she hoped she didn't.

"I just applied for a new job," she said suddenly.

His blue eyes flashed surprise.

She wouldn't tell him what the job was or her profession. But they were two attracted strangers who'd agreed to first names only and who'd established a strange but trusting intimacy. There was freedom in spilling your secrets without the fear of repercussions.

"That's funny," he said slowly, picking up his whisky glass. He took a drink. Then he put it down again, centering it between his big hands. "I just quit a job."

"Is that why you're here?" she asked. He nodded as he stared into his glass. If she wasn't here, she realized, he'd be drowning himself in it.

"Is that why you're here?" he asked, turning to look at her.

She nodded too. "I'm terrified I'm going to get it," she said, shoving all the truth out there.

The side of his mouth lifted, showing that dimple. "I can't imagine much scaring you," he said. "Why are you terrified?"

"If I get it, it will blow up my life."

His eyes touched her naked shoulders, her hair tickling them. Her eyes. Then her mouth.

"Yeah," he said, low and deep in his mammoth chest. "That's what I did by quitting."

She pressed her lips together as she looked at him, trying to resist the urge to comfort. "You don't seem happy about it," she said.

"I'm not."

"Then why did you quit?" She shouldn't have asked. It was too close to real, too close to transforming them from strangers to people with information that could be traced.

He looked at her without answering, long and lazy, with all the time in the world. When he opened those nice, pink lips to respond, she didn't know if it was the boldness of the question or the heat of his gaze that had her heart picking up its pace.

"How long do we have to sit here before I can kiss you?"

## 8.

Gina breathed out, and Henry hoped it was because the request he couldn't keep inside anymore made her hot.

"You haven't finished your drink yet," she said. But those honey-brown eyes dipping over his lips and down his chest, they didn't say no to his request for a kiss.

He picked up his glass and, without taking his eyes off her, downed it in one gulp.

Her black lashes flashed wide, and she huffed a laugh. "Well...I haven't finished mine."

He reached for her glass.

Those eyes flashed again, and she grabbed his wrist. "Don't you dare."

Her grip was surprisingly strong. It jacked up his desire to eleven. Her smile was outraged. He wondered if she had siblings like he did, a couple of brothers who made pranks and sarcasm and giving as good as you got part of daily life.

Or a couple of royal pseudo-sisters whose hearts she was about to break.

He let go of her glass. But she didn't let go of his wrist.

Instead, Gina crossed her other arm over theirs to pick up the glass—tempting him with that stretch of lean muscle and gorgeous skin—then lifted it to her lips and took the tiniest sip. She didn't drop her eyes. Or let go of him.

His blood pounded in his ears.

"Am I going too fast?" he asked. He didn't want his avoidance of her question—Then why did you quit?—make her go away.

"No," she said against the glass, taking another little sip. The amber liquid wet her lip. "I'm just appreciating the view."

God. He was a couple years shy of forty, and she had him as desperate as a kid. There was nothing he liked better than a nice, long tease.

"I can improve it," he said, giving her his dumb, cocky grin. He was never shy about what the good Lord gave him. "There's a lot under these clothes you're missing out on."

Rather than the grin he was expecting in return, she took a real slug of her drink. "I...um..." She tapped the glass against her lip. "I don't have a lot of experience taking men back to my room."

Oh. Fuck. She was so good at winding him up, he'd assumed it was a skill she'd practiced as much as he had. The realization that this was just her, responding to him, did not help him gain the calm he needed right now.

Her transparency deserved some truth in return.

"Look," he said, gently turning his wrist over so he could stroke the underside of hers with his fingers. "Even with sticking to first names and staying under each other's radar, you've been more honest with me than...well...let's just say that your straightforwardness is like a great big present under the Christmas tree. We can stay here. We can go on a walk. We can...we can go upstairs and do as much or as little as you want. I can sit and watch you paint your toes. I don't care. I don't know you from Eve, but...but I like everything about you. I don't want anything from you but your company, as much of it as you're willing to give me."

He was ready for a lot of responses. Her getting up and leaving. Her ordering another round. Her pulling out a microphone as a camera crew jumped out from under the bar and announced that Henry had been punked, because of course the most perfect woman for him in creation hadn't stumbled into the bar right when he needed her.

What he wasn't ready for was for her to pick up her glass and throw back twenty dollars of whisky in one swallow.

Still holding on to his wrist, she banged the glass back down on the bar. "Let's go," she said.

9.

Gina hauled the big man behind her down the elegant, marble-tiled hallway to the elevators like he was one of her girls. Or one of her kid sisters. When she realized she was doing it, using his arm as a leash while she walked at her normal ground-chewing pace and her nerves rang like a gong, she let go of his wrist and whirled around, pressing the back of her hand to her mouth.

"I'm sorry," she said, eyes wide.

"I'm not," he answered immediately. He definitely didn't look upset. He stepped a half step closer—and, wow, he was huge—and pulled her hand from her mouth. "I've been wanting you to drag me someplace private since the second I saw you."

He kissed the back of her hand while making promises with his eyes, then entwined his fingers with hers. "Lead on, boss."

He was easily a foot taller than she was and twice as wide as her stave-cutting, iron-welding, mallet-pounding shoulders. But the way he said "boss" made her feel like he meant it. It calmed her nerves about inadequacies and made her realize—as they stepped into the elevator and the doors slid closed—that her concerns had never once been about being alone with a stranger in her room.

A gigantic stranger.

Still holding his hand, she watched the numbers slowly tick higher.

"So...you're definitely not a serial killer?" she asked, the speed of the elevator confirming that this hotel was indeed historic.

"Definitely," he said.

God, it was like it rose a floor a minute. "And do you have something? I mean...protection. I have protection, but maybe they're not the brand you like or maybe they're not big enough, or…not to pass judgment, I mean, who knows, maybe it's really small, and that's okay…I mean, women shouldn't be judged by the size of their breasts, so why should I judge you if you have a tiny c—"

She was suddenly tugged into the hot wall of his body as his mammoth, muscled arm hugged her waist.

"Hey," he said, his finger gently pushing up her chin so she was looking at him. "Let's go back down."

"What?" He felt incredible, smelled amazing, looked like a dream. "Why?"

He grinned helplessly. "You're spiraling, sweetie. I don't want to make you nervous."

"That can't be helped."

Oh, she thought as she watched his smile disappear. She hadn't meant to make this huge, sunny Texan sad.

"Let's head back down," he said as his hand dropped from her face and that glorious arm started to slide from her body.

"No, no, no," she said, shaking her head as she gripped his neck and kept him close. "It can't be helped because…it's been a while." Since her divorce. She didn't sleep with men in wine country because—like her ex—they just seemed to want her for the connections she could bring them. She traveled a little to source timber for their barrels, but she was too busy looking for one kind of wood to make time for the other.

"And look at you. You're…" She sighed as she looked him over. "You're perfect. Being naked…with all of this. Yeah, it's got me nervous. Trust me, I'll get over it."

His smile was like the sun breaking through clouds.

"Yeah?"

She nodded like a fool. "Yes."

"Then..." His arm was pulling her close again. His eyes were a true and startling blue—no green, no gray, just a touch of icier blue around the black pupil. "Maybe I could distract you from your nerves? Since I promised and all."

"Okay," she breathed when what she really meant was yes, please, now, as those nicely shaped lips were coming closer, and then he kissed her, once, softly, sending tingles down to her toes. He paused, then did it again, just as soft.

"Damn," he murmured. But again, he waited.

Maybe he was giving her a chance to pull back. She didn't know. Her eyes were closed and her grip around his neck was tight, pulling him toward her.

Then he kissed her...yes...for real, with a lingering press, before he tipped his head and tickled the sensitive corner of her mouth. When she opened, he licked in, so gentle but compelling. His big hand held her head and his arm lowered to capture her under her butt and he lifted her, slowly, so steadily and majestically, up into the air and against his giant, He-Man, panty-drenching body while he continued to savor her mouth.

He made her feel like she was top-shelf whisky.

She wrapped her legs around his waist and her arms around his neck, and when she rotated her hips against him, just to get some relief, he made this He-Man groan.

The bell of her floor dinged. The doors slid open. Then Gina Pérez, who'd spent her life with the weight of the world on her shoulders, whispered her room number into a stranger's ear and let him carry her to it, feeling as light as a feather.

## 10.

Thank Christ, everything in this hotel wasn't as old as that elevator.

Henry didn't have to let go of her incredible mouth to angle the key card in her dress's hidden pocket against the lock or to activate the motion-detection entry light to her room. He opened his eyes just long enough to chart the room—bathroom door, big armchair (yes!), huge bed (nope, not yet), open window giving a spectacular view of San Francisco—before he let the door close behind them, turned and pressed her back against it.

He just…needed to… That mouth…that body…

Pressing hard against her strong, dense curves was as mind-blowingly pleasurable as the eagerness of her wet, agile, excited mouth. He once again thanked the good Lord that he'd stumbled into this bar on this night.

After making his boss–slash–pseudo-sister tear up.

Roxanne Medina had immediately apologized, had declared it "unprofessional" and wiped her eyes. She'd said, "Of course, you should explore new opportunities," and then gone over hiring procedures for his replacement and his truly astonishing exit package.

He'd said he didn't want it. She said if he didn't take it, she'd send her twins to his door with a suitcase of cash. Henry had been with the six-year-old twins almost every day of their lives. He hoped to escape this job without looking into their big, adorable eyes calling him out for his betrayal.

"You doing okay?" Gina whispered.

Fuck.

He let go of her mouth. What a waste to do a half-hearted job with such a beauty in his arms. He slid her a little up the door and leaned his forehead against her chest. Her legs squeezed him tighter and, Jesus Christ, those thighs.

"Sorry," he muttered. "Thought sticking to first names would keep me from wallowin'."

"Do you…do you want to talk about it?"

God, she was a sweetheart. And yeah, he kind of wanted to. He wanted to be that sad sack who turned a one-night stand into an opportunity to unburden himself to a sweet, hot babe with strong shoulders and straightforward honesty and good listening ears. After, he'd apologize by lovin' her body senseless.

But he didn't know what revealing himself to her would do. Would she still be so focused on his eyes, his body, his mouth? Or would she start looking past him, start dreaming about those powerful people around him?

It was exhausting and demoralizing with others. With her, it would break him.

He opened his eyes and tilted his head, inhaled that spicy-sweet campfire smell of her while glimpsing the gleam of her shiny, golden shoulder. What was he doing wasting this one night with her feeling sorry for himself?

"No," he growled against her, sliding his lips over until finally, finally, he was getting to taste that shoulder that had been driving him crazy all night. It was as tight and muscular and edible as he'd fantasized it would be. Bitable. He nipped it with his teeth, sucked on her bicep, tongued the sensitive skin inside her elbow. There was a burn mark on her forearm, and he licked at it.

When he looked at her again, her head was against the door and her eyes were closed and her back was arched and she was panting and holding her powerful arm out to him like an offering. And her hips, her hips were moving in little It's been a while circles against his rib cage.

He wasn't going to make her wait any longer.

"No," he growled again. "The only thing I want to be doin' with my mouth is pleasurin' you."

He palmed her lush, satin-covered ass under her flippy skirt, lifted her away from the door and carried her to that oversize armchair, big enough for a giant Texan and his tight, ripped, moaning sweetheart.

## *11.*

He made her feel like chocolates in a Valentine's box, like every piece of her—her lips, her neck, her shoulder, her arm, her elbow—was a distinct morsel he wanted to lick and taste and savor.

He made her feel small. Tender. She was short, yes. But never small. Never delicate.

But she felt like she was flying across the room as he buried his tongue in her mouth and squeezed her butt with huge, strong hands and then sat in the overstuffed brown leather armchair in the corner, the lights of San Francisco stretched out in the window just behind it.

She was just settling on her knees in his lap, just got a tease of the glorious long-and-hard of him to settle onto, when he let go of her mouth with a wet suck then lifted her—lifted her!—straight over his head, planted her knees on the back of the armchair and her shins on his shoulders, then slid down to kiss her between her legs through her underwear.

"Oh shit," she cried, grabbing his hair with one hand and slapping her hand against the glass with the other.

He laughed! That big, domineering, carry-you-around-like-you're-a-Barbie-doll jerk laughed, sending vibrations right up her thighs, kissed those quivering thighs—rubbing rough scruff and soft hair against them—then licked in hard through her underwear against her clit.

She gave some kind of dumb, not-sexy sound—it had been so long—with her forehead pressed against her hand on the glass, but apparently he didn't hate that sound, because he cursed then grabbed her underwear at her hip and tore them at the seam.

"That's my one pair of sexy panties," she gasped.

"Don't need 'em," he growled against her, making her gasp again, his muscular arms wrapped around her thighs as he pulled the satin out of the way, then separated her lips. "There's nothing sexier than your sweet, pretty, wet pus—"

Then his tongue, it just went to work, licking at her then sucking then flicking then moving around and tasting, holding her ass in his hands so she couldn't get away, all the delicacy he'd shown with the rest of her parts hijacked by his desire to beat her pussy with his tongue.

She gathered his hair into her fist. "Yeah," he moaned against her. "Take it." And she did; she just started, oh...oh...she just started rubbing herself against this gorgeous stranger's mouth.

She didn't feel small anymore. She felt enormous—tough and strong and wild enough to take his giant desire for her. She pressed her forehead against the cool of the glass and opened her eyes to imagine she was some titan about to orgasm all over San Francisco.

One of his big, cheek-rubbing hands moved, and his thumb fingered her entrance. "Oh God," she cried, knocking her head into the glass. She didn't feel it with the explosive thing growing in her pelvis. "Suck...lick my—"

"Yeah, yeah," he said, "tell me," as his soft lips surrounded her clit, as he sucked and tongued at her.

"Suck my pussy, lick me, eat me...yes, yes, yes, Henry!" she cried as he fucked her with his thumb and feasted on her clitoris and she clenched a handful of hair and squeezed his head with her thighs and came all over his face and lurched forward and again knocked her head into the glass.

This time she saw stars.

## 12.

He swooped her down into his lap.

"Are you okay?" he asked. Her fantastic thighs had been muzzling his ears, but he'd still heard the gong of her hitting her forehead against the glass.

She pressed her fist against her forehead, her eyes scrunched. "Ow," she said. Her voice was a little hoarse. He'd done that to her. It was just too bad he hadn't done that while she'd been safely stretched on the bed. He was so big, he'd gotten used to putting women on top.

He wiped his face on his sleeve then said, "Here, let me see."

Concern about a possible concussion was the only thing quieting his bellowing penis. The way this woman came...

When she pulled her fist from her forehead, she stared at what was gripped in it. It was a decent tuft of Henry's blond hair. "Oh my God," she said, horror ringing in her voice. Then she looked at him. At his still-wet cheeks. "Oh my God," she said, covering her eyes.

"Hey, hey, don't..." He picked her up, sat her on the edge of the bed, then hurried to the bathroom to swipe his face with a wet washcloth. Then he came back and kneeled in front of her. She was still covering her eyes. "Gina, sweetie, look at me. Let me check you out."

He wanted to make sure they didn't need a hospital visit before he convinced her how unbelievably turned on her abandon made him. He tugged her hands down and pulled the tuft of hair out of it. A couple of strands got caught in her calluses.

There was a red mark on her tanned forehead and mortification in her eyes. But her eyes tracked him smoothly, and her pupils weren't unnaturally dilated. "Headache?" he asked her.

She shook her head. "No. Just an overall burning sensation that I wish I could die."

"Look at me?" he asked.

She did, pressing the back of her hand to her mouth.

He looked at the crime of that beautiful mouth being covered. "Why do you do that?" he asked.

She pulled her hand away and looked at it like she was surprised to find it there. "I guess..." She folded it into her lap. "I guess I usually feel there's a lot I shouldn't say."

"Not tonight," he answered immediately. "Not with me."

He ran his hands up her firm thighs and squeezed. "We said no last names. Outside of that, you can tell me every dirty fantasy or your entire life's story. But don't cover your mouth with me." Her beautiful eyes were getting honey soft as he spoke. "The way you came, what you said, the way you...demanded me to please you, it was the single most exciting thing that's ever happened to me. Sweetie, when I tell you a lot of exciting things have happened to me, I mean it. I haven't been wanted that way, just for me, in...ever. I've never been wanted that way."

There it was, the shine of her smile in her white teeth and pretty cheeks. "And the only reason I am not on you like a beast right now is because I want to make sure you're okay. And I don't want to scare you. But, Gina, the things I want to do to you, the way I want to tear this body up—" God, just talking about it was making him lose it. "I...I'm holding on by a tiny little string, sweetheart, so if you don't want to spend the night with me making you crazy like that..."

Thank Christ, she put him out of his misery, grabbed him, and kissed him.

She made him start on his back. With her head in his lap. He didn't know what "I knew it" meant when she pulled down his slacks, but the way she was cooing to his dick, whatever she'd known, she liked it. Her mouth was warm and happy to be filled.

He hauled her up on him before she made him soak her like she'd soaked him, got on a condom, then got up inside that fabulous tight body. Her waist was squeezable and soft and strong as she rode him.

She didn't ride for long though.

"Fuck me on my back," she said, flopping to the bed and pulling and demanding.

"I don't want to…" He could barely think, much less talk. "I don't want to be too much for you."

She gave that seductive chuckling rasp, and he had to choke off his orgasm in his dick as he moved over her. "I want it," she purred, squeezing his hips with her thighs and sliding her pussy back onto him. "I want all of you pounding into me. I can take it. Make me feel it. I want to feel this one-night stand with you for a year."

That's when Henry kind of lost his mind.

### *13.*

It had been a long, long…long, long, long time since Henry had had the ability or inclination to spend the whole night fuckin'.

At thirty-seven, he figured it was just the special provenance of a college boy who was a walking erection or a wet-behind-the-ears SEAL on shore leave or shoulda-known-better bodyguard who thought the truly spectacular women suddenly slipping him their numbers were interested in *him*.

But the sky revealed by the curtains they never closed was getting brighter by the time he slipped out of her body for the final time. And the box of condoms was empty.

He moved his shoulder out from under her head and took a quick shower, then pulled on his clothes and looked at her big, brown whirlpool eyes staring up at him from bed and said "Goodbye," even though he didn't want to.

He'd promised her they'd stick to first names.

She'd pulled the blanket up to her chin. All he could see was her face and her hand, a hand that gave more pleasure than he could have dreamed, slowly curling a lock of her thick, messy hair. He'd done that.

"'Bye," she said softly. "And…thank you. For the…um…distraction."

He would've given his last eleven years of amazing memories for one last look at her gloriously soft-tough body.

"Gina," he breathed out, trying to cement her and this room and this feeling in his brain.

"Henry," she sighed in return. And that. That's what he needed to get out the door.

He'd gotten a taste of exactly what he wanted—a woman who wanted him for him, who appreciated him for him, who looked at him like he was a mountain and not a stepping-stone. He couldn't have that in real time, not yet, but in six months… He wouldn't go looking for Gina. He'd promised her first names and one night, and never once had she hinted she wanted more.

But tonight proved to him that he'd made the right decision, he told himself as he stepped into the elevator and jabbed the "L." Yeah. In six months, he'd walk away from the family that wasn't his family and find a woman who didn't want anything more glamorous than the big, brawny, uncomplicated Texan she saw when she looked at him.

He regretted not begging for Gina's last name and number the second the doors closed.

*

Gina ran down the hall of the old San Francisco hotel in nothing but a one-button-buttoned chambray shirt and not-sexy panties, the first two things she grabbed as she realized she was about to let the most incredible man she'd ever met walk out of her life.

She heard the elevator door creak closed just as she was tearing around the corner.

She bolted down the hall and smacked the down arrow.

And jabbed. And poked. And prodded.

Then prayed.

She prayed as she watched the numbers crawl down that Henry was having the same second thoughts that she was. She prayed as the numbers—finally!—began to move at an impossible-to-believe slower pace back up that he hadn't stepped out of the elevator, that he wasn't right now walking out of the lobby and hailing a cab. She prayed that, as complicated as it would be, that he was returning to her with the same desire to see if they could make this once-in-a-lifetime connection more than a one-night stand.

When the elevator doors slipped open to reveal an empty car, she knew that even tearing down the infinitely faster stairs in her underwear wouldn't help her retrieve her big, brawny, want-her-just-for-her Texan.

That didn't mean she didn't try.

She careened into the lobby—gasping, her heart on fire and clutching her shirt down around her thighs—only to discover that she'd already lost him to the San Francisco streets.

***14.***

Gina got the job.

Of course she got the job, her two younger sisters told her a month later, pulling her into their arms after they recovered from the shock that their big sister, who always was the good daughter, was making a change. She'd told Marissa and Elizabeta first, since their lives would be most fundamentally altered by her decision to step away from the company and move to Spain.

Their support and relief—they'd worried about how unhappy she was—forced her to muffle her tears against her middle sister Marissa's shoulder. She didn't want to wake the girls. Marissa and Elizabeta agreed immediately that they would be co-owners of La Niña Cooperage once—if—their mom retired. But when they began to bicker over whose name would be listed on the website first, Gina started to cry again.

This was real. As the new cooper for the Monte del Vino Real, she would be part of an exciting transformation of an ancient kingdom. Her decisions—which forest, which grove of trees, how long to cure the staves, how deep to char them—would determine the quality of the kingdom's wines for years to come.

And to make these decisions, she would leave her company, her community, her sisters, her mother. She needed to go. And she would miss them like losing a lung.

Her mother took the news about as well as Gina had anticipated.

There was shouting. Then tears. A couple of barrel hoops were thrown, but not in Gina's direction.

Gina had coached herself not to rise to Josefina's bait or be wounded by her accusations. Despite it all, she believed her mother loved her. When Josefina's voice grew quiet and most cutting, Gina battled her own temper and hurt. But the only reason she hadn't slipped off to Spain with her girls and left a "Dear John" letter was that she wanted to have a relationship with her mother after all of this. She needed it. And yet she still needed to go.

Josefina didn't declare Gina dead to her. But it was a near thing.

At the huge going-away banquet three months later at the Gary Farrell winery high atop a hill overlooking this gorgeous corner of Sonoma County, her mother gave her a goodbye kiss on her cheek and didn't say a word.

Gina let the whirlwind of moving her family to a little kingdom in Spain ease half of her heartache. Her daughters, four-year-old Josie and three-year-old Skye, were certain just landing at the airport turned them into princesses. She'd rented a small cottage just outside the village with a phenomenal view of the castle and vineyards and an above-ground pool, but when she saw it—big windows, thick stone walls, trailing red fuchsias exploding out of the window boxes—she made the owner a cash offer on it the same day.

She wouldn't be leaving anytime soon.

The other half of her heartache was eased by the excitement and wonder of establishing her own cooperage. It should have been overwhelming. In the first month, Gina assessed and updated the ancient barrel-creation and storage facilities in the onetime monastery that was now home to Princesa Sofia's winery, Bodega Sofia. She hired a crew. She visited sites where her predecessors had sourced wood and made a couple of trips to new sites. Most importantly, she absorbed every ounce of information that Sofia shared with her about the kingdom's famous Tempranillo grape and visited the region's winemakers and growers to learn more.

The prince and his billionaire wife were out of the country for the month, and she was glad she had an opportunity to get herself established before she met and accidentally fangirled over the famous couple.

When she lay down at night, she was certain she vibrated with the anticipation of finally being the captain of her own ship.

But it was also at night that she unfolded the tiny corner of her heart where she'd preserved her heartache for Henry.

For the first four months after she'd let him slip away, she'd tried to convince herself he was a mirage: a shimmering image of a man she'd squinted at during an emotionally fraught time and called perfect. No one could be that open. That kind. That beautiful. That fantastic in bed.

No one could enjoy her for herself, without any credentials, as much as he had.

But with the miracle of the last month—she lived in a kingdom, her boss was a princess, and she had a title: La Tonelera del Monte—she worked to stop thinking about Henry as a mirage and instead started considering him a promise. The promise of the love she could have.

She crossed her fingers that if she could find a man who delighted in who she innately was once, she could find a man like that again.

Five months after she'd met him, she turned over in bed and snuggled into the dream of Henry—a man just like him—and looked forward to tomorrow, anticipating her first day of building barrels for a kingdom.

**15.**

Henry made it one week before he was back at the hotel bar.

He would have been there the next day, except Roxanne had needed to travel to her Hong Kong headquarters. But a week still wasn't soon enough—the bartender had been fired, the new bartender whispered, and the hotel manager refused to share personnel records, even when Henry started name-dropping.

He was going to have to recommend the stiff-jawed hotel manager to Roxanne's recruiting team.

Henry then started googling Ginas.

Unfortunately, "San Francisco Gina," "gleaming-shoulder Gina" and "dream girl Gina" didn't get him anywhere. He could have done more; he had access to the kind of surveillance, technology and intelligence that would allow him to track Gina from the hotel lobby to her home. But he'd endure a thousand nights of sweat-soaked dreams and a million days of debilitating heartache before he allowed a crush to transform him into a stalker who abused his power and security clearance.

Five months later, he still tossed and turned in bed at the memory of what he'd let slip through his fingers. By now, she certainly had some guy distracting her who'd had the good sense to prize what he'd found.

Back in the Monte del Vino Real, as he walked across the Bodega Sofia courtyard behind Sofia, the fact that he still hadn't told his best friend or the rest of her family that he'd be abandoning his place in their lives in a month was probably another reason for his tossing and turning.

"...so much fun because she's just soaking up everything like a sponge," Sofia was saying animatedly, looking all winemaker and none of the princess in her stained overalls with a long braid down her back. "It's so easy to take for granted what you have until you appreciate it through a new person's eyes."

Henry hadn't heard a word. "Uh...sorry, lost the thread."

She stopped in the middle of the four-hundred-year-old courtyard and put her hands on her hips. "Talking to you recently has been like talking to fog. You're never here. I was telling you about our new cooper. I want to introduce you. With you and the family in Argentina for the last month, you've missed all the excitement of her getting the cooperage set up."

While Roxanne had been working out of her South American head-quarters and Príncipe Mateo had been advising Chilean winegrowers, Henry had tried to focus and find his replacement. But after seventy-five interviews, he still didn't have a list of top choices to show Roxanne.

She'd put her foot down yesterday before they'd gotten on the plane: come up with a list. Tell the family. Stop making her suffer through this alone.

She'd been angry, and this time she hadn't apologized for her emotion.

He was here to tell Sofia. It felt like he was about to cut off a limb.

Her bossy hands and huge smile didn't make it easier as she hustled him toward one of the small outbuildings on the monastery grounds and talked about wine barrels.

"...never in my wildest dreams would I have hoped to get her," Sofia was saying. "Her family's cooperage is one of the top in the US, and she was set to run it. But she's already bought a house near Rúa Trujillo for her and her two daughters. I think she's said goodbye to Sonoma County for good!"

That snagged into Henry's misery as they approached the open door leading to the monastery cooperage. "She's from California?" he asked.

"Yes," Sofia said as they stepped over the lintel into a stone-walled entry room. Oak planks left to cure were stacked to the ceiling along one wall. "In fact, I interviewed her when I went with you and Roxanne to San Francisco five months ago. You might have checked her in to the Medina Now building."

Henry shivered when he walked into the next, larger room, although heat from the back room was making the place toasty.

An older man was using a buzz saw to carve oak planks into the distinctive shape of a barrel stave. A young woman was using a mallet to level staves already inserted into an iron hoop, creating one end of the barrel. Sofia said buenos días but, obviously excited, led Henry into the back room.

It was like walking into Hades. The propane burners on the ground were currently roaring, and two of them were covered with barrels bound with iron on one end. A woman was rolling the splayed end of a barrel off the third burner. A short woman. A short woman with her back to him, her killer body outlined in a skintight tank top, bike shorts, tight ankle socks, and clunky, fire-retardant shoes.

Henry had once asked a cooper why he worked around fire with his shirt off. The cooper had explained that fewer clothes meant fewer places for ashes to get caught.

He couldn't see her hair; it was all pulled into a tight, black beanie. But her wide, formidable shoulders—shoulders that flexed and gleamed gorgeously with sweat while she rolled that barrel—were a perfect golden brown. He'd recognize those shoulders anywhere.

She turned to face him.

She blinked her thick, dark lashes a few times. Then she looked at him like she was waking up from the very best dream. "You?" she said.

It was the perfect mimic of someone faking surprise.

Henry was the one who should be surprised. Surprised that he actually believed that someone would want him for him and not the access he could provide. The job he could help secure.

"You!" he snarled.

## 16.

She'd fantasized a million scenarios about running into Henry—at an airport, in the hotdog line of a college football game, on a sunset beach, after he'd revealed himself to be a superspy and shown up in her bed to torture her with a night of tied-to-the-headboard pleasure.

But never once had the scenario involved seeing his gorgeous, thick-boned, dreamed-about face twisted up in fury at her.

Maybe it was a trick of the flames and the smoke? A bit of oak ash in her eye?

"What are you doing here?" she asked, stunned.

"Like you don't know," he snapped back.

She'd been drinking water all day, hadn't fainted from dehydration since she'd been an apprentice. But maybe she was hallucinating.

Her Henry hallucination turned to her boss, who looked in-real-life confused. "What did she tell you to get this job?" he demanded.

Princesa *Sofia* put her hands up. "Henry, I don't— What's going on?"

"Look, if she used anything about me to get this job, I want you to know I had nothin' to do with it," Henry said, that Texas accent she loved sounding foreign and grating. Those big biceps she'd adored were flinging out his arms in accusation. "I don't know her from a hole in the wall."

Gina looked at him in astonishment. He'd said— He'd done— After they'd—

Wait...used him?

Josefina Pérez had taught her daughters many things. One of them was to never let a big man make them feel small.

She drew herself up and wiped her brain clean of fantasies. "I don't know what you're insinuating," she said, quietly and distinctly, a contrast to his drawling and hand slinging. "But I didn't use anyone to get this job."

Speaking of the job...she turned and hit the kill switch for the propane to prevent the half-finished barrels from overcharring.

"Oh, sure," he spat as the flames snapped out, quieting their roar and making his disdain that much more audible. "Little Miss-Gina-don't-ask-me-who-I-am-but-I-just-applied-for-a-job. Shoulda known you were too good to be true."

Her scorching anger replaced the heat of flames. He was doing this in front of her new boss. With her employees in the next room.

Gina Pérez had been taught not to take shit from anyone.

"You want to know more than my first name?" she hissed, putting her hands on her hips. She loved making this big man visibly pull back. "I'm Gina fucking Pérez." And she wasn't going to hide anymore. "Trained at the knee of the formidable Josefina Pérez." She took a step toward him. "Adored by every winemaker in the US." Then another. "And mother of two incredible girls who will learn to kick ass and take names."

His eyes snapped wide as she stepped close enough to touch him.

"I was brave enough to blow up my world to become La Tonalera del Monte, and I didn't need any help from you." She poked his sternum, hard enough to bruise. "You're right. I am too good for you. I'm the best there is."

Sofia stepped in before Gina's temper burned down her new cooperage. "Mira, I don't know what's going on, but it appears you both are missing some important information. Henry, this is Gina Pérez, a world-renowned cooper who, as she aptly stated, did not need a reference from you. Gina, this is Henry Walker, a man who is my dearest friend when he isn't behaving como un burro, and the head of security for my sister-in-law for the last eleven years."

Henry's drawn-up, huge-chested, raised-chin glare continued to rake Gina with suspicion.

She couldn't believe she'd thought about him every day for the last five months. What a waste of time. "Well, good thing you quit that job so we can minimize these fun interactions."

His expression instantly transformed to one of shock and shame.

"What?" Sofia said, cool and deathly quiet in the still-warm room.

Henry closed his eyes.

Ten minutes ago, Gina would have begged, bartered and stolen to erase that look off his face.

"I came here to tell you," he said quietly.

She didn't know him, even though she'd convinced herself that she did. She wouldn't let her pitiful, deluded heart feel sorry for him. Not when Sofia, who'd welcomed Gina like an exciting co-conspirator into her new world order, looked at Henry like he'd punched her in the gut.

This man, this stranger, was apparently good at hurting the women who cared about him.

"We'll go," Gina said. "You can have the cooperage to talk—"

"No," Sofia said, jaw stiff. "We'll go. I need to explain some things to Henry. And apparently he needs to explain some things to me."

She took a moment to meet Gina's eyes. "This is not how we behave in my winery, our community, or this kingdom. Even if Henry won't say it, let me. I'm so sorry."

"Of course, alteza," Gina said, the highness just naturally rolling out.

She had nothing to say to Henry.

### 17.

Running over the scorching-hot sands of the Coronado beach in full gear during Hell Week was more pleasant than following Sofia back across the courtyard to her glassed-in office in the winery processing facility.

The glass rattled when she slammed the door.

"I knew it," Sofia shouted, starting at full volume, her tawny braid flying. "I knew something was off. I even…" She added a good helping of hurt to the mad on her pretty face. "I even asked you if something was wrong. I even had Aish ask you."

That awkward conversation a couple of months ago when Sofia's rock-star husband asked about Henry's "feelings" was an experience Henry hoped to never relive.

"When did you quit?" she asked, pain etching a divot between her brows.

"Same day you interviewed Gina."

Her forehead went marble smooth. "You've known for five months you were leaving and you're just now telling me." This was the voice of a queen about to make some heads roll.

This was the voice of his best friend and almost-sister for the last eight years.

Henry dropped his forehead into his hands. "I know," he moaned, letting all the misery he'd been hiding for the last five months flail out. "I'm a piece of shit." Here, he could say all the things that had been keeping him up at night. "The thing is, I don't want to go."

"What's going on?" she whispered. Her hand on his shoulder—supportive, loving, despite what he'd done, was why he told her.

He told her how women coming on to him because of who he guarded became the rule instead of the exception. He told her how some longtime guy friends he'd invited for a deep-sea fishing trip had trapped him on his boat in the Gulf for a three-hour-long presentation they wanted him to share with Roxanne. He told her how humiliated he'd been at his birthday party.

He told her he was lonely.

"The thing is, I love y'all," he said, raising his face from his hands, hating the tears he caused in her eyes. "And I'm so goddamn happy for you. But lovin' you and seein' how happy you are just makes me feel worse, because I can't have it. I don't want to go. But I feel like I'm just gonna to be more and more miserable if I stay."

Sofia, ever the problem solver, wiped her eyes. "Have you shared this with Roxanne?"

Henry shook his head.

She sighed deeply. "So what happened with Gina?"

And he told her that story too. He told her about the insta-lust and the hints from the bartender and the promise to stick to first names and the unexpected revelations about jobs hoped for and lost. He stayed away from the time in Gina's hotel room, but he was sure it was obvious in the way his voice got deeper and dreamier.

He told her about feeling adored and adoring and knew from the way Sofia rubbed a tattoo on her hip dedicated to her husband that she understood. He told her about the obsessive googling.

"You know she didn't use your one-night stand to get this job," Sofia said with a forbearing smile.

Henry nodded, shame a warm coal that was building into a bonfire. "I just...I couldn't believe it. What are the chances my dream girl was gonna show up in the Monte?"

"Yeah, what are the chances," Sofia said, her smile turning bright and prodding. "A woman who appreciates you just for you, without a care for who your family is—because we are your family—shows up in the place you don't want to leave. What in the world will you do?"

The possibilities, the potential, raced through Henry's brain.

He knew what he needed to do. He got down on his knees to start.

Sofia looked down at him in humor and surprise.

Henry took her hand in his. "What am I gonna do? Practice my grovel," he told her. "Forgive me, Sofia?"

His best friend in the world kissed his forehead, pulled him up off his knees—after a bit—gave him a big hug and then began helping him figure out how to get his dream job and dream girl back.


## 18.


After work that evening, while her girls played outside, Gina called her mother.

"Dime," Josefina said when she picked up, sounding cool as a cucumber. The only people she immediately spoke to in Spanish were her girls.

"Hola, Mami," Gina said, leaning her hip against the kitchen cabinet, letting the sight of the girls conspiring out on the green lawn, a freaking castle as their backdrop, soothe her nerves.

"I was wondering if phones stopped working once you crossed the Spanish border," Josefina said.

"No," Gina said. "But my caller ID must be acting up, because I apparently missed all the calls you made."

Her mother made a humming sound, and Gina took a sip of her wine.

"How's it going?" Josefina asked simply. But it was better than accusations or her mother hanging up on her, so with no small relief, Gina told her. She gave her a stripped-down version, not wanting to sound too excited. But still, it was exciting starting out on a new trail like the one a young Josefina Pérez had blazed into California forty years ago.

Without any intention of going into the topic, Gina found herself mentioning her concerns about filling the demand for barrels in a kingdom where new wineries were going up every day. Her mother reminded her that she could recoop existing barrels—removing the wine-soaked interior wood with a planer—thereby providing quickly produced barrels for lower-price-point wines and increasing her output.

It would have been a solution that eventually came to her. But the fact that her mother provided it without judgment, as a peer, had tears popping into her eyes.

"I wanted to say thank you," Gina said.

"¿Por qué?"

Gina took a deep breath. She saw herself poking Henry in the sternum, that stunned blue-eyed look on his face. *I am too good for you. I'm the best there is.*

"For this profession you taught me." Her eyes wandered over the fuchsias in the window box, the vine rows, the castle. "This life you gave me. Someone...questioned my abilities today, and I realized that's the first time that's happened in a long time. You raised me to strive and gave me the tools and the confidence to reach excellence, and I'd gotten so accustomed to people thinking highly of me that I took it for granted. It felt like a weight. Here, I guess, I can learn to appreciate it again. I can stand up for myself and on my own two feet, and I'm grateful you taught me that."

It was no easy thing, being a mother trying to raise strong women in a world opposed to them. Her daughters, too, she imagined, would have their got-to-get-away-from-Mom moments.

"Are you grateful enough to come back?" Josefina asked.

"Mami..."

"I have to ask, mija," her mother said unapologetically. But then her voice gentled. "I miss you."

Gina wiped her eyes. "I miss you too." She stared again at the castle. "But you know this is a great opportunity to for La Niña Cooperage to associate itself with an extremely popular kingdom."

Her mother chuckled. "I would love to see the face of the person who questioned your abilities. Are they still standing?"

Henry was a difficult monolith to push down. All day her five-month dream of him had collided with today's reality. She wouldn't mourn him, not with the jerk he'd turned out to be. But she'd mourn the dream she'd promised herself.

He was right about one thing—it had all been too good to be true.

But she had her gorgeous cooperage and a new adventure and her mom on the phone and her little girls... She looked out at the lawn. Where were the girls?

She pulled the phone from her ear. Heard their giggles.

Then heard a deep, drawling voice.

"Mami, I love you. Thank you for loving me back. But I gotta go."

She hung up and ran to the door.

***19.***

Henry pulled up to the little house with its red-tiled roof and terra-cotta planters of red and white flowers spilling all over the place and...Jesus...two adorable brown-haired little girls playing on the green lawn, and his heart seized.

It was perfect. It was his dream come true.

Get a handle on yourself, sailor, he reprimanded himself.

There was a good chance Gina was going to set the hose on him the instant she saw him. She certainly had a reason.

He turned off his truck, checked his reflection in the rearview mirror, and grabbed the gift bag from the front seat. Outside the truck, he checked his reflection again in the window and buttoned the sport coat he'd changed into specifically because it made him look massive. She'd liked his brawn, and he was going to use all the tools he had while he groveled.

He turned around and startled back to find the two little girls, the oldest in a flowered T-shirt and green shorts, the littlest in Superman pajamas, staring up at him with huge brown eyes. Sneaky little bugs. He was afraid he was going to crush them.

"Who's that for?" the tallest of them squeaked, her eyes covetous on the polka-dotted gift bag.

"Shit," he said. She'd said she had girls—he should've remembered, he should've brought them...

The little one covered her mouth with her red cape and started giggling. The older girl looked scandalized. "You can't say that word!"

Oh God. "You're right, sorry...I..."

But she had other priorities. She pointed her tiny finger—how could anything be so small and still talk and walk?—at the bag. "Who's that for?"

"Your mom," he said miserably. He squatted down to stop lording over them. "I'm sorry. I forgot to bring y'all something."

He'd been around the royal twins their whole lives, but these two girls, with their brown skin and honey eyes and mini-me expressions, still seemed like a miracle of biology and evolution.

"That's okay," the oldest said solemnly. She put her hand on his big shoulder. He didn't understand how something so tiny could make him feel so good. Her little sister nodded in sympathy. "Do you have any gum?"

"I do," he said, brightening up. He'd been chewing on a stick coming over here. He dug into his coat pocket. "I got Doublemint..."

He was pulling out the pack when he heard a sharp, "Girls!"

He looked up and saw her—Gina Pérez, he'd been whispering over and over again—standing furious with her hand holding open the screen door as he, a huge stranger, gave candy to her babies.

Shit.

"Josie, Skye, get in here right this second," she said quietly. And although they looked at the gum forlornly, they hustled across the lawn to do what their mama said. She held the screen door open wider to let them through, then glared at him.

"What do you want?"

He stood but stayed where he was. "To say I'm sorry." He had to raise his voice to be sure she heard him from across the lawn. "To apologize for acting like a horse's as—" He cut himself off when he saw the girls peering around her hips. "Elbow. For acting like a horse's elbow today."

Those thin pink lips he'd kissed and coveted, lips he thought he'd never get to see again, fell open in surprise before she firmed them up and raised her chin.

A woman like her didn't take shit from anybody.

He barreled on. "Gina, I'm so sorry. Saying what I said to you, making the assumptions I made when you'd been so open and straightforward and kind, that was awful. But saying them in front of Sofia, at your place of work, that was unforgivable."

Her expression hadn't changed, but she still hadn't gotten out the hose. He took a few steps onto the green grass of her lawn. "I ruined in under a minute the ten hours that we had together. But those ten hours are all I've been thinking about for five months. I've missed you every second since I got in the elevator."

Bare-*culo* honesty, Sofia had advised. It was the only way. And if those big eyes weren't staring around Gina's hips, he would have gotten bare-ass naked if it would help his cause.

He cautiously took a few more steps closer. Her chin had softened. Maybe. She still looked as tough as nails.

"I'm here to beg you for a chance to show you that I usually keep my horse's-elbow moments to a minimum. Even if we can only be...acquaintances..."

He lowered his head to protect his soft parts from the unbearable thought. It was still more bearable than having none of her at all.

"I just hate the idea of knowing where my dream girl is but only getting to see her in my dreams."

Knees. He should have said that from his knees. Roxanne, whom he'd gone to see before he came here, had thought that was an appropriate place for him after the five months he'd put her through.

About to bend, Gina's words, her voice, stopped him.

"This is crazy, Henry," she said, shaking her head. But she didn't close the door against him. She pressed her free hand against her mouth, then seemed to realize she was doing it. She dropped her hand and looked directly at him, a double-barrel brown-eyed blast to his heart.

"How can we be each other's dreams when we don't know a thing about each other?" she asked.

**20.**

Henry Walker had performed some delicate operations in his time as a Navy SEAL and as head of security for one of the world's wealthiest women. But none as delicate as convincing one Gina Pérez to trust him, a stranger she'd spent ten wild hours with five months ago. A stranger who'd been cruel the second he'd seen her again.

She'd said he was her dream too. And if he hadn't been such an incredible horse's elbow, he could have savored and treasured the look of wondrous joy on her face when he'd first stepped into her cooperage.

"I know a lot about you." He couldn't help but grin at the instant scrunch of skepticism on her face. "I do," he said, taking careful steps forward like he was feeling for land mines. "You're smart and funny and kind. You have great taste in liquor. You say what's on your mind, even when you're trying to hold back. You have the whitest teeth and good, rough hands and an awesome laugh and…"

He noticed the littlest girl was smiling at him like he was a lovable idiot. "And, thank Christ, I finally know where you got those shoulders that've been hauntin' me. I know if I make you mad, which I'm gonna try real hard not to do, I'm gonna hear about it. I like that…" He slapped his chest. "I like that your feelings toward me, good or bad, they're about me, not the people I'm around."

She tilted her head at him. He was now a couple of yards from her. Sunlight played in her hair, which was wavy like she'd just washed it. She was wearing old jeans and a slouchy sweatshirt, no makeup, and he wanted her worse now than he had when she'd been in her flippy skirt.

He pulled an envelope out of the gift bag. "I brought you this. So you can learn about me too."

"What is it?" She wasn't reaching to take it.

"My résumé." He held it out. "You actually will need to look at it. The cooperage falls under the royal family's purview, and all department heads will have to sign off on hiring me as head of royal security."

She reached out and—just for a second—they were connected by an eight-inch stretch of paper while their eyes met. "So you…won't be leaving?"

"You were the only person that knew the truth for five months. I never wanted to quit my job protecting Roxanne and her family. These people are my family. But everyone I met kept looking straight past me to them, and I got afraid I'd never be able to find someone who saw me."

When he came clean to Roxanne and her prince husband, Mateo, she'd raged over what he'd put her through, and Mateo had raged over being the last to know, and then they'd both excitedly talked about a castle security reorganization.

It was always a bit of a roller coaster with the royal family.

"You saw me," Henry said. "I saw you. Without either of us caring about what's on our pieces of paper."

His heart pounded as she looked him over. There'd never been a moment when the measure of him had been more important.

"What else is in the bag?" she said. And she looked exactly like her oldest right then.

Henry tried to hide his grin as he named the $250 Japanese whisky they'd enjoyed together. "I figure, if nothing else worked, I could ply you with expensive whisky."

She looked at him, still not smiling. "You would have to come in..."

"To be plied?" he said.

But she continued to study him. He stuck out his chest and let her beautiful brown eyes look. She had a lot riding on this decision.

So did he.

"Josie, Skye." She put a gentle hand on each girl's head as she said their names. "What do you think? Should we let him in?"

"He seems nice," said Josie, the oldest.

"He's got gum," sighed Skye, the baby.

Henry bit his lips against laughing, because Gina still hadn't smiled.

"I've been hurt too," she said, "by people more interested in what I represent or what I can do for them than who I am." She lifted her chin and pressed her daughter against her leg. "And I've never felt more seen or valued for myself than I did that night with you."

His chest was big. But right now, it felt like it could barely contain his heart. He'd given her the power to leave it bleeding.

Instead, she opened her screen door just a touch wider.

"Yeah?" he asked.

"Yes," she said.

And she answered a lifetime's worth of prayers when she gave him a warm, white-toothed, round-cheeked, she-couldn't-be-lieve-he-was-at-her-door smile.

On legs he hoped like hell didn't show they were shaking, he stepped up to her door. And held out his hand.

"Henry Walker. It's sure nice to meet the woman of my dreams."

She slid her hand—small, tough, hot and beloved—into his.

"Gina Pérez," she said, her gaze on his lips before drifting up to meet his eyes. "It's nice to meet the man of mine."

He held the door open for her and followed his love and her baby girls inside.


**THE END**


Enter the sensual word of royalty, billionaires, and moun-
tain vineyards in the *Filthy Rich* series.
*Lush Money*
*Hate Crush*
*Serving Sin*


*"Lopez successfully flips the gender switch on the wealthy
CEO trope while at the same time incorporating a generous
dash of fairy-tale glitz and glam into the captivating sto-
ryline of her marvelous debut. And when these elements are
combined with engaging characters and an abundance of
boldly sensual, vividly rendered love scenes, you have every-*

*thing fans of sexy contemporary romances could ever crave.*
"—Booklist ★ (Starred Review)

# Chapter Nine

# Crack in the Plaster

*What would it take for the average woman, just a lady you pass at the grocery store, to enter into a threesome? In what circumstances would it jump off the pages of a steamy story into something fathomable? Or even comfortable?*

*When would it be a welcome respite?*

*I had an idea and a spare weekend. This is my answer to that question.*

***

In a ratty, oversize sweatshirt she'd reclaimed from her son and worn workout shorts, Beth Hernandez pounded on the motel door. It was 3 a.m. and she'd only checked in to this fleabag motel two hours ago after the airline finally confirmed that she wasn't making it out tonight. Every decent hotel was booked because of the summer thunderstorm that had closed JFK and stranded her in DC. She really needed to get a few hours' sleep before she made her way back to the airport at the break of dawn to jockey for a flight. But she couldn't sleep because two people—two men, it sounded like—were having waaaaaay too much fun slamming their headboard into the wall next to her head.

She pounded again, feeling the exhaustion and anger and injustice rising through her fist. What she wouldn't give for a little time and space and energy to allow a man to slam her headboard. She was prepared to break her hand through the door to get these guys to shut the fu—

Her fist flew through the air as the door lurched open.

"What?!" a husky voice barked.

It must have been the sex smell. It wafted out into the stormy night, deep and bitter, musky and rich and familiar; she might be forty-two and single, but she still remembered the sex marathons she and her ex-husband had when they were in their twenties. With it also came the scent of Irish Spring and oil, like the men inside had worked on a car and then showered it off before they...got to work.

So it must have been the sex smell that paralyzed her brain and stopped up her words and left her frozen, fist still in the air. Her eyes took a deep, pornographic gulp of the scene.

The big man filling the doorway in front of her might have been the prettiest man she'd ever seen. He was shirtless—naked, actually—with his hips wrapped in a sheet and his thick, muscular torso covered in nicks and scars and tattoos. His plush lips and bright blue eyes were such a contrast to that workman's body; his short blond hair was a sweaty mess. Behind him—oh, thank the good Lord she could see just between his shoulder and the doorjamb—a second pretty man was stretched under the covers. It was ridiculous to call such a long, wide-shouldered man pretty. But he was, his dark wavy hair equally sweaty, watching her with suspicion.

She looked above his head and bit her lip to keep from whimpering. There was a crack in the plaster, the result of one of these pretty, giant men pounding his penis into the other.

"Holy crap," she breathed, feeling true awe for the first time in a long time.

That made the hulking man in the doorway lose his scowl. His face eased into a soft smile. This time, she did whimper, watching what a smile did to those blood-red lips. Lips abused by what he and the other man did to each other.

"Yes?" he asked. His voice was whiskey fumes. She didn't even care that he was laughing at her, laughing at the tired soccer mom in her sexless pajamas gawking at him.

"I..."

"What's she need, Max?" That one's voice, from the bed, was tender in its gruffness. Max. She met the man's blue eyes and felt a *zing* of want. He saw her. This was Max. Hi, Max.

"Not sure yet, Johnny," he called back and her mouth went as dry as a summer sidewalk. How long had it been since someone had said her name like that? Johnny.

Max's smile went up another notch, and he leaned on the door, calling attention to his big, beautiful shoulder. "Whatcha need, sweetheart?"

"I..." She couldn't catch her breath; she felt like she'd just finished one of those HIIT workout classes she despised. The quick breaths filled her lungs with the Max-and-sex smell; she fed on them like an addict. "I...was going to tell you to keep it down."

"Yeah?" He was nothing but delighted. "And now?" He'd called her sweetheart in that gravel-strewn voice.

"Now? I, um..." She laughed. What else could she do, barely protected from a rainstorm by a cheap metal awning, under the gaze of a beautiful stranger, more aroused than she'd been in a spate of angry then lonely years. "I'm probably...um...I'll probably just go back to my room and join in."

Max chuckled and it was syrup over the secret parts of her. "Sure, sweetie, you can go back to your room," he said as he walked back, slowly opening the door. "Or you can join us in here."

"Max!" the man growled from the bed.

Jaw on the floor, she stared at the man in the bed who'd shot up to sitting. The blanket was at his waist, but everything above it was exposed. Every inch of glorious, bronzed, muscled shoulders, chest, and abs like masculine beauty heightened with magic and steroids and wishing well dreams. He pushed back a lock of dark, wavy hair, exposing a mile-wide bicep. His dark, dark eyes touched her, and her insides gave a hard squeeze.

"Sorry 'bout him," Johnny said with chagrin. The other one, Max, was her age. But this one was younger, sweeter. His voice was warm honey. "He confuses real life with porn."

Beth put a hand in her messy hair, pressed against her temple. "I seem to be having the same problem right now."

To her astonishment, Johnny's apologetic gaze turned from kind to considering. His eyes traveled over her, from her face, over her breasts, down legs that suddenly felt very naked. She was in her glasses and an old sweatshirt that her ex-husband had said added ten years and twenty pounds. But when his eyes met her again, she felt sexier than she had since the last anniversary she'd shared with her husband. The last anniversary before he threw away fifteen years and what she'd thought was a true partnership without a backward glance.

The devil was suddenly in Johnny's sweet smile. "I guess it's only a problem if someone's offended," he said, and she wondered where they learned to talk like that, like they were using their voices to stroke skin. "If there's no offense, then it's an opportunity." He patted the mattress with a big hand. "Wanna come in?"

She knew there was oxygen in the rain-drenched air, knew there was sound as the storm pounded against the roof, knew there'd been strength in her knees when she'd marched furiously around the motel to bang on their door. But right now, she couldn't breathe, couldn't hear, and had to lean her shoulder against the doorjamb to stay upright.

"Johnny, I—"

"It's John," he said, not unkindly, that damp curl of hair again falling onto his broad forehead as he nodded his head at the other man. "Only he calls me Johnny."

She leaned her back against the jamb and let it support all of her weight as she looked at Max. He stood there watching her, his thick fingers around the edge of the door, his big beautiful body just there, right there, mirroring hers as the sheet dipped just enough for her to see the muscle that started at the top of his pale hip and disappeared down into the mysteries beneath his cover. There, on the silky skin that covered muscle, was a perfect purple bloom. A hard, focused mouth had sucked him there. She could imagine him rolling and gripping the sheet white-knuckled while it happened. She wanted to create a twin.

She met his eyes again, those heavy-lidded, focused eyes, and had to lean her head back against the frame as lust sluiced down her body from the tips of her ears to her toes. Did anyone ever say "no" to those eyes?

"You're gorgeous," he rumbled, the words slipping from his lips like sweets.

"I am?" Beth replied, mystified. She'd known she was, a lifetime ago. But that confidence had grown weaker with the slow dawning understanding that her husband no longer wanted to share a home or a life with her and breathed its last breath when he left her for his spin instructor.

He'd no longer been able to see her. He hadn't wanted to look.

But these two men were looking now. Max grinned wider. "Yeah, sweetheart, you're beautiful." She loved delighting him. "And you're sad."

Beth nodded without meaning to. She was so glad he was able to see her through her shroud of unhappiness.

Max leaned toward her. "You call or text or email whoever you want to let them know you're in here. You can take a picture of our licenses. We'll give you our socials." He grinned and purred, a stranger offering the very best candy. "But come in. You don't have to do nothin'. Come in and watch. Or just lay back and let us put our mouths on you." The mind-shattering mental image would have put her on her knees if not for the doorjamb at her back. "We'll only do what you want. But...come in. Let us show you some fun."

She hiccupped a half laugh, half sob, and wasn't that a sexy reaction to a proposed threesome? When was the last time she'd had some fun? Between the deadlines and the book tours and the college visits and the house and the glacier-slow healing of her shattered heart, when had there been space or energy for it? Or even a desire?

But here, tonight, she felt like she'd stepped through a rip in her universe: into a motel she wasn't sleeping in, a city she wasn't supposed to be in, and a pummeling rainstorm that would keep whatever they did in this room secret. Into the bedroom of two gorgeous, obviously in-love and open-spirited men who made her feel safe and seen and sexy and who just wanted to give her "some fun."

Fun? Hell, they might be saving her life.

"Okay," she got out, jittery but fervently glad that she'd showered off a day of frustrating travel before she'd gone to bed. "Okay. Okay, I—"

Johnny—John—wrapped his hips in the blanket and levered himself off the bed. He was bigger and even more beautifully blinding stretched vertical. As he approached her, trapping the blanket around his narrow hips with one hand, he held out his free hand. She didn't understand how someone could look so sweet yet tempting at the same time.

Max also stretched a hand out. His smile commanded.

Just inside the doorway of this fleabag motel room, two stroke-inducing men held their hands out because they saw her and wanted to include her in their fantasy. But they weren't going to pressure her. She had to choose.

Beth didn't take their hands. Instead, she pushed away from the frame. Tucked her hand into their covers. And tugged them off.

As a sheet and a blanket fluttered to the floor, one forty-two-year-old woman stepped into a fleabag motel room and kicked the door shut behind her.

**THE END**

# Chapter Ten

# Touch Me

*This is another story I wrote for the **Read Me Romance** podcast. I asked for it to be read by Stacy Gonzalez, the award-winning narrator of both of my books in the Milagro Street series. Because of Stacy's narration, **Full Moon Over Freedom** was given an Earphones Award from AudioFile Magazine and named one of its top audiobooks of 2023!*

*"Stacy Gonzalez's fierce narration of Lopez's second-chance romance is a stormy yet satisfying listen....Gonzalez's boundless sensitivity to the longings of the heart completely transforms the story through her audio performance ."—**AudioFile Magazine**.*

*You can listen to her narration of **Touch Me** here.*

**Content warning: surprise massage, tease of infidelity**

***

Marisol Gutierrez had it all.

That was what everyone told her.

Head of her own wildly successful investment fund, a husband who loved her to his mild-mannered Midwestern bones, two talented and thriving children, and a cadre of employees, friends, family, and organizations who valued her and needed her.

Even her dog, her little brother teased, was perfect. A perfectly behaved and adorable junkyard mutt.

But what she never told anyone—no journalist or entertainment news reporter or business associate or friend or, even, her staunchly supportive husband—was that having it all meant bearing it all. It all was in your possession. Your safekeeping. It meant you were a possessor of all of these loving, beautiful, smart, talented, valuable entities full of potential and if you dropped one of them—if you got frigging exhausted and it went tumbling out of your over-burdened arms—then...well....

Marisol didn't like to think about the "then well."

Instead, Marisol Gutierrez allowed herself a good, hard, half-hour cry every Thursday evening in her corner office's private bathroom, then she washed her face, took off her clothes, and emerged promptly at 6 p.m. for her one-hour massage with Rhondel. Marisol paid handsomely for the best hands in San Francisco. While Marisol cried, Rhondel set up his massage table, pulled the shades on her floor-to-ceiling windows, and lit aromatherapy candles, all in blessed, undemanding silence. In fact, Rhondel never uttered a word except the rare times when they would grab a drink after the massage when her husband was at his class and the kids were busy with their own plans.

So when Marisol stepped into her elegant office, she was fine that she was still hiccupping a little, her face blotchy and eyes red. She knew Rhondel, tinkering behind the screen he set up, would say nothing. Marisol breathed in the light scent of sandalwood (her favorite) and crossed to the massage table.

She took off her robe, slid between the warmed heavy flannel sheets, and laid her face into the doughnut at the end of the table that allowed her to keep her spine straight. She inhaled deep, then let it all out. For one hour, she'd put her worries and anxieties and terrors into Rhondel's capable hands.

"I'm ready," she called, closing her eyes.

She heard him come around the screen and stop at the head of the table. Big male hands pressed against her flannel-covered back. A greeting. She smiled, eyes still closed, breathing deeply. His hands rose and fell with her breaths. That was different, but she liked it.

He circled to her side and folded the sheet down to expose her naked back, picked up her arm, and placed it back down to trap the sheet just above her ass. His touch felt more tentative than normal. Rhondel had worked on her glutes when she'd been deluded enough to train for a marathon; they weren't shy with each other.

She heard the *snick* of a bottle, the rub of palms warming up the massage oil. He stood at the head of the table again.

The instant the man put his hands on her shoulder blades and slid them down the planes of her back, Marisol knew this wasn't Rhondel.

Her head shot up, out of the doughnut.

She was looking directly into the world-famous bedroom eyes of Hollywood superstar Ray Morgan.

***

It would be a massive understatement to say it was a surprise when Ray Morgan's newly developed production company made an appointment with Marisol's group to discuss managing the assets of their first production fund. Marisol hadn't known a thing about their interest until the appointment was already made. Her 38th-floor office full of wicked-smart women superb at putting on the airs of disaffected hipsters had been in an uproar. As their boss and mentor, a Latina in a role few thought she could manage and some refused to believe she deserved, she couldn't reveal the intensity of her long-time crush on the gorgeous celebrity. But when she'd met his chestnut-dark eyes across her conference table, it'd done nothing to staunch the way she felt about him.

"My people compared your firm with ten others and made this meeting based on the returns on your investments in companies owned by BIPOC women," he said in his chest-deep voice, so low it was like a lullaby even when he was talking about her company's mission. He'd been wearing a white shirt and a silver-gray suit that looked like tailored moonlight over his mahogany skin and wide shoulders. "When I saw the numbers, I was impressed too."

She couldn't imagine Ray Morgan, with his superhero cape and his Oscar, looking at her numbers. It was the last thing he needed to be looking at.

When her second-in-command dimmed the lights and began the presentation on precisely how they would invest his hard-earned money, she saw something else he didn't need to be looking at.

Using the folder of documents they'd prepared as cover, the man was surreptitiously staring at her—instead of the documents—over the rim of his ridiculously sexy black-framed reading glasses. She'd recently started wearing them as well. But they didn't look like that on her.

He met her eyes and she stared determinedly back, challenging any man—even this beautiful creature—who thought he could ogle her in her place of work. She forced herself to call it ogling. But he was shameless. He met her eyes with a tiny smile before he turned his gaze back to the presentation.

Some men were turned on by power and it appeared Ray Morgan was one of them.

***

Now, the movie star who'd been voted the sexiest man of the year two years ago looked back at her, his hands on her naked body, without blinking. His bottomless eyes were resolute. Challenging. And his hands—hard, hot, massive—slowly slid up her skin as he straightened. At her shoulders, he gently pressed her down against the table.

"What're you doing?" she hissed, looking through the doughnut hole at bare feet—his feet were long, sleek marble—and jeans. Rhondel wore expensive kicks and the latest leggings.

"Helping you relax," he murmured, the gravel in his voice like a San Francisco tremor in the quiet room.

"You don't—"

"Shhhh..." he hushed, moving to her side to sweep one strong hand down the right side of her back. Marisol's mouth opened involuntarily at the warm stroke into her skin and muscles. "You know I've wanted to take care of you for a while. Let me."

He used both hands to slowly sweep from her spine to her side, an inch at a time, like he was scooping tension off her back and down to the floor. Her eyes stuttered wider at the shocking pleasure of it. Acclaimed movie star Ray Morgan, with his simmering dark glances and come-hither grins, had wanted to do this to her for a while? Since when? When had he learned to rub muscle and skin like he was channeling ecstasy right into her bloodstream?

Was she a role he was practicing for?

Whatever feeble objection Marisol was going to try got eaten up by her involuntary moan when his big thumbs worked in between her shoulder blades and spine.

"Good?"

She could just hear that cocky grin that got panties flung at him when he walked the red carpet.

"Shut up," she whimpered.

His chuckle—chest deep and window rattling—had her curling her toes around each other as he circled to her other side and began working the left side of her back.

"This can be as little or as much as you want it to be," he said, bent to her, his breath near her ear. "Your husband never needs to know."

She stiffened even though everything in her was melting at his touch. That *definitely* was not part of the masseuse handbook. It blurred the line about what this could be. She wanted to get up and leave. She wanted to have multiple backs for him to rub with his huge hands.

"I miss seeing you at the conference table," he said. "I miss being the only one who makes you smile when we sit there."

*I never*, she wanted to hiss. She smiled during positive performance reviews and at the office Christmas party and during the office-funded happy hour she attended once a month. She smiled excessively in the comfort and privacy of her home. But she never smiled at the conference table, not after the partner of the first financial group she'd interned for—a man she'd thought of as a mentor—had told her she should smile more as he put his hand on her thigh.

The fact that she'd been giving Ray Morgan unknown-to-her smiles at the conference table was just one more reason for her to tell him to stop and leave. She knew he'd comply in an instant.

She muffled a groan as his cupped palm slid warmth and magic down the muscles of her side.

***

After the end of that first meeting, he'd asked her to lunch as she'd been making pleasantries with his team. The lunch was obviously supposed to be just him and her. The room had waited with bated breath for her answer.

She'd invited her assistant, her second-in-command, and the lead for their fund in Kenya, and he'd invited a corresponding number of his own people.

It didn't prevent everyone from seating them next to each other.

At the sun-soaked La Mar, a Peruvian cebichería, everyone seemed to go out of their way to talk to the person sitting next to them and leave Ray and Marisol to their own devices on their side of the circular table.

"I hope you don't mind that I invited you to lunch," he murmured.

She gave him a cool, polite smile. "Of course not. Why would I? Lunch is necessary during work hours and we are work associates."

That made his sculpted jaw beneath his trim black beard firm. She'd seen that look when he was eyeing a bad guy.

"Right, work associates." He tapped his middle finger against the lunch table, a sign he was annoyed. "What do you like to do in your downtime, Mrs. Gutierrez?"

She liked attending her son's theater rehearsals, driving her daughter to fencing lessons, watching old episodes of *Dallas*, *Falcon's Crest* and *Corazón Salvaje* on YouTube, and FaceTiming with her brother, a professor at the University of Kansas. Oh, and she liked fucking her husband.

She never discussed any of that at work.

She couldn't be that part of herself—wife and mother and sister—during business hours. In front of all these people depending on her.

"This and that," she said as she sipped on her ice water with lemon. "You, Mr. Morgan?"

He said something about golf and working out when she knew—he'd declared it in his *Rolling Stone* cover interview—that he hated both.

From the end of that uncomfortable lunch to the finalization of their working agreement, he never again tried to spend time alone with her during business hours.

That in no way impeded her intense, fangirling, hang-his-poster-on-her-wall attraction to him. Or his attraction to her.

*****

"Why were you crying?" he murmured as his thumb did something along the wing of her right shoulder blade that made her spine tingle.

"You can massage me," she told the man initially made famous by his art-house love scenes. Ray Morgan had a great ass. "But that's it. I'm not discussing that with you. That wasn't for you to hear."

Without comment, his hand moved to her arms. At five eight, she wasn't a small woman. Her absent dad's Swedish heritage helped to defy her mom's Mexican height limits, and she'd inherited her tías' formidable hips and ass and shoulders. But when his big hands circled her biceps, he made her feel wispy. She turned her head on the doughnut to look down at his hands, dark against her olive-tan skin. His hands looked mammoth against her, with long fingers and wide, manicured nail beds. He'd once been a young man who'd worked landscaping to help support his family. She wondered if that guy knew that manicures were in his future.

She hid her face in the doughnut again.

When his hands smoothed down to her forearms, when he worked the tendons that would ache with carpal tunnel, the carpal tunnel she developed working too long on her laptop, working at theater rehearsals and fencing practices and in bed until her husband pulled the laptop away from her, working to keep paychecks flowing to the people she employed and dollars earning for the people who invested in her fund for college and retirement, she had the sudden impulse to cry again. When he used those thumbs to rub into her palms, her hands involuntarily constricted to grip his.

This wasn't okay. Movie star Ray Morgan wasn't her masseuse. He wasn't meant to manage her worries this way. She couldn't…

Still holding her hand, movie star Ray Morgan ran a gripping hand down the length of her entire arm, just so right, and she gasped at the sensation.

"Do you like it?" he asked, teasing and tempting.

"It's fine," she said through a strangled voice, yanked from sorrow to temptation so quickly that her pussy tingled. Her pussy was naked there beneath the heavy flannel sheet, waiting there with a growing impatience about when it would be her turn, not yet understanding she wasn't going to get one.

"Fine?" he said. He said it much too close to the shell of her ear, like he knew how sensitive it was. "I'm sure we can do better than fine."

He professionally, competently, dominantly pulled the flannel up to tuck it around her neck and cover her torso completely.

Then he reached under the sheet to touch her leg.

Ray Morgan was touching her right leg. He pulled it out from beneath the sheet, held it between his hard body and bicep, then flipped the covers under while securing her leg on top and modestly keeping her ass covered. When had Ray Morgan, a working actor since he followed his wife to California, learned the impersonal-yet-personal skills of an expert masseuse?

His touch was entirely appropriate but there was nothing impersonal about it.

He held her thick thigh with the long span of both hands. When his thumbs began to work into the muscles, Marisol bit her lips against a groan.

As he stroked his way down in slow, thorough centimeters, Marisol fought against spreading her thighs and seeing where else his fingers wandered.

He skipped her knee—it was something Rhondel knew to do because of a soccer injury she'd gotten in high school—and he also skipped the bottom of her foot. Her feet were so ticklish she couldn't even wear fuzzy socks.

When he cupped his big hand over the top of her thigh, she was ready for the motion. He'd done it already to both sides of her back and both of her arms when he was done working the tension out of them, this final, big-handed, top-to-bottom stroke that no masseuse had ever given her. It was like he was giving a blessing and saying a tender goodbye to each portion of her body. It made her feel incredibly cared for. It made her want to offer him the warm inches inside her as well.

She thought she was ready.

But when that hand finally stroked down her leg from thigh to ankle in a firm, hot, unyielding caress, she moaned, helpless in her pleasure.

That asshole chuckled deep in a chest she wanted to lick.

"I knew we could do better than fine." His voice made the tiny hairs on her body stand up. "Turn the fuck over."

****

The fact that there were no more out-of-office meetups during working hours in no way impeded his long looks and heavy glances. To anyone else, Ray Morgan looked completely professional while they sat around the conference table. But no one had studied his heavy-lidded, black-lashed, bedroom eyes like Marisol had. She couldn't count how many times she'd looked up from the documents to find him running that big fingertip over his lower lip while he stared over the edge of his document at the gleam of her shoulder in a sleeveless dress, the push of her breasts against her blouse, or the stroke of her thumb over the back of her hand.

He watched her like she was a box of chocolates and he was on Keto before one of the prizefighter movies that wrecked his body.

He spoke to her about anything other than the deal they were working on whenever the ebb and flow of their staff allowed him to.

Once, while waiting for documents to be checked and signed and photocopied and notarized, they'd ended up alone at the conference table.

"Your staff..." he began, tilting that perfectly shaped skull at her. His hair and beard were speckled with silver that his stylists wisely convinced him not to cover. "How do you maintain a mythic status with them while getting them to adore you?"

She focused on the page in front of her to avoid letting him see how his admiration fed her. "I pay them well, praise them, work to make sure they have room for healthy personal lives, offer them appropriate guidance on new challenges, and trust them to do their jobs."

"Can I send a few directors your way? I've never worked with anyone so talented."

The warm glow of his praise felt like a beam of sunlight. She didn't want that here.

Another time, they'd both been late for one of their meetings. While the team had waited upstairs, they'd ridden up the thirty-eight floors together in an empty elevator.

"You ever think about making one of those smart women who work for you a partner?" he said, leaning on the side wall, watching her unabashedly. "Sharing some of the load?"

"Why would I do that?" she asked sharply, keeping her eyes on the rising numbers.

"You work very hard," he said quietly. His voice could have vibrated apart the elevator cables. "I bet your husband doesn't even know how hard."

"He's busy working hard too," she said. *8...9...10...* "He's never needed to know. Work stays at work."

"He's very successful."

*That* drew her eyes on him. "So?"

He stopped a moment. He was a big, muscular man behind whom she could barely see the elevator wall. He still looked wary. "You two have plenty of resources if you wanted to take it a little easier—"

She turned to face him fully and put her hands on her hips. She would have hefted her tits at him if not for the security cameras in the elevator. Security could not hear her words. "Would you say that to me if I wasn't the spouse with a vagina, Mr. Morgan? Would you recommend that he step back from his career so that he could *take it easy* like all he was good for was eating bonbons and watching telenovelas?"

"Hey," he said, pushing off the elevator wall to step up to her. "That's not what I was suggesting at all."

"Then what were you suggesting?" She had to tilt her head back to look up into his scowling face. It shouldn't have aroused her.

"You're stressed," he said. "I don't like seeing you stressed."

"You wouldn't *see* me stressed if you didn't insist on coming to every meeting with your team," she said. "You're the one who keeps putting us in that conference room together." He was the one that kept forcing this situation, forcing his way into her work life and forcing her to like him seeing her there.

Forcing her to say things she didn't want to say. "The cold, hard truth, Mr. Morgan, is that nothing in this life is guaranteed."

Her hard-working single mother's death when she was sixteen, obliging her to juggle work and school and taking care of her younger brother since they were an expense none of their extended family could afford, certainly had taught her that.

"We could have another 2008 crash," she said. "My husband's career might go belly up. He could decide to trade me in for a younger model."

Ray Morgan's expressive face hardened impressively. "He would never be that stupid."

"*Nothing* is guaranteed," she purred.

If he'd grabbed her to kiss her then, she would have let him. Hi broad hands twitched at his sides with the impulse. But the kiss wouldn't have been about passion. It would have been about control. His effort to wrench it from her. Her desire to trust him with it, if only for the span of an elevator ride.

"The only variable I can predict is me," she said. "What I do. How hard I work. You don't like to see it? Then stop coming here."

The elevator doors dinged, and she stepped away from movie star Ray Morgan before someone besides the building's well-paid and discreet security guards could see them panting on each other.

He did not stop coming to their meetings. He didn't stop watching her and idly playing with his bottom lip when he did so. He didn't stop asking about who she, Marisol Gutierrez, was as a woman and boss and master of her own ship.

But he never suggested again that she "take it easy."

***

The movie star's husky words, *Turn the fuck over*, rocketed down her spine.

Trembling, she stayed where she was. "We shouldn't do this," she whispered, her face still in the doughnut.

"Why?" His growl was like his big finger running up between her legs.

"I like my marriage the way it is," she said. "I don't want anything to change."

"Fuck that," he cursed. "I want to shake up your marriage."

Part of her wanted him to grab. Part of her wanted him to dominate and free her from the decision.

His hands settled on the bed next to her body.

He sighed heavily through his teeth. "Let me finish the massage," he said. "Just let me finish. If this is the only way you'll let me take care of you, let me do this."

Who was strong enough to say no when Ray Morgan begged?

The quick nod of her head was the only consent he was getting.

With a caring touch, he untucked the heavy flannel from around her body, held it high so that her nakedness was blocked from his view, and waited for her to turn over onto her back. She scooted down until her head was on the bed before he folded the sheets over her then tucked her in.

She kept her eyes closed.

She heard the squeak of the stool as his weight settled on it. He detached the doughnut. Then he rolled closer, slid his hands under her head and cradled it.

He held her head for a long moment and it took everything in her not to open her eyes.

This was totally normal. She'd had masseuses hold her head in their hands as a way to center them and herself. As a way to express their intentions.

What did Ray Morgan intend?

He straightened, the stool creaking beneath him, and breathed out a long, deep breath.

Then Ray Morgan's huge, hot hands slid slowly under her shoulders and down her back, using her own weight to press her against the massage of his palms and fingers, until he reached her waist, fingers spread and thumbs in the curve of her. She was all but cradled in his superhero arms.

Near her ear, he said, "I heard your husband is a good guy."

She could smell his cologne, a light sandalwood.

"The best," she whimpered, her head lolling, as Ray Morgan began a slow and erotic stroking up her back.

"Then why do you cry alone in your office?"

"That was private," she moaned. When his thumbs stroked lightly against her sides, they sent a pleasurable threat that had her hips rolling.

"There's private and then there's you working yourself into an early stroke like your mom," he growled against her ear. "I could kick his ass for not looking out for you better."

"He's busy," she tried again. "He took care of us when I was in school and then getting my career up and running. It's my turn."

At her shoulder blades, rather than easing up and giving her poor shivering body a break, he pushed his hands back down again, back down to hold the small of her back in his hands.

His trim beard brushed her cheek. "Baby, you take all the turns you want." He worked her flesh and muscle. "Just lean on him a little more." He moved so slow; he felt like the continental plates shifting beneath her. "He's a big guy. He can take it." She felt like she was floating. "And if you can't lean on him at home…" His fingers came up over her shoulder blades, rubbed over her shoulders, trailed up her neck, and combed through her short curls as he lifted her head. "Lean on me here," he growled into her ear.

She literally flailed at the pleasure. "I think my hour's up," she gasped.

If he dragged his hands down her back one more time, she was going to come. If he held her one more time, she was going to cry.

"Don't," he said, desperate. She could feel his breath on her lips, knew if she opened her eyes, she would see his gorgeous face hovering over hers.

"Please, don't. Let me touch you. Let me take care of you. I don't want to change anything, I just…let me give you what you need. At least right now. At least tonight."

He was extracting her control, not with his huge body or dominant commands, but with the naked hunger in his voice.

"What do you think I need?" she whispered.

"A break." He nuzzled her cheek. "With someone you can let go with. Someone you can trust."

Trust.

She opened her eyes to stare into his midnight ones.

"I hate that you fucking cry alone in this office. But if that's what you need, let me make you cry in a different way. Just tonight. Let me be the best fucking fantasy of your life. Then you can go home and forget. Kiss your husband and act like nothing ever happened. Like nothing's changed."

Ray Morgan had come digging into her life in a way she'd never expected him to. He had a comfortable existence. There had been no reason for him to come to her conference room, to work so hard to get to know her there.

She could never go home and forget the man who'd worked to get to know her inside and out, then secretly learned a skill so he could offer her relief.

Nothing was guaranteed.

But she could no longer deny him.

She laughed like a sob. "You've been the *only* fucking fantasy I've had since I was eighteen," she said. "Sometimes I think I dreamed you up from staring too long at my *Teen Beat* magazines. Touch me, Ray. Please touch me."

The restraint the massive man who'd played a superhero and prizefighter had held himself back with snapped as he kicked away the stool—she heard it crash against a file cabinet—circled around the massage table and took her mouth, lush and unapologetic, big fingers under her neck and tongue tasting her like it was how he could breathe again. With her arms trapped under the heavy flannel, all she could do was tilt up her head and give up her mouth, let him lick and fuck it.

She opened her eyes and saw how beautifully his thick black lashes lay against his cheeks, how painfully his brow was furrowed, like kissing her was so good that it hurt him. She gave a groan into his open mouth, helpless at the roar of want in her, and the hand beneath her neck dragged down between her breasts, hooked into the flannel, and pulled it down and off of her.

He pushed off the massage table and looked down at her naked body, possibly deciding which inch to defile first. When he licked over that full bottom lip he'd made into her favorite kink, she whimpered, raised up her knees, and squeezed her thick thighs together.

"Fuck, yes," he growled.

Without permission or hesitation, he shoved his hot hands between her knees and spread them, leaned over from where he stood near her torso and licked into her wet pussy.

"Oh my God," she yelped, slapping her hands down, one against his broad back, one against the massage table.

He gripped her under the knee, his hand so big he could hold her leg like it was her wrist, and growled into her cunt, "Stay still." When he fit his mouth to her rose and wetness, there was no way she way staying still. She tried to grab on to the slick of the table the way she was gripping his T-shirt as she arched her hips up against his mouth.

"Ray, Ray, Jesus," she called. It felt like he was trying to lick her soul out of her cunt.

She always scheduled her massage during the office-funded happy hour she didn't attend, ensuring the office would be empty. She was so glad for it now; as she arched her back, nearly blind with the pleasure he was inflicting between her legs, she was certain she was about to come loud enough to break eardrums.

"Ray," she whispered, trying to warn him. There was nothing she could do about the nails she was digging into his back. "*Amor...*"

"Get it," he said, dirty, between flat-tongue licks. "Do it." He added one of those thick fingers she'd watch trail across his lip in the conference room and...Oh God...the deep, penetration of it. He crooked it as he sucked—

"Ray!" she screamed, hoping she didn't shatter the glass of her 38th floor office as she came. It would be a long way to fall.

She knew movie star Ray Morgan would be there to catch her.

"Fuckfuckfuckfuckfuckfuckbaby," he cooed, honey voiced and hurting into her pussy, licking up what he'd done to her. "Why do you always taste so good?"

Nothing got her movie star more desperate than getting her off.

"Fuck me, *mi amor*," she panted, the orgasm still trembling through her. "I need you inside."

He dug his fingers into her thigh hard enough to bruise. "Goddamn," he groaned. "If my dick brushes my jeans, I'm gonna come."

"Then just turn toward me. Let me suck on it."

She yelped a laugh when he bit her thigh. "I'm a good Kansas boy who doesn't believe in spanking, but you make me change my mind." His drawl came out when he was worked up. "You and your dirty mouth."

She closed her eyes and shoved a hand under his T-shirt to trace over his magnificent back. "You love my dirty mouth."

"Yes, I do," he said.

He did straighten then, and moved away from her, her hand trailing away from his body in an echo of the way his hands had trailed over her.

"That private instructor hasn't been teaching you Pilates, has he?" she murmured.

"Why would I need to learn Pilates?" His big hands wrapped around her thighs, gently this time, and he began to effortlessly pull her to the bottom edge of the table.

It was a measure of their twenty-two-year marriage that she'd never once questioned what he was doing at his twice-a-week class.

"Your doctor said it would be good for your back." She lay there, still glowing with her orgasm, as she heard him unzip his jeans.

"My doctor said less stress would be good for my back. And stepping away from punishing my body with an unnatural weightlifting regimen." She heard the strain in his voice as he got himself out of his boxer briefs. They always loved to talk through their lovemaking and the banality of marriage talk—for two kids from broken homes—somehow was always hot.

He hooked her knees over his bent arms. "Getting your high-octane brain to power down makes me less stressed." She opened her eyes as she felt him trace her seam with the smooth, hard head of his dick. The high table made her a perfect height to receive him.

She looked at the gorgeous, thick-muscled, slopey-eyed man who graced magazine covers and inspired slash fan fiction and fathered her two children. "I can't believe you did all of this for me."

"I didn't." He moved just the tip inside her and knew to stop. That was her favorite part. "We wouldn't have gone with your group if it wasn't the best one." Movie star Ray Morgan had filmed his final superhero movie and had decided to take the first break from acting he'd taken since he'd arrived in California with his wife, who'd come to attend graduate school, and new baby twenty years ago. For his health and the health of his family, he was pivoting to a less demanding acting schedule and a newly formed production company.

A production company his wife's investment group was now a partner in.

As he took the first gentle pulse inside her, Marisol sucked in a breath.

"It was a gift to me..." His penis pulsed deeper and deeper into her. "To see what you've accomplished here..." He closed his eyes with a mild snarl and pushed with a grunt. "To see how much your employees admire you." Her body was lulled by the slide of his words and cock. "I'm not asking you to step away from this."

He hit deep and she ground herself on him.

He pulled her hips into his body, unwound his arms so she could wrap her thighs around his jean-clad hips, and leaned over to cover her torso.

He licked at her nipple before he kissed her lips.

He pushed up as if to keep talking, took a look at her mouth, then dove back down. He kissed her as he moved inside her, deep and wet and stroking, and she held him tight against her.

With a hard thrust of his hips that made them both groan with pleasure, he pushed up onto his forearms. "I would never ask you to step away from what you've worked so hard for," he panted, meeting her eyes. "What I ask is that..." He surged those powerful hips into her. "You do whatever you need to do to make sure you live a long..." He gripped her shoulders. "Long life with me." She clenched on to him hard and he moaned. "You can't—can't take care of any of us..." He dipped his head and licked between her breasts, as close as he could get to her heart. "You can't take care of me or the kids or...*unh*...your employees or the investments or...*damn, damn, baby*...your brother or...*shit*...not even the dog, if you're not here."

She sobbed into his pleasure-pained face and urged him to go faster with the movement of her hips.

He shoved his arms under her body, cradled her head, and kissed her as he gave it to her without relenting.

Her doctor had flagged her high blood pressure a year ago, concerned because of her relatively young age and family history. Marisol had barely had time to think about it. Didn't want to think about it.

But Ray had asked about the new medication she was taking.

Then he started his "Pilates" class. Five months later, the assistant from his newly developed production company had made an appointment with her group.

The wall that Marisol had originally established to keep Hollywood separate from her business—wives of successful actors were discounted as nothing more than pretty accessories—had become a wall she thought her worry could live behind, siloed off so the glorious, glamorous husband she adored would never have to see it.

But before he'd become glamorous, her husband had been the boy who'd delivered a cheese-only pizza to the crappy off-campus apartment she could afford for her and her brother her first day of her freshman year. He'd taken one look at her and brought them every mis-ordered or wrong ingredient pizza he could get his hands on for five days.

On the fifth day, while her brother was at school, she'd taken Ray's hand, walked him to her bedroom, and made him the first and only man she'd ever given her body to.

He'd always been glorious.

She cried as she came now, her arms wrapped around his huge, supportive shoulders.

The sound he made as he pulsed and lurched inside her was somewhere between a groan and a sob and a laugh.

"Why're you laughing," she said, tears streaming down her face.

He rubbed his own tears into her neck, his beard so beloved against her skin. "You yelled 'reallocate resources' when you were coming."

She punched his shoulder. "I was trying to tell you I think I can share some of the load."

"Good," he said, breathing relief into her neck as he kissed it. "Good. Lean on me, baby."

She rubbed her hands up and down where she'd punched and held him close. "I'm not giving up Rhondel," she said.

"Who do you think hooked me up with lessons?" he murmured into her ear between licks. "He'd be pissed if I put him out of a job."

She'd still have her Rhondel, and she'd still have it all, and she'd still have the tendency to try to carry too much.

But now she would do more to lean—for the sake of all that she carried—on the strong superhero shoulders and occasionally aching thirty-eight-year-old's back of her mild-mannered, movie star, Midwestern masseuse husband.

**THE END**

# CHAPTER ELEVEN

# A Good Man

*I love the romance genre, but unfortunately, as an author of color writing characters of color, the genre hasn't loved me and other authors who look like me back. You only need to look at who is dominating the bestseller lists in romance to see that is true.*

*So, I am trying my hand at other things. This is an "other thing," an original story written for this collection. This story is hot. There's a great steamy scene. But this is not a romance story. If you're willing to try it, I hope you like it.*

**Content warning: This is not a romance story**

***

Summer in a college town was a young man's paradise, but it was hell on a man in a suit.

After a day of roaming up and down Lawrence, Kansas's Mass Street and not getting a decent lead until the sun was mellowing on the horizon,

Jake Travelstead walked into the Tex-Mex café sweaty, rumpled, and eager for the end of his day. It was 7 p.m. and well past quitting time. He said a little prayer that his next conversation would make his long day tramping through thick July humidity worthwhile.

Coco Loco was a small place, booths on each side and tables in the middle, with a colorful bar under a stucco arch at the back. The smell of grease and cumin made his stomach howl as he walked toward the bar. Tuesday summer nights in a college town were quiet, and only three of the booths were full. He hoped this worked in his favor as he began to slip the folded-up paper, tearing at the creases after a day of showing it off, out of his humid inner pocket.

"Hello," said a girl standing at the end of the row of bar stools. She had dark eyes with long lashes, her black hair was pulled back in a high ponytail, she carried a basket of salty chips and a frosted glass of beer, and she wore a sky-blue T-shirt with "Coco Loco" printed in a half circle over one perfect breast.

She looked as good as air conditioning.

When Jake focused on her face, he was surprised to see that she was scanning his body in a slow, interested once-over. Her heavy-lidded eyes traveled across his suit jacket, from one shoulder to the other, before they paused on his lips.

When her eyes finally met his, her smile wasn't shy. "You want a table or do you want to join me at the bar?"

The paper was stuck in his pocket. "I...uh...bar?"

Her smile went wider. Her lips were a deep rose without the shine of lipstick. "I'll be right there."

Jake pulled out a barstool, feeling heat-stroked.

He knew what he looked like on a good day—a fit six two, dark-blond hair, light green eyes, a good nose, full lips, and a jawline that was only starting to soften a little from his thirty-two years. As a kid, Jake had been in JCPenney ads until the teasing and his dad's quiet made him refuse his mom's pleas to continue modeling and instead pour all that energy into baseball.

But today had not been a good day and the average Kansas woman liked to be chased. Seldom were the women as straightforward as this strikingly pretty girl.

She came to him from behind the bar and put chips and salsa, a menu, and a sparkling glass of ice water in front of him.

He grabbed the glass and emptied it.

"Thirsty?" she asked, a husky laugh in her word.

"Yeah."

"What else can I get you to drink?"

"Water's fine."

She tilted her head as she re-filled his water glass with the gun. "You look like you've had a day." The tip of her long ponytail brushed her brown, gleaming arm. She lowered her voice to a whisper. "You want something stronger, I'll only charge you half price."

Technically, he was still on the clock. Realistically, he *had* had one hell of a day. And this would be his final interview.

"How's the margarita?"

"We make them in a bucket."

"I'll get a Tecate."

"Good choice." When she smiled, she had twin dimples in her baby-soft cheeks.

They worked out what he should order—a black bean and white queso burrito even though it would mean salads and protein shakes for the rest of the week—and then she told him, "Sit tight, handsome," in that husky voice of hers as she went to check on her tables.

*Chill the fuck out*, he admonished his ice-cold beer. She was far below the appropriate hit-on age, she was a possible witness, and she was doing what every smart waitress, bartender, and barista did: She was being friendly to increase her tip. It was only because he was tired, his hunch on this investigation seemed to be going nowhere, his entire fucking career as a Kansas City field agent seemed to be going nowhere, that her direct-eyed admiration was hitting him in the gut.

When she got back, he'd pull out that damp piece of paper and his badge, get his info, eat his burrito, and get the hell out of here.

He heard her chatting with a couple as she walked them to the door. When she'd dropped off their dirty dishes in the kitchen and again stood in front of him, she said, "They come in once a week and always leave me twelve percent. To the penny. They left me twelve percent on Christmas Eve."

That bit of ballsiness stalled his hand in his pocket. "You were nicer to them than they had a right to," he said.

"They're as kind as can be," she said. "You can't presuppose someone's intentions. People are inscrutable. All that's predictable is pattern, and I know they're going to be great guests who tip poorly. My pattern is to complain about them when they leave. If I don't, the injustice of it'll make me do something nasty to their food."

He pulled out the paper because if he didn't, he was going to ask for her number.

He spread the photocopied photo out on the bar then pulled out his FBI wallet. "I'm Agent Jack Travelstead," he said as he flashed his badge and credentials. Her eyes went wide. "Do you recognize this man?"

She gave a throaty laugh. "Are you serious?"

"As a heart attack," he said grimly.

Her smile fading, she took the identification out of his hand like it might bite her. When she dropped her head to study it, she nibbled on her rose-colored lip. Then she looked up at him to compare. "You don't look like a cop."

He'd disappointed her, and he withheld his *I'm an agent, not a cop* because she didn't care.

Her eyes were like deep alleys of darkness in the forest, the places you stayed away from when you had to take a leak. She had wide, strong cheekbones to offset those dimples.

She looked over his shoulder. "Have a good night," she called. The restaurant door closed with a *whump*. There were only a couple of guys sitting on the same side of the booth still in the restaurant.

A ding came from the kitchen. She tossed his ID wallet at him. "Order's up," she said and disappeared around the corner.

He hoped she was coming back.

She returned carrying a large plate. The burrito, blanketed in green sauce and white queso, was as big as a baby and sent up jets of steam. She opened the cooler one-handed, grabbed another Tecate, and used the opener mounted on the side to uncap it.

His body begged *want* and *now* and *mine* as she placed the huge burrito with contrails, the beer with ice sliding down the bottle, and her perfect five-foot-four curves right in front of him. "All yours."

He dug in and instantly burned the roof of his mouth, which was better than saying whatever fool thing was on the tip of his tongue.

"So, Mr. FBI Man, you want to know if I've seen this guy?" She straightened pretend glasses on her nose and picked up the paper with her pinkies extended, like she was on a PBS show. She looked at him over the edge of the paper. "Generally, I don't like cops—"

"Yeah, I got that," he mumbled through his full mouth.

"But this is pretty exciting. I'm an idiot for true crime."

That was one way she was like every woman he knew.

The silly expression on her face faded as she looked at the picture. "Oh my God, yeah, he came in here."

Everything in him that had been flaring since he'd walked through the door of this dumpy Tex-Mex restaurant dinged and flashed like he'd just hit the jackpot. Jake wiped his mouth with his hand and grabbed his notebook out of his jacket pocket. "When?"

"Last week. Last Tuesday. I've been hoping he wouldn't come back tonight." She grimaced as she held the paper in one hand. "Is he dead?"

Jake stopped writing. "Why would you ask that?"

She put the paper on the bar and wiped her hand on her shirt, down the in-and-out curve of her waist. "Because if he's dead, I'm going to feel really bad about all the times I've called him an asshole in my mind."

"Why? What happened?"

"He was *such* an asshole," she said. "He came in drunk and got drunker, then started bothering two girls trying to eat. I told him I'd call the cops if he didn't leave."

"What time was this?" he asked, scribbling like mad. This was great. This was everything. She was giving him exactly what he needed. "Did you call the police?"

"No, he left after he called me a 'cunt.' Do you know how many people I let call me the c-word?" Absolutely zero, he imagined. "He came in around eight, after the little bit of dinner rush, and left maybe around eight thirty. I know I had enough time to worry that he'd come back."

That perfectly fit Jake's timeline. "Was anyone with him? Did you notice anyone following him?"

She shook her head then stopped. Cocked it. That long ponytail tick-tocked behind her.

"I think a guy *did* come in soon after him," she said slowly. "He ordered a Coke and a burrito, but he wanted his check early, before his food arrived. I think...yeah, he left right after the guy."

Good Lord, it couldn't be this easy. "Any chance the second guy paid with a credit card?"

"Cash," she said, poking a pin in his excitement.

But then she pointed over Jake's shoulder. She had long, thin fingers and no-nonsense nails. "We've got a security camera. The owner is out of state until Thursday, but if you come back then, he can show you the video from that night."

Jesus fucking Christ. In two days, he could have video of the man his colleagues called his boogeyman, the monster only Jake could see hiding under the bed.

That was still two days off. "What'd the second guy look like?" he asked.

She shrugged. "White. Maybe in his early thirties? Brown hair. Not too tall or short. Pretty typical looking guy."

"Is there any way to get at that video before the owner returns?"

She shook her head.

"If I showed you some mug shots, do you think you'd be able to identify him?"

Her eyes went wide when he said "mug shots" and he realized again how much younger than him she was. He'd seen that look on many civilians' faces when their lives brushed the ugliness of his world.

"I don't know," she said. "Why? Is the asshole dead?"

Jake studied her. Bright, beautiful, endearing, she'd make a stunning witness. He had to ensure she kept working with the cops she didn't like. "For now, all we know is that Tommy Lansing—the asshole—is missing. But you're the last person who saw him so far. He's a twenty-two-year-old pre-law student at KU."

"Oh my God." Her hand covered her mouth. "He's my age."

She *was* too young for him.

"I might've passed him on campus." Her hand dragged down her long ponytail like the silky feel of it provided comfort. "He still has time to have the asshole redeemed out of him."

If she'd seen the charges against Thomas Lansing III, she might re-think that notion. "His frat brothers contacted campus police on Thursday," Jake told her. "His parents and the university filed a missing persons report the same day. No one was able to find any trace of him after his last class on Tuesday until today. A Tuesday regular over at Louise's told me Tommy was doing shots and said he was going to go get a burrito."

The disturbed look evaporated off her face. "Is that how you found me?" she asked. "You showed that picture to enough people until a drunk regular told you about a burrito?"

He opened his mouth, didn't know what to say, so closed it again. He gave a quick nod.

Without a word, she turned around to grab a bottle of tequila off a high shelf. He looked anywhere but at her curvy body stretching long to reach it. She set two shot glasses on the bar then filled them both.

"What's this?" he asked.

"For you. To toast your hard work." Her eyes were deep, shining wells of gladness. He'd been hugged and kissed on the top of his head by his coach after a grand slam in Little League. This was better.

She raised her glass. "¡Salud!" She leaned across the bar, close to him, before they drank. "That means to your health."

The tequila went down sweet.

"Can I talk to your cook? See if he heard or saw anything that night?"

"The regular Tuesday cook called in sick today," she said. "I can give you his number."

He readied his pen over his notepad.

She met his eyes with a soft smile. "I'm going to close up early. Want to get a beer?"

He'd noted the opening and closing of the restaurant door. Her last table had left. They were alone.

"I can't." She was now part of the investigation. She was a witness. "You're too young for me."

Her grin—that wide, bright, lush, dimpled grin—grew. "I'm not asking you to father my children."

His grip on the pen grew sweaty.

"It's just one night—" She blanched. "I meant-I mean...it's just one *beer*."

The femme fatale had fallen right off of her.

He had to keep her cooperative, he told himself.

It was just one night.

"What's one beer?" he asked, clicking his pen, tucking his notebook back in his pocket, and hiding the photo away.

*

Mass Street was quiet and still hot as they walked two blocks in the final fading rays of a spectacular sunset—sunsets were easier to notice when you were walking with a beautiful girl—but it was busy and cool at the Jazzhaus, a second-story, low-roofed, long-bar club where a band with a stand-up bass was gearing up to play.

He got a draft beer, she got a bourbon on the rocks, and he paid for them both before they found a table in a far back corner. He wheedled around his discomfort about buying whiskey for a witness by insisting on repaying her for all the free drinks at the restaurant. He looked like a serious tool in this college hipster bar; he had to keep on his jacket to hide his sidearm in the shoulder holster. They hunched down to hear each other below the noise.

"So what are you studying?" he asked. If he kept reminding himself that she was a student, that she was ten years younger than he was, then everything would be fine.

"Majoring in psychology. Minoring in Latinx Studies." She took a sip of bourbon then shrugged. "Still not sure what I want to do with myself."

She'd gone down to a basement office at the restaurant to change, and she'd come up in a button-up white shirt, the same salsa-splattered jeans, and a worn Kansas Jayhawks baseball cap. *You don't want to see the state of my roots after a night in the restaurant,* she said. But she'd combed out her hair and, beneath the cap, it waved long and deep-brown to the middle of her back.

The cap kept her eyes, her face, her words just for him. All of her was just inches away if he leaned his forearms on the table.

He sat back in his seat. "I didn't know what I wanted to do when I was your age either."

She snorted. "You always knew you wanted to be a cop."

How did she know that? "I...wasn't sure which branch I wanted to work for. Local police, county sheriff's office, FBI, military law enforcement. There're a lot of options." He leaned forward, his beer against his thigh, honestly curious. "Do I come off like an authoritarian dick?"

Her smile faded into something so sweet and soft that it was almost sad. She looked at him for a long minute. "No," she said finally. "You're a good man."

He could hear his heartbeat in his ears. He felt like everything—this case, this night, his career—was finally going to start going his way.

He raised his glass and tapped it against hers. "Thank you..." He stared at her blankly.

"What?"

"I don't know your name."

She stretched her hand over the table. "Agent Jake Travelstead, I'm Clara Conejo."

He took her hand. It felt warm and steely beneath silky skin. "Isn't conejo the word for..." He thought for a second. "For rabbit?"

"Very good," Clara said, her voice like the fur she was named after.

She didn't pull away. He held on.

A girl heading to the bathroom bumped him, and Jake finally let go of Clara's hand. Jesus. The two beers and a tequila shot were treating him too fine right now. He pushed his beer away. He needed to wrap this up and go.

"You know, maybe I've watched too many *Law & Orders*, but doesn't the FBI stay away from local cases unless it's a bigger deal? Like a...a kidnapping or a drug cartel thing?" She held the bourbon glass in both hands and tapped it thoughtfully against her lower lip, a lip that was wet and ripe. "Why is the FBI looking into one missing student?"

Jake cleared his throat. "Some believe there are markers that connect the Tommy Lansing case to other crimes."

"What markers?" She licked that bottom lip.

He reached for his beer. "I really can't discuss that."

"Oh," she said, straightening. "Will you get in trouble with your task force?" Her eyes grew wary. "Are a bunch of Feds going to bust in here, wondering where you are?"

He wished. He gave a humorless laugh as he leaned back in his seat and took a long drink from his glass. "Nobody cares where I am. They've about had it with my wild theories. My boss gave me until today to find something concrete. Which you, sweetheart"—he raised his glass and tipped his head at her—"have helped me do. I'll write up my report in the morning and shove it in his face."

Clara smiled. "So they don't already know about you, me, and a clandestine burrito?"

He shook his head and put his beer over his heart. "I'm taking that tequila shot to my grave."

"I know that's lonely." Her smile wandered off. "It's hard when no one believes you."

The warmth of being seen spread like good whiskey. He rubbed his sternum with the heel of his hand and searched for something else to talk about. "I'm actually surprised you didn't recognize Tommy Lansing. He was in the news before he disappeared."

She pulled all that long, silky hair over one shoulder and it swept the table when she shrugged. "Between work and school, I keep my eyes on my business. Why was he in the papers?"

Most college-aged girls in Lawrence had known to look out for Tommy Lansing.

"After the Jayhawks won the tournament last year, he was accused of raping two different passed-out girls at two different celebrations. One of the girls was raped behind a dumpster here on Mass, but the case was thrown out for lack of evidence. He raped the other girl at his frat. But the prosecutor was no match for the attorney his parents provided. Thomas Lansing III was given a not guilty verdict."

Clara looked green. "That sonofabitch. He didn't even change schools?"

Jake shook his head. "Both girls have moved away. There are rumors that there might be others..."

Clara emptied her bourbon glass then banged it down on the table. "So, a serial rapist goes missing and the FBI is all concerned for him?" Those soft, seductive, heavy-lidded eyes pinned him. "Why weren't you concerned about Thomas Lansing III *before* he went missing? Why weren't you concerned about the lives he was destroying? If the guy in the restaurant did something about him, then he deserves a medal, not being caught by you."

Her *you* dripped with contempt. That warmth she had could burn him to a crisp.

"Keep your voice down," he said sharply. "I get it. I'm telling you this because..." He leaned closer. "Because I think that's what connects Tommy's disappearance to the other crimes. That's what I'm investigating. I believe somebody's eliminating sexual abusers in the region."

Her eyes went huge. "Really?"

"Yeah." A waitress put down two more drinks Jake hadn't signaled for. He picked up the fresh glass of beer. "Some of the murdered were on the sexual offender's registry after serving time. But others—I only found out about accusations against them when I went digging. There was a girls' volleyball coach in Clay Center who had a goddamn Coach of the Year plaque behind the girl who broke down in his office when I interviewed her. She said she didn't think anyone else knew."

"This is crazy," she said. *Crazy*, she called the situation. But she didn't look at him like he was crazy. "Why won't your bosses listen to you?"

Her belief rocketed through his veins.

"There's no symmetry to the killings," he said. "Serial killers like it one way but this guy—a couple of the murders didn't even look like murder until I investigated them. There was a car accident with messed-up breaks, poisonings, suspicious suicides, a few stabbings, and some guys in the woods so long the animals made it hard to figure out who they were or what had happened to them."

The words, the triumph of them, poured out of him. He'd done this, he'd done almost nothing but this for over nine months, sacrificing his free time, a relationship that could have gone somewhere, and—almost—his career. But he'd figured it out. Now he had a lead and a witness and an image of his suspect sitting on the security video of a Tex-Mex restaurant.

"The only pattern is the sexual assault and the fact that they were in situations, like renting near a school or newly married with a young step-daughter, that would make it easy to assault again."

He was the only one who'd seen the pattern. He'd been right all along.

She looked at him like she was astonished by him. He didn't need to be astonishing. He just wanted to do his goddamn job and be believed. "Tommy Lansing was the most high-profile victim yet." Jake said. "I think the guy's escalating."

"Maybe it was just a crime of opportunity," she murmured.

Jake frowned and took a deep drink. "Then that means he's getting messy and that's worse," he said. "Innocent people could get in his way. I want to stop him before he kills another victim."

She traced the rim of her glass with her no-nonsense fingertip. "It's gross to hear you call them victims."

"Trust me, I don't have any sympathy for them."

"No?" Her eyes were heavy on him. He could tell her what she wanted to hear, keep those dimples and her sexy glances, or tell her the truth.

"Regardless how I feel about the men being killed, we have a system for a reason."

"A system that lets rapists go free."

"An imperfect system," he said. He couldn't solve this for her. All he could do was be straight with her while trusting she'd still agree to testify and wanting her more every second.

He was about to pick up his beer for the last swallow when she put her hand over his glass. She met his eyes and he didn't blink. "If you found the guy, if you were alone in an alley with him, what would you do?"

Right or wrong, he wanted to touch her skin. He wanted to turn her palm over and rest his head in it. "Do you think I'm a good man?"

She took her time considering.

Then she inhaled a big, sad, chest-filling breath, and he wondered how hard her twenty-two years had been. "Yes." She moved her hand away.

She said nothing more. Nervous in her quiet, he finished his beer.

Clara stood. Jake felt her rip away from him like a cabin door had opened mid-flight. "Tomorrow, I'll help you as much as I said I would. I'll give you the number of the cook and, on Thursday, introduce you to my boss. I'll look through your mug shots."

She circled the table until she loomed over him. He had to tilt his head up to meet eyes he could barely see under her ball cap. Her breasts, her salsa-and-dandelion smell, the warmth of her, were inches away. "But that's it. No more. Tomorrow, we're just going to be the FBI agent and his witness."

He nodded. His chin almost brushed the button of her shirt.

"Tonight, you should walk me home."

He wanted to bite that button off. "I really shouldn't."

"I weigh a buck and a quarter, and I've had two whiskeys and a tequila shot." He could feel her breath on his face. "You know what's out there in the shadows. Are you really okay with me walking alone?"

He closed his eyes, lowered his chin, and rested his forehead against her body. If he could spend the rest of his life right here, right in this moment, he would.

He felt her step back. Even though the band had started, even though his eyes were still closed, he knew she was walking away. He could let her go. He could show up at the restaurant tomorrow and pretend that no line had been crossed. He could bring her some mugshots, interview the cook, and get the video from her boss. If he got his man—he knew he was so close to getting his man—he would one day see her in court. Then she would earn her degree and go on with her life, and he would forget that he'd once been tempted to be a very bad man.

He stood, pulled cash out of his money clip, and threw it on the table. He shoved past the crowd waiting to pay the cover at the entrance—"tie-wearing motherfucker" one kid yelled—and barreled down the steps. Outside, in the velvet blue summer night that had finally cooled, she was waiting for him.

She grabbed for his hand and he squeezed hers. The touch of her fingers pulled at strings in his gut. Every sensorial nerve between his head and toes jangled. She had to tug on him to get him walking.

"This is fucking insane," he said as they turned the corner onto a side street. He was a walking hard-on. He hoped to Christ her place wasn't far.

"This is insane," she echoed, and thank God this little girl was breathless. "I want to pull you between the cars and go down on you."

He stumbled on a crack. "Fuck."

"We shouldn't be doing this," she said, pulling him faster beside her. "I shouldn't be doing this to you."

"No, you shouldn't."

"Do you want to do this with me?"

He twirled her toward him and kissed her, pushed up her chin and swooped under her cap and kissed her. Her lips were as soft as he'd dreamed and she gasped against his mouth. He doubted much surprised this brilliant little girl.

"C'mon," she said. She grabbed his hand and they ran.

It was only half a block to outdoor steps they stumbled down to reach the door of her basement apartment in an old, broken-up Victorian. He swept her hair to the side and buried his nose in her neck, inhaling her as she fumbled to unlock her door.

"Fuckfuckfuck," she moaned, tilting her forehead against the peeling wood and grabbing one of his hands to shove it between her legs. He wrapped his free arm around her and cradled the apex of her in his hands.

"Open the damn door," he demanded in her ear.

She pawed at the dented knob halfheartedly and he carried her inside.

Once in, he kicked the door closed behind him, spun her around, and flicked off her baseball cap to get his hands in her hair. He tilted her mouth up to him as she grabbed his tie. "Tie-wearing motherfucker," she growled into his mouth before she filled it with her tongue. He held her to him as she held him to her and the wet, reckless, uninhibited kiss knocked any thought of age and station out of Jake's mind. He'd never felt consumed before. He'd never wanted to eat a woman alive.

Her kiss slid to his ear then his neck then those hard-working hands were unbuckling the leather belt holding up his suit pants. He got his hands in the open collar of her shirt and tugged. Buttons pinged across the concrete floor.

When he looked at her face above a boring beige bra that cupped her fabulous breasts, she looked halfway to coming. "I didn't think you'd do that," she gasped, sipping at the air. "You keep being different than I expect."

He swept his big hand over all of that silky, golden-brown skin. "Is that good?

Her hand slid down the front of his slacks and squeezed. "It's awful."

Kissing and greedy, it was a jumble of hands and fingers as they got each other's pants open. "Are you fucking kidding me?" he begged as he slid to his knees to kiss the little ribbon at the waistband of her white cotton panties. He couldn't believe the woman who was his sexual catnip had the world's most boring underwear. He would've kept kissing—she smelled like a cinnamon roll down here—but she fell to her knees and pulled his cock out of his black boxer briefs.

"Oh God," she moaned, almost like a sob, as she held his heft in her hand. She scooched back to lean forward and put her mouth around the head. He kept himself still for a second, just a few seconds, knees spread and weight back on his hands, still wearing his coat and tie and feeling heaven. But this act, as a first act, reminded him too much that he was much older and she was much younger. Reminded him too much of the men who were being killed and what they forced their victims to do. He pulled her up by her shoulders and kissed her, slipping his fingers into those plain cotton panties.

He groaned at the feel of her. "You're so wet, sweetheart. Thank you for being so wet for me." She gave another half tearful sound into his mouth as she used the saliva she'd left on him to work his cock. He leaked for her—he'd give it all up for her—and she rubbed her thumb over the tip of him and squeezed tighter.

"You're so good," she said like a prayer, thrusting on his hand. Her sweet little pussy milked at his finger. "You're so, so good."

He pulled them both up to kneeling so he could take her mouth while he got his finger as deep as it would go. She wailed into his mouth as she came all over his hand. He came on her stomach and rubbed it into her skin, kissed her neck and whispered love words and rubbed himself into her skin.

When he finally lifted his head and opened his eyes, the room slid sideways.

"Whoa," he said, putting his hand on the back of the sofa to steady himself. They were on the floor between a wooden table and an ugly couch; they hadn't even made it to the living area of what looked like a one-room apartment.

"You okay?" she asked.

"Yeah, just..." He gripped his forehead. His knees felt like they were moving, like he was on the deck of a ship. "Just had a lot of drinks. Where's the bathroom?"

"Here." She helped him up and that boat kept rocking. She wrapped an arm around him and he slid his arm over her shoulder. "I'll help you."

"Jesus, I'm..." Spots were forming around the edge of his vision and he squeezed his temple with one hand.

"Sorry," he croaked as she guided him to a closed door. All the time he was worried about the age difference and he was the one acting like a drunk kid.

"Don't be," she said. She kissed him gently on the cheek. "I'm the one that fed you all those drinks. Bathroom is here."

She opened a door into a dark room. He put his hand out to feel the doorjamb—his migraine was getting worse and it was getting harder to see—and stepped inside. He refused to puke in front of her.

The door closed behind him. The room smelled like dirt and mold. She had a seriously shitty apartment. He patted the wall for a light switch and only felt the rough scrape of brick.

He had to plant both hands against it. His stomach was about to go. "Clara," he croaked, the sound making his head split. "Where's the light switch?"

She didn't answer.

"Clara?" he called again, desperate, bile crawling up his throat.

"I'm sorry, Jake," she finally said, right at the door.

His knees wouldn't hold him anymore. He slumped to the floor and collapsed onto his back.

"I think I need help, Clara," he said from the dirt floor.

"I'm sorry." Why was she crying?

His head wanted to explode.

"I have to stop them."

Jake rolled to his side. He didn't want to choke when he hurled. As the darkness gathered, he felt it. His sidearm was gone.

"No one else will stop them, Jake. So I can't let you stop me."

Clara had known, probably had known from the instant Jake had walked into the restaurant, what he would do if he got the guy in his sights.

He was, after all, a good man.

The darkness closed around him and swallowed him whole.

**THE END**

# CHAPTER TWELVE

# A Mermaid and Her Star

*When I wrote this story for **Aloha: An Anthology for Maui,** which raised money for Maui relief and is no longer available, I was hoping to be the first to write a love scene on a paddleboard. Alas, when I put the question out to social media, I discovered that others had rocked that ocean before me.*

*My two series, Filthy Rich and Milagro Street, intermingle in this story. I hope you enjoy the Easter eggs!*

***

Marina Torres didn't know how she got here.

She floated cheek-down on the paddleboard, her toes trailing in the water as the gentle sun warmed her back and the tender breeze wandered over her skin. She didn't think she'd ever felt anything as delicious as a Hawaiian summer day.

She opened her eyes. Across the expanse of teal blue water, a voluptuous green-blue she couldn't believe was real, she stared at the Mokes, tiny twin islands of sand and yellow grasses, rising out of the water like the undulating humps of a sea monster. In the twenty-one years of her life, this was the farthest she'd ever been from her hometown of Freedom, Kansas.

How in the world, she thought again as she dabbled her fingers through the water, did she end up here?

She knew the steps. She'd filled out the application last fall for the Medina-Esperanza Internship Program, which connected talented citizens from billionaire Roxanne Medina's hometown of Freedom with paid, temporary opportunities in her global organization. Marina got her reply while she was still at KU finishing her fall-semester finals: She'd been invited to use her soon-to-be degree in journalism with a minor in music to create social media and content for rock star Aish Salinger, Roxanne Medina's brother-in-law, who would be recording an album that summer at the world-famous Island Sound Studios in Honolulu.

Marina had cried, nearly thrown up, called her mom, then her Grandmo Loretta, then been bombarded by calls, texts, Instagram DMs, and Snapchats from everyone in her family. She'd responded to the invitation and accepted the position.

Over the course of the spring, she'd received the plane ticket, location of the huge beach house where the whole team chronicling the making of the new album—including Aish Salinger and his wife, winemaker Princesa Sofia—would be staying, and suggestions on what to bring for their two-month stay on Oahu. In Hawaii.

Hawaii!

Physically, she knew how she'd gotten here. A week ago, she'd stumbled out of the plane after a nine-hour flight, bumping her guitar case into everything before a flight attendant had steadied her and then slipped a flower lei over her head. They'd driven across the island from the airport, through the lushest green with the world's tallest, most-terrifying cliffs, to emerge on the other side in front of the world's longest, most beautiful shoreline.

It was her first cliffs and her first shoreline, but she was certain they were the world's mosts. The driver had driven them until the road ran out at a gate. When the gate rumbled back, it revealed two many-decked beach houses separated by a bridge of black lava rocks, a stretch of sand, palm trees hanging over the water, and the Mokes. Their little corner of paradise came with tiny islands.

How in the world did she get here?

Today was her first day off after three days chronicling Aish in the studio, and while she wanted to explore Oahu, she figured she would spend the day drowsing on the paddleboard that she'd gotten pretty good at as a first-timer and adjusting to the fact that she was hanging out with a rock star and a princess. When was someone going to pinch her and wake her up?

Her board bumped into the black, jagged lava rocks that made up the jetty between the beach houses that were in sight of each other but spaced far enough apart to provide privacy. A shadow fell over her.

"You're trespassing on my beach," a gruff voice said.

She yelped with surprise, dropped the paddle she'd been hanging on to, and scrambled up on her hands. Above her, a man stood on the levee like Poseidon risen up from the water. He was a solid shadow outlined by the sun, but the perimeter of him showed turquoise board shorts, well-defined biceps, broad brown shoulders, a trim black scruff over a square jaw, and a thick swoop of black hair as he looked down at her.

She should be inoculated to shocks by now, but she still felt little spots around the edge of her vision. There was no way it was him. But it was him. She knew that outline like the back of her hand.

She saw she had bobbed farther over to the other beach house's side of the cove than she'd realized. "Sorry," she coughed out through her shock, pushing herself fully up and straddling the board. She began to pull the paddle back to her with the line strapped to it, anything to avoid looking at him and full-on freaking out. "We were told the other house was empty."

"It isn't," he said, low and growly. Her toes curled in the warm water. "I'm gonna have to call security."

"*What?*" Now she did look up at him. "Why?"

She wanted to point out that there were no private beaches in Hawaii, but she swallowed that along with her crushing disappointment. He wasn't a sexy, avenging sea god. The man whose picture was her screensaver and whose hit show she'd bought Blu-rays of even though she didn't have a Blu-ray player was an asshole. "I'll just go back to the house and let Aish and Sofia know—"

"You're with Aish and Sofia? Shit. Well, now I'm going to have to kick all of y'all out."

"*What?*" she screeched. Javier Campos wasn't a good guy or a laid-back Texan, no matter what all the costars and charitable event organizers and the head of his foundation said. He was a big stupid jerk who she'd spent too much of the last five years adoring. He was no better than the farmer who'd called the cops on her and her cousins for picking blackberries out of the thorny ditch on the edge of his property.

"That's ridiculous. You're going to evict us because I touched your side of the ocean?" God, how would Aish and Sofia take it when they discovered their intern got them kicked out of their summer house? "There has to be something I can do!"

He stayed quiet as he continued to lord over her. She'd jammed her paddle against the levee to keep from scraping against it; the only sound was the lap of the water against the black, sharp rocks. He slid his hands into his shorts as he watched her. Prickles rippled over Marina's skin.

Without warning, he squatted down. Now she could see his face fully. She was a yard away from Javier Campos, staring up into the face she'd spent hours staring at, and helplessly her eyes wandered over his dark summer scruff, his bossy nose with that slight ding to the left, his overlong black hair moving in the breeze, until they looked into hazel-gold eyes as unreal as the ocean and as bright as sea glass. Those eyes, with the intensity of an oncoming storm, were looking right back into hers.

She prayed he didn't notice what was happening in her bikini top.

"You could sing me a song," he said.

The easy waves rolled beneath her, sending her closer to the rocks. "You heard me?"

There was a deck across the road from the beach house, and every night since she'd arrived, after spending the whole day surrounded by people, Marina had taken her guitar to the deck and sung to the sea and the endless stars and the dark outline of the Mokes. She'd minored in music because she wanted to go into music journalism. But the music, her music, was only for her.

He nodded, making his straight black hair fall across those golden eyes as he squatted there. "I've started drinking my whiskey outside to listen." The slight drawl that never showed in his voice when he played a thirty-second-century space detective, the drawl of a twenty-six-year-old man from the oil fields of West Texas, sounded weirdly familiar. He sounded like the boys she'd grown up with. "I woke up on the porch this morning. You lullabied me right to sleep." He pushed his hair back, showing off that incredible face. "You could be a mermaid lurin' me into the ocean. I should kick you out just for that."

He was as bad as her cousins or the boys on the playground who'd chase her, pull her ponytail, then wonder why she didn't chase them back.

She shook her head, trying to make what was happening align with a world that made sense, but didn't look away from him. "I can't believe you're just screwing with me," she said as the board rolled on a wave and her bikini-ed body rolled with it. His eyes flicked down before they met hers again. "You should know better than to screw with people with less power than you."

She couldn't believe *that* was what made him smile. It was a big smile, as bright-white as the sun and crinkling his cheeks, and it made him look less hot and so much sweeter. He seldom smiled in pictures.

"Want to call my mama and tell on me?" He pushed to standing and, without warning, dove over the front end of her board into the water. Astonished, she watched the ripple and eel of him in the perfectly clear Pacific water as he swam away then back. He popped up at her knee.

"She'd like you," he said, sleeking his hair back from his broad forehead as he floated there. "Want to talk to my mama?"

TV-star Javier Campos—his face wet and strong and handsome, his shoulders brown and sleek and muscular, his body naked except for turquoise shorts—bobbed in the Pacific Ocean half a foot from her left knee. Every centimeter of skin from her knee to the edge of her black bikini felt like it was sizzling like a sparkler.

She tucked her drying, short, brown curls behind her ear so she could look her fill. "Your mom should know that her son who owns fancy beach houses and fights book banning and has two Emmys is still a big jerk."

He smiled at her like she'd pull down her bikini top. He smiled at her like *he* was about to pull down her bikini top. "Oh yeah," he said on a drawling laugh. "Now *I'm* starting to like you. What's your story, Ms. Mermaid?"

"No way," she said. "You first. Aish and Sofia said the other house was empty."

Although he still smiled, the tease fell out of his expression. His eyes wandered away then settled back on her. She wondered what could make him look that way in the middle of paradise.

Finally, as he treaded in the teal-blue water, he said, "I walked off set a week ago. That's where I was supposed to be for the summer."

She couldn't believe it. The big-budget film, with its acclaimed director, amazing costars, and super-cool mystery-noir plot, was going to be Javier Campos's launch into movie fame. He'd had offers before, but had always said in interviews that, as the highest-paid Latino in television, the role had to be just right. That he'd walked away from such a well-publicized moment was actually harder to believe than the reality that she was sleeping in a beach house he owned.

"I'm so sorry," she said. "Here..." She leaned carefully back on the board. "Grab onto the nose." When he did, she adjusted her weight so the paddleboard was balanced as it carried them both. She was glad to see his shoulders relax as he watched her curiously, the sun gleaming in his sleek, black hair.

"I thought mermaids wanted to drown their victims," he said.

"That's one way to make sure you don't kick us out."

They floated quietly and Marina marveled that the same water moving over his naked body flowed over her calves and between her toes.

He ran his teeth over his bottom lip. It made her lick hers.

"You're the first person I've talked to who hasn't asked why I quit," he said.

Marina thought of NDAs and lawsuits and unnamed sources. She thought of the noise of his phone and email and social media, and his beach house on the tip of Oahu that was so quiet a woman could be heard singing down the road.

She wondered if this wealthy, much-watched man felt as small as she did in this big ocean. "Although you're a jerk in person, you've always seemed like a pretty decent guy on paper," she said. "I'm sure you had your reasons."

His face as he stared at her stole the rest of her words.

Marina's parents had divorced when she was young and they'd both quickly married again into okay relationships. Still, she'd always felt the only benefit of coupling up was that it made it easier to raise kids and buy a house. That was until she'd gone home post-graduation and visited the family's bar on Milagro Street to see her favorite cousin, Alex, who was back in town.

When Marina walked in, there'd been a huge white guy sitting at the bar with floppy dark hair and glasses and a button-up shirt tucked into jeans that were ironed. The way he was looking at Alex...Marina felt like she'd walked into their bedroom. She would have snuck back out if the cowbells over the door hadn't given her away.

Javier Campos had just looked at her with a hint of the way that professor had looked at her cousin. It made Marina feel like a miracle and a gift and a puzzle all at the same time.

Just as quickly, Javier Campos shifted to stare at the Mokes. Marina heard the caw of island birds above them.

"I didn't know they were gonna expect me to speak with an accent," he said, his voice coming from way down deep in his chest. "They insisted it was more 'realistic.' I didn't know they were going to have me eat salsa and give me a throwaway line about my sister's quinceañera without any respectful Latinidad in the rest of the story." His knuckles flexed where they gripped her board. "It's so easy for them to look through white. But they behave like melanin is a fucking force field—the more there is, the harder it is for them to see the person and the actor."

He sounded exhausted by the battle. "I couldn't..." He ran his hand over his eyes, then scrubbed it over his head, making his black hair stand in wet peaks. "I wasn't going to fuck this up for every Latine actor who comes after me."

With no other person in sight and without a peep from civilization—no planes roared overhead, no boat sped across the water—they could have been the last two people on earth. It gave her the strength, the imperative, to do what she was about to do.

She leaned forward on one arm, reached out her hand, and touched Javier Campos. She combed her fingers through his thick hair, settling it down where he'd made it wild, smoothing it as she gently raked her fingernails over his scalp, then combed her fingers around his ear. When she ran her palm across the scruff of his cheek, the sandpaper shush of it lit up her arm.

"It's okay to take a break so you can keep fighting," she said softly.

He looked at her like she'd shoved him under the water. "Fuck," he breathed, grabbing her hand and dragging it to his mouth. Staring at her like she was keeping him from drowning, Javier Campos kissed her palm, then pressed the hot tip of his tongue to the exact center of it, tasting her.

Her hand spasmed around his hard jaw as her pussy squeezed. He lifted his chin and freed his mouth. "Why does your sweetness make me want to take a bite out of you?" he asked, his eyes like lightning.

"That's my job," she said, running her thumb over the divot in his chin, now that she had free rein of it. "I lured you into the water. Now I get to eat you up."

Was that *her* talking?

"Fuck," he spat again, his black brows scrunching together. "Let me up there with you."

She nodded fast and desperate because if this was all a dream, she wanted to get to the good part before she woke up. "Just..." She leaned far back onto her elbows as he pushed down on the nose, tested it, then popped himself up and straddled the board, never taking his eyes off of her. Sunlight sparkled in the water dripping down his brown skin and taut muscles, and she started to push up so she could grab him before he disappeared.

"Wait," he rushed out, stopping her. His eyes raced over her and she saw herself through them—girl stretched back on the board, skin just as brown as his, thighs and tummy and breasts offered up with only little scraps of black bikini to interrupt the view. He reached out then hesitated, squeezing his hand into a fist before he stretched it back out and pressed it to her stomach. "You're real," he said, like there'd been a doubt.

She sucked in her belly at the sensation of his hot hand covering her from waist dip to waist dip.

"I can't believe you're real," he said, and they both stared as his hand moved with her breath.

This was a fantasy, but not a dream.

Still back on an elbow, she pushed his hand down until his palm held the heart of her. "I'm real," she said. "I want you."

He groaned like she was electrocuting the water, and he pressed his palm between her thighs, shoving just right, and Marina's head fell back on a moan-gasp as she widened her thighs and rolled her hips to meet the pressure, the board helping her as the water lapped over her thighs. An orgasm usually took intense mental concentration and half an hour and enough friction on her clitoris to start a fire, but since it also usually involved Javier Campos's face, she was already half there.

When he growled, "Pretty girl," deep and low, Marina whimpered, and that was before she felt him tug her bikini bottom to one side and stroke two fingers between her folds, grunt at how juicy she was for him, then twist his hand to pet her clit with his thumb. Her stomach jumped at the sensation. "Jesus, you're pretty."

He gently pushed those two fingers inside, and Marina gritted her teeth and whined through them at the pleasure.

She forced her head up on her neck so she could watch. This brown, sun-soaked man had his hands between her legs, was staring where he held her suit to one side while his fingers pulsed inside of her and his thumb thrummed over her clit. Her thighs trembled against the water, and his cock was a thick rod in his turquoise swim trunks.

He looked up and caught her staring at it. Trapping her in his gaze, he let go of her suit and gripped his cock through his shorts. He stroked it slowly. Then he slipped his fingers out of her body, raised them to his lips, and slid them into his mouth. His eyes closed and he clenched the head of his dick as he sucked them clean.

"Oh my God," she cried, feeling the want of her rush out, a tidal wave of welcome. None of this could be happening. "Oh my God, I need you inside me."

She shoved up as he grabbed for her and the board beneath them rocked dangerously, but then he lifted her and slung her thighs over his and she clung to his biceps and he shifted to the center of the board, steadying it even as her brain exploded into a million stars as she realized she was pressed skin to skin, pussy to cock, with this beautiful man. Javier Campos met her eyes then bit her chin then her bottom lip then, eyes still open, pushed his tongue into her mouth and Marina drowned in him.

He tasted like the whiskey he'd talked about. He tasted like seawater and man. She never wanted anything else in her mouth as Javier Campos squeezed her ass and ran his hands over her naked back and shoved down a bikini cup so her nipple pressed against his chest, then clenched her head so he could fully own her mouth. The whole time, she was grinding and grinding and grinding against his hard, hard—

"I'm gonna—"

"Like hell you are." He lifted her up, off the ridge of his cock, and leaned slightly back to keep them steady on the paddleboard as she trembled. When she saw the tensed muscles of his abs, however, she gave up restraint and eagerly rubbed her pussy against that washboard. He smacked her ass, so loud it echoed over the water, and she squealed as the board tilted precariously and they were almost tossed into the drink.

She laughed as he squeezed his thighs around the board to steady them, then moaned when he slipped his hand between her legs from behind to pull her bottoms to one side.

Below and above, he teased her lips. "How much are you going to hate me if I tell you I brought a condom?" he asked against her mouth.

She sighed in relief as he pushed a finger inside. "How could I hate you?" she breathed. "Who wouldn't want to have sex with a mermaid?"

She wasn't a mermaid. A week ago, she'd never even been in the ocean. She was just Marina Torres from Freedom, Kansas, a newly minted college graduate who was in the middle of a fever dream. But when Javier Campos growled, "Get my cock out," before he sucked on her tongue, she felt like a mythical creature as she reached into his suit, stroked her hand down hard, hot skin before she pulled him out, long and thick in her hand, then snatched the condom packet he'd taken out of the back pocket of his trunks. She ripped it open with her teeth, pulled the latex out, then, as he kissed her and got her ready with his fingers, she slid the condom over his cock.

She bit his nose when he chuckled at her for sliding the torn wrapper into the bikini cup still covering her right boob. "No one's littering in my ocean," she said.

He stopped laughing when his mouth wandered over to her left nipple, heaving there right in front of his face, and she stopped chiding when he lifted her and slowly lowered her down onto his cock. She rocked her hips to ease the way, but being filled with him felt like the inevitability of the water meeting the sand.

When she was fully settled against him, when he was fully inside her, they both stilled. He panted against her breast. Her lips pressed into his hair. She could feel the wet bunch of his swimsuit beneath her, the corded muscles of his hips against the give of her thighs, the sculpted body his job demanded supporting hers. Floating in the Pacific Ocean with a man inside her shouldn't have felt like coming home.

"Sweetheart," he whispered against her skin. She heard him swallow, and then he kissed her nipple. "Sweetheart, you feel so good." He rubbed his thumb over the small of her back like he already knew that was one of her most sensitive spots and she full-body shivered. He deep-belly groaned and she squeezed him inside her.

They moaned in unison.

She was instantly, desperately hungry and so was he by the way he buried his hand in her curls and dragged her mouth to his, claiming it as he lifted her up with an arm around her hips then pushed inside as he let her back down, demanding and urgent. She dug her nails into his shoulders and back, clinging with the muscles inside her, gripping as tightly as she could to give pleasure and to demand it back. The water churned around him as they kissed and grabbed, both selfish and desperate and generous, and the foaming water felt like it washed them clean, washed away the TV star and the mermaid and left two skin-and-bone souls who had the incredible luck of finding each other.

He fucked her so good. When she started to vibrate on top of him, when she felt like nothing but ecstasy from her mouth to her toes in the warm water, he cupped her head and stared into her eyes.

"Do I call you my mermaid?" he said between gritted teeth, shoving in and holding her so close.

She was blinded by pleasure and his gorgeous sunset eyes. "Marina," she moaned out. She might never see him again. She didn't care. "Your Marina."

Her orgasm was volcanic and, dimly through the explosion in her own brain and body, she heard him give a sob of surrender and relief, like he was throwing himself into her fire. She shook on top of him, surely evaporating the water around them for miles.

Minutes later, wrapped around him and holding him close, her feet up on the board and heels resting against his bare butt, she began to cry.

"Hey, hey," he said, rubbing her back and squeezing her even closer. "Hey, what's wrong, I—"

She raised her head from the crook of his neck so he could see her smile as tears dripped into her mouth.

"I just..." Joy throbbed in her tear-choked voice. She motioned at the islands, the water, the endlessly blue sky, and then down at their laps, where he was still inside her. "Look at where we are. Look at what just happened." She wiped at her cheeks and for the rest of her days, her tears would taste like this ocean. "This is the most magical moment of my life so far."

She focused on his impossibly handsome face. "Thank you for being here for it," she said. "Thank you for sharing it with me."

She saw again that mystified and amazed look flash across his face as he stared back at her. His fingers flexed into her hips, like he was keeping her from swimming away.

Finally, he said, "I like that. The most magical moment of your life 'so far.'" He gave the dimple in her left cheek the softest kiss. "Thank you for giving me magic too. I needed it."

He kissed the dimple in her other cheek before he said, "Want to go for a swim?"

Without warning and still inside her, he tipped them both over into the water, used himself as her paddleboard for a few strokes, then finally slipped out to deal with the condom, which he shoved into his zippered back pocket along with the wrapper. When she began to rearrange her bikini top, he asked for it as a souvenir, so then she demanded his trunks, which he gladly handed over because of its "gross DNA pocket," and soon, they were two naked people paddling after each other in the Pacific, with no destination or goal, no background or consequences, simply a mermaid and a star who didn't know how they'd gotten there, but who both wanted to make this fantasy last as long as they could.

A nighttime, a summer, or a lifetime all seemed like very real possibilities.

## THE END

# Harvest Time

*In 2019, my debut book, **Lush Money**, launched my romance career. With a self-made Mexican American billionaire businesswoman who makes a baby deal with an impoverished Spanish winegrowing prince, the book was as bonkers as I could make it. That book—and the entire Filthy Rich series—also included my central message: women can claim their space and find good and worthy men who love them that way.*

*This brand-new story I wrote for this collection falls between **Lush Money** and the second book in the series, **Hate Crush**. It's only spoilery if you believe the billionaire and the prince ending up together is a surprise.*

*¡Salud!*

***

"Stop!" screeched Roxanne Medina, self-made billionaire and future queen of the Monte del Vino Real.

The Mercedes S580e tearing down the road between two vineyards skidded to a stop in the gravel. "Jesus H. Christ," yelled her bodyguard, clutching the steering wheel with one hand and his heart with the other. "What?"

"Did you see that?" Roxanne asked, scootching to the right passenger side and rolling down the tinted window.

"If I'd seen something, I wouldn't be having a heart attack right now!"

Henry, the big blond Texan that Roxanne depended on to coordinate her safety on three continents, was as cool as a cucumber when it came to true emergencies. He was a bit of a drama queen the rest of the time.

"Back up," she said, shoving her Prada sunglasses up on her head as she peered through the green-and-rust foliage of the vineyard rows.

"*Back up, speed up, pedal to the metal, Henry,*" he mimicked. "Pick a direction already." With a put-upon sigh, Henry put the car in reverse and began driving backward as effortlessly as he drove the car forward.

Henry had a right to his bad attitude. The final, crucial steps in establishing a woman-led tech company out of Shenzhen had kept her at her Hong Kong headquarters for the last two weeks, and with harvest in the Monte at its height, her husband had been unable to come to her. It'd been fourteen days since she'd seen Mateo Ferdinand Juan Carlos de Esperanza y Santos, one of the top viticulturists in the world and the future king of the Monte del Vino Real. It'd been 342 hours since she'd touched her Golden Prince.

So maybe she'd been a little short with Henry since...well, since she'd gotten into the back seat in Hong Kong. When she'd "visited" the cockpit of her private plane for the third time, he'd told her assistant Helen—a former Army nurse and commercial flight attendant—to tie her to the seat if she tried to check his speed again.

Once they landed, she'd demanded that Henry "step on it" even though they both knew there would be hell to pay for raising dust on the harvest-ready grapes.

Only the unlikeliness of what she'd just glimpsed could've convinced Roxanne to drive away instead of toward the man she needed like oxygen.

It was just her second harvest in the Monte del Vino Real, the Spanish principality she'd married into in the mountains of northern Spain, and none of the beauty whipping past had settled down to routine yet. The bright rust of exhausted leaves mixed with those that were still deep green, creating a gorgeous green-and-gold carpet leading up to the majestic mountains that surrounded the valley. El Castillo, the 600-year-old Moorish castle that was a gift from Reina Isabella, could be seen at the edge of the vineyards. The fact that Mateo's shitty parents still lived there, the neutered king and queen of the Monte, didn't make its crenelated walls and tall tower any less beautiful.

When they approached a gap in the vine rows, Henry slammed on the brakes. "What the...?" he breathed.

Glad she hadn't been hallucinating, Roxanne laughed as she got out of the car. "What in holy hell are you three doing?" she yelled.

A teenager from the Monte's village startled when she saw Roxanne. "Reina," she murmured, nodding her head. The other two women in the spa-sized galvanized steel tub continued to hoot and stomp.

Roxanne made her way across the shorn grass to her sister-in-law and her husband's first lover.

The grin on her face only grew as she got closer. Both her sister-in-law, Princesa Sofia Maria Isabel de Esperanza y Santos, and the winegrower who'd known the princesa and príncipe their entire lives, Carmen Louisa de Vega, had held down the fort in the Monte when Mateo had been ducking away from his father in the US. They were both serious, accomplished women working just as hard as she and Mateo were to bring the Monte back from financial ruin.

Which made seeing them like they were now, laughing, grasping at each other, their lovely faces bright with sun and exertion as they tramped around in the container and grape goop flew, that much more enjoyable.

"Are you for real with this?" Roxanne laughed as she approached the tub. Carmen was in shorts, Sofia was in overalls with rolled up pants legs, and they were both in a mash of purple-blue grape skins, glistening grape pulp and seeds, and tender green stems up to their knees.

Sofia, twenty-six, stopped and put her hands on her hips, breathing heavily and grinning. "Wanted to test...the control over the flavor pro-file...using foot stomping versus using the destemmer-crusher," she panted. Sofia had studied enology at the University of Bordeaux and planned to revolutionize winemaking here in the Monte.

Carmen Louisa, forty-three, shoved Sofia's shoulder. "Don't listen to her, *mi reina*," she said. "She was bored." Mateo's first lover had taught him some tricks Roxanne *deeply* appreciated. She also appreciated how she was a positive, calming force for all of them.

Sofia giggled like she was high. "You have to try this," she said. "It's so weird."

Roxanne knew from last year's harvest that the season was an all-hands-on-deck period for every citizen of the Monte, regardless of whether they worked in wine or not. There was a fierce rush when the grapes reached their appropriate sugars and needed to be picked, then periods of tedium as people waited for the next truckload of grapes to be brought in for processing or for the next harvest bell to go off. Mateo barely slept or ate for a month last year, only running into their mountain-side home to pound her into the mattress, pass out for two hours, down a protein shake, and run out again.

She eyed the tubful of grapes skeptically as she thought about how desperate she was to be pounded again. "I don't—"

"C'mon," Sofia wheedled, scooping her long, dark hair over her shoulder. Although Sofia was accomplished, smart-as-a-whip, and could party both Roxanne and Mateo under the table, she used her little sister skills as mercilessly against Roxanne as she did against her brother. "Por un minuto. Henry, you too!"

The teenage girl who worked at the bocadillo shop in the village was already sitting on a bench near the tub, wiping off her feet, making room for them in the tub. Roxanne turned to her bodyguard. "Henry, you comin'?"

Although he was leaning back on the sedan with his thick arms crossed, Henry looked about as relaxed as a sentry. He'd put on his midnight-black sunglasses. "Uh...I'm good," he called, waving a finger as retreated to the driver's side of the car.

Henry did not talk about his obvious crush on the princesa he was getting to know better, and Roxanne did not ask.

"The sooner in, the sooner out." She sighed theatrically, heading to the bench with a bit more enthusiasm than her words expressed as the ladies cheered. It did look like fun. As Sofia and Carmen Louisa began to tromp around again, she slipped off her mint-green Louboutins, the heels already caked in the clay-rich soil that made the Monte famous for wine grape growing, then dunked her feet in a bucket of soapy fluid. She let them soak for a second as she tied her long, dark brown hair into a knot on top of her head. Then she stood, gathered up the knee-length skirt of the Dolce & Gabbana shirtdress she wore—she thought it was the perfect dress for harvest season, a riot of cherry-red flowers on a teal background—and stepped into the tub.

She gasped as the sun-warmed grapes squished up between her toes and encased her calves. "Oh!" she gasped, startled, grimacing at the two giggling women.

"¿Qué piensas?" Carmen Louisa asked.

Roxanne didn't know what to think. "It's...disgusting," she said, sending the two into louder peals of laughter. "But also kind of..." She tentatively lifted her knee. "Kind of like the world's weirdest massage?"

Sofia held out her hand to steady Roxanne. "Walk around a little. It's harder work than I thought it would be."

Gathering more of her skirt and raising it higher in one hand—she really loved this dress—she clung to her sister-in-law and wobbled as she stepped around in the grapes, the movement beneath and around her feet a firm, mesmerizing squish. Every time she stepped down, she felt like her leg was surrounded in pulpy sunshine. She let go of Sofia, going for a little lap in the tub. Unlike the harsh stems of commercial grapes, the stems of this just-harvested fruit were tender under her heels. It was fascinating to watch the grapes mash beneath her weight.

She smiled at Sofia, who was watching for her reaction. "This can't truly be useful," she gasped, the muscles in her thighs starting to burn. "Or hygienic."

Sofia shrugged as she chuckled. The three of them looked ridiculous, stomping around. "There is bird poop and slug slime...in the grapes we gather...the fermentation process kills everything." She wiped her forehead. "I know a winemaker in Portugal who...swears by this method."

These vines, Roxanne had come to realize over the last two years, were more than plants. Their success meant the prosperity of Mateo's—and Roxanne's—people. Their demise meant the end of a legendary kingdom and way of life. Even a bad growing season, a norm in farming, was like having a child sick in bed that you fretted over. These vines and vineyards that Mateo had an encyclopedic knowledge of were like his children. Like her children.

Connecting with the grapes this way was strangely fulfilling. It was as close as she could get to them. As sweat gathered at her hairline and her thighs burned, she was using the power of her body to help the fruit evolve to its true purpose.

A throat cleared, startling all three of them.

Whirling around, Roxanne saw her husband standing ten feet away, looking like he'd just stepped out of the vineyard row. In a cream canvas shirt, dirty chinos, and tall muck boots, the afternoon sun in his gold-tipped hair, he was the most glorious sight she'd ever seen.

"Mi reina," he called through a choked voice. "Can I see you for a moment?"

***

That throaty, full laugh, floating above the vine row, beckoned him like a seafarer to a siren. That couldn't be... Wasn't she still in the air?

Mateo had come out here to check the sugars, again, even though he'd just checked this vineyard this morning and already knew it was going to be at least three days until these grapes were ready for harvest, but he needed to have something to occupy his body and mind while he was waiting for both to be consumed by his precious, amazing, gorgeous, luscious....

Joder, he missed her.

The triumph of this harvest should have been more than enough to keep him busy. His lab-made varietal was finally showing its full potential. His people were finally feeling confident about the financial footing beneath their feet. His parents' efforts to get in his way were finally no more effective than pebbles thrown at the ocean.

But this was the longest he'd been away from his billionaire queen since they'd told the world about their love a year and change ago, and missing her, wanting her, needing her, had grown from a gnat's irritating buzz fourteen days ago to, right now, a chainsaw's scream.

He could hear nothing but the rush of blood to his cock as he stared at his queen stomping grapes.

She was Demeter. She was Gaia. She was Mother Nature and Mother Earth and the holy blessed Mother and a finger-beckoning Tiacapan demanding pleasure wrapped up in one glimpse of a woman. Her thick, dark hair, tied in that knot he was fascinated by, was lolling against her neck. Her face glowed with thrilled effervescence. She held her dress, a pattern twining flowers around her full breasts and slim waist, high and showed him gorgeous, flexing brown thighs streaked with the fruits of his labor. She was essential and holy as she laughed with the two other women he loved most in the world. She was a deadly onslaught striking him like lightning, melting him to the earth of his forefathers.

He couldn't be this hard in front of his sister.

"Mi reina," he called, dropping his hand in front of his pants. "Can I see you for a moment?"

She jumped then stared, and, good Lord, the way her dark brown eyes lit up at the sight of him. There was soul-deep comfort in knowing he wasn't the only one drugged and besotted.

"Por supuesto, mi rey," she purred and no, oh no, she couldn't talk to him that way in front of his sister. He gripped his hands into fists in front of his fly.

She stepped out of the tub without any help, her skirt still held aloft, like she was stepping down from one of the ridiculous thrones his parents had purchased. Her bare feet, her muscular brown calves, were streaked with the grapes he'd grown. She swiped them with a towel, picked up deadly, spring-green heels, then sauntered toward him.

She gave him a smile as old, as knowing, as powerful, as Eve's. Her knot of hair lost its mooring and tumbled around her shoulders.

He barely swallowed his groan.

She stopped two inches away. Without her heels, standing barefoot on his land, she tilted her chin up, covering herself entirely in his looming, heaving shadow. "I've missed you, mi amor," she whispered.

He picked her up, threw her over his shoulder, spun around, and started running into the vine rows. Any concern that she was opposed to such treatment was erased when he heard the twin thunk of expensive footwear landing in the dirt, then felt powerful hands smack then squeeze his ass. Vine leaves brushed over them as he ran, as he felt her wriggle then jam a hand into the back of his chinos so her nails gripped skin and muscle. He grunted and ran and held on to those sticky, hot thighs until the peals of laughter they'd left behind became faint.

Then he slid her off his shoulder and pushed her to the dirt, dropping to cover her immediately.

"I'm sorry, I'm sorry," he groaned, taking her sweet, precious, enthusiastic mouth as he ran a hand up her legs, his fingers reveling in the sticky residue left on her silken skin. "I can't wait."

"Just like this," she moaned back, desperate, squeezing his hips with her thighs as she clawed at his fly. "I need you just like this."

The first touch of her hand on him was a shock. He jolted and twisted against her at the heat, but then he ripped down her lilac panties and flat-tongued the tacky juice at the bend of her knee. When he tried to follow the juice up her thigh, she yanked his shirt to get him back on top of her and then sucked the grape juice off of his tongue.

"No, no," she cursed and demanded, shoving down his pants. "Inside. Get you...need you..."

When he shoved into her, he hissed and squeezed his eyes closed at the overwhelming sensation. She groaned low and earthshaking and gave a voluptuous shudder beneath him.

Up on his hands, he opened his eyes to look down at her. Her hair was spread out on the earth that was their home. She'd saved this home for their people. The shadows of their vine leaves played over her skin and flower-drenched dress. She looked up at him through clear, deep-brown eyes, eyes she no longer colored because she wanted to see the world and let the world see her clearly.

She was caught in the calm of the storm just like he was. "Just like this," she whispered, her hips moving like the sea beneath him. "The second I saw you, my man, my gorgeous, perfect man, I wanted to christen our home with you."

"Fuck," he groaned, grabbing her shoulder and jolting into her. Want for her ran up his legs, into his thighs. "Fuck, home, my beautiful home." He sped up—he couldn't help it—shoving and stroking into her, all concepts of home and family and nurturing and protecting and giving coalescing into this one life-giving woman, a woman who'd planted her feet on the backs of his thighs and was careening herself up into him, opening herself up and demanding it.

"Yes," she cried. "Yes, mi querido. Make me your home. Make me..." She writhed against him, wild and earthy, leaves in her hair and royal command in the hands that gripped him.

He pounded and pounded and pounded, sure they shook the mountains and echoed in the Earth's core.

Her hips arched, almost bucking him off, and he shoved her down and shoved in and consumed her mouth and she shrieked into his, her orgasm earthquaking around him. He held her tight, shaking through every second of her pleasure, then groaned long and painfully as he flooded her with his.

He'd once hated her for her seeming ability to gather every ounce of physical satisfaction from a place and direct it into his body. Now he floated in what must be all the lusty satiation ever enjoyed in the Monte's mountain valley, and rightfully so. He was its future king after all.

When he tried to roll off the wife he had to be crushing, she huffed a complaint and squeezed him tighter against her.

"¿Estás bien?" he whispered against her cheek, stroking it with his lips.

"I feel tilled and planted," she murmured. She opened her eyes. "The dirtiest thoughts slammed into me when I saw you. I needed you just like that."

"Please never make me that hard again in front of my sister," he said, softly kissing lips that looked full and tender from what he'd done to them. "Why were you three stomping grapes?"

Roxanne's laugh sounded all used up. "It was your sister's idea."

"Joder." He sighed, looking down to see the purple stain of his fruit streaking her naked legs. He was still inside her. Unbelievably, his body stirred. "I might have to put a grape bin in our bedroom."

"Oh," Roxanne breathed, her pelvis rotating lazily against him. "I'd like to see you in the grapes. I'd like to see your hands..." Her fingers clenched his as he raised her thigh. "Your big hands squeezing them...."

They groaned as both of their bodies declared that their needs weren't quenched. Would never be quenched.

"Welcome home, mi reina," he said as he moved deep into her once again.

"Welcome home, my Mateo," she said, opening herself wide.

## THE END

Learn more about **Lush Money**, named a top 10 romance debut of 2020 by Booklist.

*"Lopez successfully flips the gender switch on the wealthy CEO trope while at the same time incorporating a generous*

*dash of fairy-tale glitz and glam into the captivating sto-ryline of her marvelous debut. And when these elements are combined with engaging characters and an abundance of boldly sensual, vividly rendered love scenes, you have every-thing fans of sexy contemporary romances could ever crave.*
*"—**Booklist** ★ (Starred review)*

*A marriage of convenience and three nights a month. That's all the sultry, self-made billionaire wants from the impover-ished prince. And at the end of the year, she'll grant him his divorce...with a settlement large enough to save his beloved kingdom.*

As a Latinx woman, Roxanne Medina has conquered small-town bullies, Ivy League snobs, and boardrooms full of men. She's earned the right to mother a princess and feel a little less lonely at the top. The offer she's made is more than generous, and when the contract's fulfilled, they'll both walk away with everything they've ever wanted.

Príncipe Mateo Ferdinand Juan Carlos de Esperanza y Santos is one of the top winegrowers in the world, and he's not marrying and having a baby with a stranger. Even if the millions she's offering could save his once-legendary wine-producing principality.

But the successful, single-minded beauty uses a weapon Prince Mateo hadn't counted on: his own desire.

***Order now***

# CHAPTER FOURTEEN

# Star *69

S ince I offered my short story **The Phone Call** *(the short story that starts this collection) as a free read to newsletter subscribers, I would every now and then get an email about "the rest" of the story. What happens when Rosemarie and Sam step inside?*

*This is that answer. I hope you've enjoyed this collection. I've enjoyed writing it for you.*

**Content warnings: Mentions death of a spouse**

***

Three years after one of them (Sam) called the other one (Rosemarie) and began their at-least once-a-day phone calls and six weeks after their first astonishing kiss on Valentine's Day and two weeks after Sam moved into his new (and hopefully temporary) apartment in Boston and four hours after dropping off the girls at her girlfriend's house for the weekend, Rosemarie fidgeted in silence across from her best friend and new love on their first date.

Not even the low candlelight and heavy rain hitting the windows of this high-end restaurant on the harbor could hide the nerves in Sam's eyes as he poked at the ice in his Old Fashioned.

If she wasn't so nervous herself, she could tease this confident, worldly man focused on his cocktail like it was a specimen in a lab. But in a new, flowy, sapphire silk dress with her hair blown out and her makeup professionally applied, she felt like a sugar skull that would crumble apart if she behaved like she usually did.

He was so gorgeous in the candlelight, a charcoal suit over his fit body, his thick dark-blond hair brushed back when she'd only seen it flicky and wavy, perfectly shaved when she liked his scruff. Rosemarie had watched the cute coat check girl eye him up and down as he'd removed his trench coat and she knew (thanks to her curiosity-killed-the-cat questions about his love life) that it'd taken less provocation for him to approach and take home a woman.

As she carefully pushed a highly sprayed curl out of her eyes, the reminder that she was finally going to make love to this man who'd experienced the act with so many didn't ease her nerves.

The movement caught his eye. He flashed a grin that didn't relax either of them and asked, "So…uh…are the girls looking forward to their weekend at Wendy's?"

The girls. Her girls. Soon, she hoped, their girls. Her two young girls that Sam had known since their births were the reason they hadn't made love yet. They were the reason that instead of dragging him to the foyer floor that Valentine's Day night, she and Sam had wrenched apart and talked until dawn from opposite ends of the dining room table. He'd flipped the dining room chair around and clung to its rungs as they'd said all they wanted to say to each other but didn't touch.

*I won't fuck this up for you or them or me or us* he'd said right after *I'm dying to be inside you*. His love for her and her girls had made her flip her chair around and cling too.

In the whirlwind weeks since, after deciding that a temporary apartment would be best and getting him moved across the country and carefully introducing the girls to the concept that Uncle Sam would be...Sam, there'd been a growing unease that the patience necessitated by her daughters was starting to be an excuse.

*Sex with Sam*, a concept that once buzzed her like champagne bubbles, was becoming as daunting as the electric chair.

Which was why they'd promised one thing tonight.

She leaned across the table with what she hoped was a seductive smile. "We said we wouldn't talk about the girls."

One of her big sausage curls almost plopped into her wine. She flicked it away, then grabbed the glass before it tipped over, jarring the table.

"Yeah," Sam said, throwing his stir stick into his drink, splashing the bourbon up on his snowy cuff. He wiped his palms together with a grimace. "Yeah, sorry."

What was wrong with them?

She dropped her smile. "Why is this so weird?" she whispered, trying to see his face through the flickering tapers. Thunder rumbled outside.

Sam grabbed her hand. "It's not weird."

She raised her eyebrow even as she thrilled to the heat and freedom of his thick fingers twining with hers. There'd been one erotic afternoon when they'd hid their clasped hands while watching her youngest's T-ball game.

"It's not," he insisted, green eyes showing the stubbornness that had been one of the first things she'd learned about him. "It's new. We've shoved a lot of eggs into tonight's basket."

Their first time, their relationship, and the course of their whole future felt crammed into later tonight. Whether they could overcome the reality that she was his best friend's widow would finally be confronted. And the fact that she was now his best friend—and he was hers—seemed like it could be more of a hindrance than a help when they were horizontal.

The squeeze of his hand echoed the kicked-up beat of her heart. They desperately didn't want to screw this up.

A sommelier wearing a tux appeared, holding a leather-bound wine list. He presented it with a flourish to Sam. "I understand you'd like to pair a few bottles with your five-course—"

Sam shoved the book back at him. "Give us a sec," he said without taking his eye off Rosemarie. The man faded away.

Sam gripped her fingers until they almost hurt. The candle flame made his eyes glow emerald. "Let's get out of here."

"What?" she asked.

"Let's...c'mon..."

He pulled her out of her chair.

Five minutes later, after he slapped his credit card on the hostess stand and said he'd be back for it tomorrow, after he grabbed their coats from the bewildered coat check girl but forgot to get their umbrella, after they ran two blocks in the rain looking for a cab when she hadn't hailed a cab in years, he pulled her under the awning of a closed tourist shop.

"Goddammit," he said, shoving his dripping hair back. "Isn't there a hole-in-the-wall chowder place around here?"

His trench coat had slipped open and his white shirt was plastered against his skin. She was certain her silk dress was ruined beneath her soaked coat.

She didn't care. "Those are more legend than reality," she said, leaning her forearms against his chest and nestling up against his heat.

His big hands came up to surround her biceps. "How hungry are you?" he asked, searching her eyes.

For food? "Not at all."

His hands squeezed her arms. "Let's...let's get room service. I can't—" He blinked and took in her ruined makeup, her destroyed hair-do, and their devastated first date. "Jesus. What have I—?"

"I'm glad," she said, pushing her hand into his wet hair. It was going to dry wavy and flicky, just as she liked it. "I'm so glad we're out of there." She pressed against him and went up on her tiptoes to nuzzle his warm, wet earlobe. "I'll get us a car."

He groaned as she sucked, but she stepped away when he tried to draw her closer. She pulled out her phone.

Sam had fallen in love—she thrilled at the notion—but he'd never been in love. She had. Sam was impulsive in a way Philip hadn't been and she embraced the Sam-ness of it. But her years of a loving, dependable marriage could steady them when the seas got unexpectedly choppy.

Although what she did when the car was just around the corner wasn't going to help Sam feel steady.

She pulled a black sleeping mask out of her purse and held it up to him. "Could you put this on?" she asked as his eyes widened.

This wasn't the first time he'd been blindfolded, but Rosemarie knew she didn't seem like the type. It was a measure of the years they'd known each other that he put it on without question.

"Thank you," she whispered, kissing his cheek just as the Uber pulled up to the curb. She led Sam to the car and cautioned him to duck his head.

"We're not getting weird back here," she told the driver as she slid into the Prius. "I just want it to be a surprise."

She'd told Sam she'd made a hotel reservation.

The woman chuckled. "Sweetheart, I'd let you get as weird as you want if I didn't need a clean car to make some money tonight." She reassured Rosemarie that she had towels in her trunk; she and Sam were dripping all over the seats.

Rosemarie resisted making small talk during the twenty-five-minute drive. They'd failed at it all night anyway. She settled her hand over his on his thigh, idly ran her fingers over the solid muscle of it, thumbed the scar he'd gotten on a cross-country bicycle tour, but after a few minutes, he squeezed her hand and moved it to the seat between them. When he shifted and a traffic light highlighted his lap, she saw why.

She bit her lip and looked out her window, sending up a silent prayer that she—a woman who'd only had sex with one man for years and then no sex for the last three—could live up to the expectations in his fitted charcoal slacks.

When the Uber deposited them where they would be spending the weekend, Rosemarie wondered if the sightless Sam recognized the walk as she led him up the drive, the whine of the front door she'd risked leaving unlocked so she wouldn't have to use her keys, and the creak of the third and thirteenth steps she'd learned to avoid when putting down babies who were horrible sleepers.

By the time they reached their destination, her heart was beating so fast that all she could get out was a weak "Ta-da!" as she pulled the sleeping mask off his head.

Sam's shapely mouth dropped open as he took in the redecorated bedroom. During the last two weeks of keeping her hands off him, she'd started obsessing over that sexy dip at the top of his lip. Now, as she waited for his reaction, her fantasy of licking it was her focal point.

He finally asked "When did you...?"

"This week." The new dimmer switch was set to keep the lights low and, she hoped, sexy. Their coats were dripping on the new bedroom carpet. "That's why I made up that thing about being on keto when you tried to bring over doughnuts on Monday."

There'd also been a desperate and ultimately fruitless effort to lose five pounds before they ended up here.

He stayed in the doorway of the bedroom as he took in the walls re-painted a soft gray, the new bedding similar to the high-end comforter and pillows he had on his own bachelor bed, and the rearranged furniture. The overnight bags she'd said that Wendy was going to drop off at the hotel were tucked into a corner. She didn't tell him there was a new mattress.

His silence was daunting. "I want you to feel like this is your home," she said. She hoped he understood. "I want you to...know that this is your bedroom."

For the girls, the quality of the schools, the location of their friends, and consistency in young lives that had already had so much change with the death of their father, they'd decided not to sell the house. Rosemarie had brought it up, even though Sam had never once suggested that it would be difficult to step into the role of husband and father in the house his best friend had picked out and painted. Sam had helped Philip put up the fence.

But because self-sacrificing Sam had hidden his love for her out of a fear that it was inappropriate and unwanted, Rosemarie knew that moving in here wouldn't be without its echoes. In her bedroom that she hoped to transform into their bedroom, she wanted to welcome Sam to make his mark.

As he continued to say nothing, her boldness shrank.

"I hope this is okay," she murmured, twining a finger into her hair when she remembered how soaked she was. Her expertly applied eye makeup was probably streaked down her face. She felt as attractive as a drowned rat. "We can...we can go to a hotel. If this is too...I'm sorry if I rushed—"

Sam grabbed her, kissed her as he kicked the bedroom door closed, then shoved her back against it and surrounded her, taking over her mouth like it was the way he was going to get inside. She moaned, shocked and pleasured, around the hot, deep thrusts of his tongue as Sam kissed her like a man who'd waited eight years to do it.

He slid his mouth across her cheek to her jaw. "I'm going to break you open like a champagne bottle," he growled into the thin skin of her neck as he inhaled her. "Love of mine, I'm going to drink you up."

The greed that rose in her was monstrous. She dug her fingers into his wet hair and jerked him back to her lips. There was wild freedom in exploring this mouth that was new and yet so precious as she licked and sucked and fondled. The hunger she'd had when she'd started them down this path—*I think we should have sex*—hadn't been appeased and had, instead, been given a growth serum. Her hunger could demolish a city.

She twined a leg around his thigh as her blue high heel clunked to the carpet and sucked on his eager, agile tongue. There was a fire between her legs and she needed him to quench it.

Still kissing her, he grabbed her coat and ripped it down her arms. She did the same for him, rubbing her palms down his big shoulders and strong biceps as he shrugged out of the wet trench coat. Sam didn't carry himself like a big man because he didn't have to. But he was.

"This dress was the meanest thing you've ever done," he moaned into her cleavage as he stooped down, nuzzling her, gathered the hem of the ruined blue silk in his fingers, then slowly, slowly, pulled it up. "How was I supposed to be a nice guy when this delicate dress was just taunting me to rip it off you?"

When his fingers traveled from sheer nylon to banded lace, he groaned, "Goddamn," then stepped back to look. She kicked off her other heel and leaned back against the door so he could see the black thigh-high stockings.

"That run in the rain ruined this dress," she promised as he made a guttural sound when the slow climb of her dress and his fingertips showed black lace panties. "You'll never have to see it again."

"I'll buy you another one," he swore as his hands and eyes traveled up her bare belly. She spread her fingers against the wooden door instead of covering her stretch marks. "I'll buy you two so I can do all the nasty things I imagined doing to you in it and still rip it off."

As she raised her arms over her head so he could pull the dress off, then settled her arms loosely over her wet hair, she closed her eyes and bit her lip and squeezed her thighs together. She knew he was…a dog. She never imagined he'd be a dog for her.

He made another desperate sound before jerking her away from the door, picking her up, then throwing her—throwing her—onto the bed. She bounced, getting her elbows under her, which put her in perfect position to stare down at the top of his dark blond head as he nuzzled the bare skin of her thigh above the lace band. His light-licked hair was drying into the waves she loved.

"Is this new too?" he asked against her skin.

"This?" His lips burned like sun-heated silk.

"All of…" His fingers trailed over her black thigh highs, along the hip of her panties, up her ribs to the bottom of one lacy cup. "Jesus."

It was miraculous to see his hand on her body. "Of course," she said, still looking at the top of his head. It came out like a coo. "It's all yours."

"Mine," he said, deep and low, as he kissed her thigh, following the trail of her nylons as he pulled them down, kissing her knee and her shin and even her toes. He gave the same treatment to her other leg, declaring, "Mine," as he picked it up and licked the shivering skin at the back of her knee.

"Mine," he repeated as he moved up to get to her mouth, a big man in a fine, damp suit pushing her into the mattress, giving her deep, drugging kisses while she wrapped her arms around his neck until she had to relinquish her hold as he worked his way down to her breasts. He turned her over and said it again, "Mine," as he bit and kissed down the knobs of her spine, each lick making her quiver harder until he undid her bra. The trail of his tongue over her ribs was torture as he turned her, tasting, then pausing to look, then moving back in to call her "mine" and "mine" and "mine" as he licked at her nipples then pulled with his teeth, measuring her reaction and the agonized pant of her mouth with those smoky green eyes.

"Mine," he whispered to her black lace panties. He bit her hip bone, making her wrench her hips on the new comforter. He nuzzled at her plushness around her belly button as he drew her panties down her legs.

"Mine," he said as he placed each bare foot on the brace of the mattress frame, spread her thighs, then straightened to stare.

A gorgeous bachelor from L.A. stood in a damp designer suit in front of her, staring at her naked body. Her naked, mom-of-two body. A painful self-consciousness began to overcome how desperately she wanted him. She could feel an embarrassed flush creeping over her. She put her hand between her legs, covering herself.

Instantly, he squeezed her knee. "What's wrong?"

"I-I just..." She pressed her other hand over her stretch marks. She was one second from hiding under the comforter and grabbing the bedside remote to turn off the lights. "I...I don't think you've been with many moms. I'm not going to look like those other women you've—"

"Jesus," he cursed, scooping her up and against him, getting a big hand under her butt and around her nape. "Don't you get it?" he said, searching her eyes. "There *was* no woman before you. I'm grateful as fuck for the time of day they gave me, but for years, for years..." She heard the agony of his long wait as he squeezed her nape and forced her to meet his passionate green gaze.

"You'd wander into my thoughts, and the pain I would feel to see you, to hear you, to touch you would make me deaf and blind to everything else. Don't act like this is a one-night stand and I'm going to compare your thighs to others I've had wrapped around me. Be glad I haven't tied you down and pulled up a chair to study your pretty pussy. You're going to let me, some other weekend when the girls are gone, let me worship your sweet, wet cunt, make me a slave to it all weekend long."

"Oh my God," she gasped at his breath-stealing words.

He shook his head. "How's that for exposed, Rosemarie? You don't think I'm fucking petrified?" His hand was so hot, so steadying at the back of her neck. But he was afraid too. "You're giving me this chance and, Christ, the fear that I'm going to fuck it up has made me act like a..." He shook his head again and the slope of his gorgeous green eyes made him look so sad. "Look at your poor dress. Look what I did to our first date."

He looked down at her breasts crushed against his rain-wet suit. She was naked and he was fully dressed. He still had on the deep-green tie the girls had demanded to buy him for his birthday. "Look...look what I'm doing to you right now."

"Sam," she said softly, putting her hands on the shaved planes of his face so he'd meet her eyes again.

Sam. Now her Sam. Her Sam who thought—after years of knowing him, after everything they'd been through, aware of how much she loved him—that there was something he could do to ruin this or change her mind or make her regret.

"Sam..." she beckoned again.

When he looked at her, full of caution and hope and lust and terror, it was like looking in a mirror.

"Sam, did you see how wet I was when you spread my legs?"

He inhaled sharply. "Yeah," he replied, guttural.

Still holding his face, she leaned forward to kiss him. "You did that," she said between kisses he gently returned. "Nervous and self-conscious, I'm still so wet because of you." She kissed that sexy dip above his lip—since she could now, she could kiss it all weekend long—then licked his top lip.

"Don't you want to feel how wet you've made me?" she breathed against it.

"Fuck," he groaned like a sob, his hand clenching hard on her butt cheek.

"Thank you, honey," she said, kissing and kissing her Sam, sweet and delicate to tempt him to tear her apart. "I don't want you different either, Sam. My Sam. Can you please take your clothes off?"

This time when he put her down, he did it like she was porcelain. But Rosemarie grabbed one of her new pillows and shoved it under her head and spread her legs, ready to revel in one of her favorite fantasies happening in real time—the fantasy of Sam taking off his clothes for her.

He groaned chest deep, like he tore something loose, as he stripped off his tie and Rosemarie began to circle her clit with one manicured finger.

"You're a fucking menace," he growled as the strip tease became the frantic destruction of a tailored suit. But the see-through shirt, then his hairy chest and treasure trail and mounded biceps and the hiss of his belt yanking out of the loops and...God, she was already so close as he panted through his open mouth and watched her rub her own clit.

"Sam!" she demanded as he dropped his slacks.

"What?" he barked, not raising his eyes from her busy hand.

She stared at the gorgeous tent of his boxer briefs. "That's mine," she said, pleasuring herself to the length and heft of him. "And these are the last thighs you're going to sink between. Don't you forget it."

"Fuck," he spat as he grabbed himself and squeezed, jerking back his head to glare at the ceiling. "Goddammit, Rosemarie!"

She watched the white-knuckled grip that he could take and felt herself burn. She was so close. If he'd just pull down that black cotton and give her a peek—

He grabbed her around her knee and began pulling her to the edge of the bed.

"Wait," she said, wiggling. "Let me see—"

"Good girls get to see," he growled. "Bad girls get fucked."

She slapped a hand over her mouth to hold back her thrilled giggle as he pulled her thighs around his torso. Was she a bad girl?

"What, no foreplay?"

"The last month-and-a-half has been nothing but foreplay." He ripped his boxer briefs down and then she did get to see—just a glimpse—before she got to feel, that big solid head, and her smile dropped away just like his scowl and their eyes met.

In late-night, heat-soaked phone calls over the last six weeks, they'd talked about this moment. Spilled their dirty imaginings of it. Even discussed how to get ready for it. He'd had himself checked out. She'd gone back on the pill.

And now they were here. He was there, at the warm, wet, eager entrance to her, and he was hot and solid.

It'd been so long.

She wanted him so much.

This was *nothing* like cleaning the gutters.

"Yeah?" he asked, sweet and soft, as a drop that hadn't come from the rain meandered down the beloved cheek she would refuse to let him shave this weekend.

"Please," she whispered back, her answer sure even though her vision was watery.

*Thank you for him, love,* she sent up to the heavens.

Then there was no room for thoughts of before as now, right now, Sam wrapped his big hands around her hips and started to work himself in, minute and steady rocks that were easy despite her celibacy, so easy and wet and warm that quickly both of their breaths were trembling out even though he didn't speed up and she didn't want him to, wanted to watch him like he was watching her, recording every sensation of this momentous moment that felt so unbelievably good.

So unbelievably right.

When he was touching the heart of her, the muscles of his jaw jumping and his fingers squeezing desperately at her flesh, she rolled up her hips to clench him and crossed her ankles above his firm ass. He knew how to have sex with many. But she could show him how to make love to the one.

"C'mere," she said, tugging at him. "Take me in our bed."

"Woman," he groaned, covering her and sliding them both to the center of their new mattress. "My beautiful woman." He held her face in his hands and stared down at her, his dark blond hair a halo around his head. "You love me back."

"So much." She sighed, kissing the tears from his jaw and squeezing him with her body. She was going to make love to her man so good that he'd never doubt it.

This first time, neither of them were going to last long.

Sam swore it, swore he was going to come in her fast so he could get his face between her legs and live out his deepest fantasy, tasting himself on her, then he trapped her hands over her head and reared up over her and took her, took her, plunged his cock in and pulled out, delicious fucking as he feasted on her mouth, and—because she was his best friend and longtime love—she decided to let him, let him get them both off fast and hard and screaming and then, later, after he'd tasted his fill and made her scream again, she'd climb on top and pleasure him slow, ride him until he was fully adored by her and fully satiated by her for the very first time.

This was the first time with her new love who she knew to her bones. She couldn't wait to enjoy so many firsts with him for the rest of their lives.

## THE END

# Trope List

1. **The Phone Call** – Widow • Husband's best friend • "Just one time" • Secret pining • Dirty talk • No sex

2. **First Date** – Couple • First date after lots of sex and marriage proposal • Dirty talk • Edging • Instant orgasm • Bonus chapter for ***After Hours on Milagro Street***, book 1 of Milagro Street series

3. **Twelve Drummers** – Strangers • Consensual magic made them do it • Secret pining • Exhibitionism • Gangbang

4. **Too Old For You** – Younger woman-older man • Age gap • Former teacher • She pursues him • "Just one time" • Take care of her • Open pining • Car sex • Barely concealed fanfic

5. **The Proposal** – Childhood friends • Good girl and bad boy • She pursues him • Secret pining • Fingering • Dirty talk • Take care of her • Deleted chapter from ***Full Moon Over Freedom***, book 2 of the Milagro Street series

6. **Hot Pockets** – Married couple • An ottoman, a doorjamb, and bear slippers were defiled in the making of this story

7. **In the Stacks** – Strangers • Fantasizing • Exhibitionism • Masturbation • Insta-lust • Take care of her

8. **Dream Man** – Strangers • Only first names • One-night stand • Insta-love • Take care of her • Novella in the ***Filthy Rich*** universe

9. **Crack in the Plaster** – Strangers in a no-tell motel • Threesome • Two guys, one woman • Insta-lust • Take care of her • No sex

10. **Touch Me** – Movie star • Teasing at infidelity • Surprise massage • Take care of her

11. **A Good Man** – FBI agent and college-aged witness • Younger woman-older man • Age gap • She pursues him • Insta-lust • **Not a romance story**

12. **A Mermaid and Her Star** – Strangers • Movie star • Insta-lust • Paddleboard sex

13. **Harvest Time** – Married couple • Too long apart • Insta-lust • Dirty talk • Bonus chapter for ***Lush Money***, book 1 of Filthy Rich series

14. **Star *69** – Widow • Husband's best friend • Couple • First time • Dirty talk • Open pining

# Acknowledgements

First and foremost, thank you to dear friend and renown illustrator and designer John Sprengelmeyer for the fabulous cover. We'd both thought of a Rosie the Riveter homage to honor all the strong women I write about, but it was John's idea to show as many men in the stories as space would allow worshipping her. It's a brilliant concept, a powerful image, and a phenomenal representation of my writing. Check out more of John's amazing work at Sprengelmeyer.com.

Readers don't realize it, but you all owe thanks to editor Jessica Snyder. Without the copywriting help of her business HEA Author Services, you would be tripping over A LOT more commas. Jessica was wonderful about providing word-choice suggestions while letting my wild writing style fly free!

Thank you to all my Patreon subscribers who inspired me to write so many short stories with your enthusiasm and excitement every time I posted. You helped me believe these stories deserved a life beyond Patreon's (crappy) paywall!

As always, eternally grateful for the love, support, and enthusiastic cheerleading of Celeste, Clay, Gabriel, Simon, and Peter. Always Peter.

# About the author

Angelina M. Lopez has been writing professionally her whole life: first as a journalist for an acclaimed city newspaper, then as a freelance magazine writer, and now as a romance author. She writes sexy stories about strong women and the worthy men lucky to love them.

Her two latest releases in her high-heat, small town, Latinx series, ***After Hours on Milagro Street*** and ***Full Moon Over Freedom***, have received in total four starred reviews, an AudioFile Earphones award, and were named top ten romances of the year in The Washington Post, Entertainment Weekly, and the Fated Mates podcast.

Angelina lives with her family in Houston, Texas.

The best way to keep up with Angelina is to sign up for her newsletter. You can find more about her at her website, AngelinaMLopez.com, and at @AngelinaMLo on Instagram.

# Also by

## *After Hours on Milagro Street*

*The Washington Post* - Top 10 Romance Novel of 2022

*Entertainment Weekly* - 10 Best Romance Novels of 2022

*Fated Mates* podcast - Best of 2022

"Bar none, one of the best contemporaries of the year."—Sarah MacLean, co-host of Fated Mates and New York Times bestselling author of *Knockout*

## *Full Moon Over Freedom*

*The Washington Post* – Top 10 Romance Novel of 2023

*AudioFile Magazine* - Best Audiobooks of 2023 and winner of Earphones Award

"Lopez is remaking the romance genre one gorgeously sexy book at a tim e."—Sierra Simone, USA Today bestselling author of *Priest*

## *Lush Money*

*Booklist* – Top 10 Romance Debut of 2020
"Everything fans of sexy contemporary romances could ever crave." —*Booklist,* ★ Starred Review

## *Hate Crush*

"Angelina M. Lopez continues her sinfully delicious Filthy Rich series with a second novel that elevates her ability to blend soapy drama with steamy bedroom scenes and gut-wrenching emotion....Lopez keeps readers gasping with shock and pleasure in equal measure." —Maureen Lee Lenker, *Entertainment Weekly*

## *Serving Sin*

"Angelina M. Lopez' Filthy Rich series continues to take traditional romance tropes and turn them upside down. Serving Sin, her third book about mega-rich folks and the romantic misadventures they get up to, is the best one of the series, spicy, delicious, and a twist on the ordinary." —Lisa Fernandes, *All About Romance*

**Learn more about Angelina M. Lopez and her books at AngelinaMLopez.com**